# Also By Colleen Cross

*Katerina Carter Fraud Thriller Series*

*Exit Strategy*

*Game Theory*

*Blowout*

*Katerina Carter Color of Mystery Series*

*Red Handed*

*Blue Moon*

*Greenwash*

*Nonfiction*

*Anatomy of a Ponzi: Scams Past and Present*

# *Katerina Carter Color of Money Mysteries*

## *Red Handed – a short story*

When forensic accountant and fraud investigator Katerina Carter and journalist boyfriend Jace Burton accept an impromptu party invitation, crime is the last thing on their minds. Then a winning wine investment leaves a sour taste in Kat's mouth and she unravels the clues to a million-dollar wine fraud, all before dinner!

## *Blue Moon – a novelette*

Kat and boyfriend Jace's plans for a fancy dinner go awry when she discovers that her elderly neighbor Fiona has taken an ex-con into her home as a boarder. Fiona's volunteer gardening program at the local prison has changed lives, but extending her generosity further just might put her own life in jeopardy.

Kat's suspicion deepens when she learns of a recent life insurance policy. And accidental death pays double.

## *Greenwash – a novel*

Forensic accountant Katerina Carter and boyfriend Jace Burton embark on a weekend getaway at a luxury mountaintop lodge just before Christmas. While he writes the biography of a billionaire environmentalist, she explores the snowy wilderness.

Then two local protestors die under mysterious circumstances, and Kat and Jace race against time to save themselves from an even deadlier disaster.

## *Bonus! Excerpt from Game Theory, A Katerina Carter Fraud Thriller!*

# Red Handed

# Chapter 1

Some days—correction—most days—Katerina Carter questioned the wisdom of buying the old Victorian house. She and Jace had bought it, sight unseen, at the city tax sale. It had seemed too good a deal to pass up, an entire Victorian house in exchange for payment of three years' worth of unpaid taxes. But any savings had been more than eaten up in repair bills. Not to mention sweat equity.

She'd taken a rare day off work to focus on some much-needed home improvements. Fraud investigation tended to be slow in late August and she was between cases anyways. It was debatable which was harder: catching criminals or sanding away decades of paint layers on a neglected old house.

Kat laid down her paintbrush and smiled as she surveyed her work. The veranda looked stunning, the white paint gleaming in the bright afternoon light. While there were more pressing tasks around the house, they were largely invisible, like plumbing and electrical work. Doing the painting herself meant less money dropped into the insatiable money pit. She also wanted to finish before the onslaught of Vancouver's autumn rains.

Jace Burton stood in the doorway, his head almost touching the top. "Looks great."

He flashed a smile that made her forget he'd been gone almost two hours.

Kat blew him a kiss and sat down in a creaky Adirondack chair, wondering why it had taken all summer to get around to painting the railing.

Of course she knew the reason. She had been preoccupied with the endless repairs and related casualties, most recently the burst pipe that had morphed into a complete re-plumb. Not to mention the warped fir floors resulting from the leak.

"Did you get the paint?"

Jace tapped his forehead. "I knew I forgot something."

"But that's what you went for. Only one item on the list." Jace's singular focus was a boon as a journalist chasing a story, but less productive when it came to other things.

"Sorry. I ran into Kirk Evans at the hardware store and lost all track of time. But I got something else." Jace pulled his arm out from behind his back. "This."

Kat leaned forward to read the small print on the bottle. "A bottle of red wine? Uh-oh, Jace. Drinking and painting never works out for us."

He laughed. "That's not what I was thinking. Besides, this isn't just any old bottle of wine. It's Screaming Eagle Cabernet Sauvignon."

"Screaming what?"

"Eagle. Kirk's got cases of this stuff. You can't buy it anywhere. He's a wine investor now."

Kat had heard of wine investors, but she'd never met one in real life. She pictured Wall Street bankers or money managers trying to justify their overpriced drinking habits. She couldn't picture Kirk buying and holding craft beer, let alone fine wine.

"That's a switch from unemployed journalist," she said. "Don't wine investors need money for start-up capital? He's been out of work for quite a while now." Kirk had worked with Jace at *The Sentinel* until he was caught up in the downsizing last year.

"We didn't get into details, but somehow he's making it work. This baby's worth thousands. At least that's what it sells for. Kirk buys it for about five hundred bucks a bottle."

"And Kirk just gave it to you? What's the catch?"

"No catch, just showing his appreciation for me helping him out last year." Jace held out the bottle for her inspection. "Anyways, I thought we'd save it for a celebration. Once we finish with the plumbing and stuff."

"Are you crazy? We can't drink something that expensive." Kat sucked in her breath as the bottle slipped in Jace's hand. She certainly didn't want to feel indebted to Kirk Evans. "Put it down before you drop it. We've got to give it back."

Jace handed her the bottle instead. It looked like an ordinary bottle of Cabernet Sauvignon, except for the vintage year. Nineteen ninety-seven had to be expensive, even if the small monochrome label made it appear more ordinary than most. She studied the label's flying eagle motif, wondering what made it so special.

She stood to return the bottle to Jace and almost tripped.

"Yikes!" Jace's mouth dropped open as he lunged forward. "I got it."

He grabbed the bottle from her hand and placed it on the table. "This stuff goes for over two grand at auction. People would give up their firstborn for a case."

"We can't keep it, Jace. We certainly can't drink it." Odd that Kirk would just happen to carry an expensive bottle of wine with him on a trip to the hardware store. But then Kirk *was* a bit of a braggart. Kat wouldn't be surprised if he carried around a bottle as some sort of success trophy.

"I tried giving it back but he refused to take it. He wanted me to have it since he's making such a killing. Said I could sell it if I want, he wouldn't care either way."

"That was nice of him." Kirk wasn't known for favors, unless he got something in return. "Since when is he so generous? I thought he was broke since his severance pay ran out."

"He said the layoff was a blessing in disguise. Apparently wine investing is quite lucrative. He buys from the wineries, then resells it at auction. He has some kind of connection, I guess. I had no idea people even did that sort of thing." Jace sat down opposite Kat in the matching Adirondack chair. "Kirk says he's a millionaire now. He was at the hardware store looking at materials for a wine cellar in his new house."

"He has a new house?"

"He told me he's gone from broke to millionaire, just like that." Jace snapped his fingers. "Less than a year. Wouldn't it be amazing if we could do the same?"

Kirk was notoriously cheap. That was probably why he was building the wine cellar himself. But it hardly made sense to give bottles away, even to Jace. "There must be some angle, something he's not telling you."

"Doesn't seem to be. He just has good connections. Oh, and he invited us to his housewarming dinner party tonight."

Kat was surprised Kirk would risk money up front to buy the wine, let alone resell it.

"At least that way we could return the wine," she said. She was curious about Kirk's sudden change of fortune. "And investigate this wine investing further."

It sounded too good to be true, and Kat intended to find out more.

# Chapter 2

Kat stood on the deck of Kirk's brand new, eight-thousand square foot house overlooking the Vancouver harbor. She had to admit she was impressed. Gone was the old beer-guzzling, belching Kirk. New-and-improved Kirk sipped wine and wore a tailored shirt and pants that took thirty pounds off his large frame.

Suzan, Kirk's wife, materialized out of the crowd of a hundred or so guests, dressed in a low-cut shimmery cocktail dress. She beamed at Kat.

"You like?" Her wardrobe was as gaudy as ever, only more expensive gaudy, judging by the not-so-discreet designer initials on her purse and watch. It was just like Suzan to parade around her own house with her purse slung over her shoulder. She would have kept the price tags on if she could.

"Of course I like it," Kat replied. "It's absolutely beautiful." The view at least was stunning, with 180-degree views of the harbor and mountains. The house itself was a glass and metal monstrosity that sprouted like a weed from the old-money hillside.

"Kirk has done *very* well, hasn't he? That's why we wanted to have this little celebration. To thank all our friends." She waved her arm towards the expanse of lawn below them.

Kat followed her gesture and surveyed the action below. Small clusters of people mingled amongst the tables, sampling wine and canapés. Yet Kat knew none of them. Where had Kirk's new friends materialized from?

"You have to try the wine, Kat. It's amazing." Suzan sipped from her oversized goblet. "And profitable too."

"I will in a while," Kat said. "I'll stick with water for now." She wanted to stay sober until she was certain Jace had returned the bottle to Kirk, but it was tempting.

"It's a very good investment," Suzan said as she twirled her glass. "You might want to get in on it too."

Kat spotted Jace talking to Kirk on the lawn by the bar. She excused herself and made a beeline for him. Jace waved to her as she crossed the lawn.

"I told you, Kat. Kirk finally found his niche. Isn't this a great little party?" Jace smiled at her.

Their plan had been to return the wine and only stay for dinner. But Jace was already enjoying himself a little too much. He was always more animated with a drink in his hand.

"Wine?" The waiter smiled and poured a generous serving of the same Screaming Eagle Cabernet Sauvignon vintage Kirk had given them.

What the hell. She could at least grab a glass but wait to drink it. She rarely attended expensive parties like this one, so it wouldn't hurt to enjoy it. Kat took the glass and turned to Kirk. "How long have you been doing this?"

"Doing what?" Kirk's blank stare morphed into understanding. "Oh, you mean the wine investing. Isn't it great? I just started six months ago, and I've already made enough to buy this place. In cash. It's a game-changer for me."

"You buy and sell wines at auction?" Kat was dying to taste the two-thousand-dollar wine but didn't want to appear too eager. She would wait until she had finished talking to Kirk. Then she could truly savor it.

"Not exactly." Kirk waved his hand, almost knocking over a tray of drinks. "I buy from the wineries, then I sometimes sell at auction. But most of the time I sell privately, to a select group of wine collectors. I have a waiting list, you know."

"Wow, that's amazing," Kat said. But what about auction commissions? As far as she knew, they charged a pretty hefty commission. How did Kirk make substantial profits so fast? More importantly, how could something so lucrative not have a lot of competition?

"Sure is. I'll have *The Sentinel* begging me for an interview any day now. Bet they're sorry they let me go." Kirk gulped the rest of his wine and placed the empty glass on a passing waiter's tray.

"They must be kicking themselves over it," Kat said.

Suzan rematerialized at Kat's side and held out her wrist. A gaudy diamond and emerald studded bracelet glinted under the lights illuminating the yard. "Like it? Kirk just bought it for me." Suzan giggled. "For believing in him."

"Gorgeous." Kat swished the red wine in her glass, salivating at the thought of tasting it. She had researched Screaming Eagle a little before the party. It was highly-rated, at 98 points out of a hundred. She had never tried a wine rated greater than 94 points. Yet all her 90+ point wine tasting experiences had always been absolutely delicious. The law of diminishing returns must factor in. How could it taste hundreds or thousands of dollars better? Beer-guzzling Kirk couldn't tell a Zinfandel from a Cabernet six months ago. How could he suddenly have a knack for wine tasting, let alone investing? Kat was suspicious of his motives.

She also couldn't wait any longer to taste the wine. She took a small sip of the Cabernet Sauvignon and swished it in her mouth for a few seconds before swallowing. She frowned. It was nothing like what she had expected.

She wasn't exactly an expert but she appreciated a good quality Cabernet Sauvignon. It was also one of her favorite wines. While this one was full bodied, with the usual notes of black cherry, licorice, and pepper, it also had an unpleasant acidic flavor. Her taste buds weren't as sophisticated as a sommelier but this one tasted a little off.

That might be a good thing since she couldn't afford it anyway. It tasted so bad she couldn't even stomach finishing it. But this wine was supposedly worth thousands. How could she just leave it?

Suzan had drifted off to mingle with the other guests, and Jace and Kirk were engrossed in a discussion on expanding his wine business. Kat deposited her half-full glass on a table, deciding it wasn't worth finishing, no matter what the cost. She wondered when dinner would be served as she went in search of a bathroom.

The house interior was even more glitzy and spectacular than the exterior. She walked through the marble and stainless steel kitchen towards the front of the house. The living room was packed, which explained why all three restrooms were occupied. After waiting several minutes, she decided to head downstairs. There were bound to be multiple bathrooms on every floor of a house this size.

A spiral staircase descended to what could only be described as a large open gallery. Oil paintings lined the wall, broken up by a handful of doors, all closed except for one door left slightly ajar. She headed toward the door, assuming it to be the restroom.

She opened the door to find an office instead, strewn with boxes and papers. She was about to close the door when something caught her eye.

A long table ran the length of the room. Underneath were dozens of wine bottles, all empty and unlabelled. Even more concerning was what was on top of the table.

Labels.

Screaming Eagle labels, the exact same vintage of Cabernet Sauvignon Kirk was selling.

Her heart thumped in her chest as she realized it was all fake. No wonder Kirk had been so generous with the wine. He had probably hosted the party to drum up interest and find more buyers. A simple fraud, but a very lucrative one.

She turned back to the door and closed it behind her. There were hundreds of people in the house, so there was a good chance another guest might come looking for a restroom and stumble upon the room just as she had.

All the partygoers were oblivious to the fact that they were drinking cheap wine disguised as something much more expensive. She wondered how many had already placed orders with Kirk.

She surveyed the room and walked over to the floor-to-ceiling wine cases stacked against the far wall. At twelve bottles a case, it was a significant amount. She bent down to pull a bottle out of an open case at her feet. Sure enough, it was identical to the bottle Kirk had given them.

She did a quick tally in her head. Assuming Kirk sold these for a few thousand per bottle, the room held over a million dollars' worth of inventory.

Unbelievable.

Jace wouldn't believe it either, unless she provided evidence. She fumbled in her purse for her cell phone, finally locating it.

She snapped photographs of the table, labels, and the bottles with her cell phone. The supplies in the room explained the source of Kirk's sudden wealth beyond a doubt. Kirk was relabeling cheap wine and passing it off as more expensive vintages. No wonder he had profited so quickly.

It also explained why her wine had tasted so bad. She bent down and opened a case of wine. It was Cabernet Sauvignon all right, but a different brand, one she had seen selling for under ten dollars a bottle. No wonder Kirk was living large. He could re-label and sell these fake bottles at auction and count on hardly anyone sampling them. They were considered investments, after all.

Screaming Eagle was so popular that collectors rarely resold their treasures. The tiny Napa Valley winery only produced a few hundred cases a year at best, and they were immediately snapped up by collectors. She had even heard of people who photographed their wine in family photos each year, the bottle present each year as their babies grew into adults. One fan had positioned the bottle in his baby's bassinet, with the same bottle reappearing years later in his son's graduation photograph.

Kirk had picked the perfect wine to knock off, provided he didn't saturate the market with too many bottles at once. That would arouse suspicion.

But it also raised another point. Kirk needed to sell wine on a much larger scale to make millions. That meant he had to be counterfeiting and selling other wines too. Why else would he serve thousand dollar wines to his many guests tonight? If it were truly rare, he wouldn't pour so much of it. And he certainly wouldn't have given a bottle to Jace.

Maybe photos weren't enough proof. She grabbed a label from the table just as she heard footsteps. She quickly exited and closed the door behind her. It closed with a loud click. She realized now why the door had been slightly ajar when she had found it. It had an automatic lock and she had just locked it.

"Why are you down here?" Kirk stood at the foot of the stairs, his large frame blocking her escape.

She had been caught, red-handed, with the label in her hand.

# Chapter 3

"Are you lost or something?" Kirk crossed his arms, his gregarious mood of just moments ago replaced with an accusatory tone.

Had he seen her emerge from the room? She didn't think so, but she had been in the vicinity of the office door when he spotted her. Why else the sudden mood change?

Kat remembered the label in her hand and stuffed it into her pocket. "Uh, no. Just needed the restroom."

His gaze drifted down to her hand. Had he seen the label?

"Down here's my man cave. What's wrong with the bathroom upstairs? Not private enough for you?"

Kat took a deep breath and laughed. "You're just too popular. With so many guests, I mean. I guess the bathrooms fill up fast."

His shoulders relaxed slightly, but he didn't budge from the staircase.

All she could think of was how to get up those stairs as fast as possible. But Kirk was immobile. "I should really find Jace. We've got a lot of painting to do tomorrow."

Kirk nodded, but the closed door caught his eye. "That's funny. I'm sure I left that door partially open."

Kat shrugged as she walked toward Kirk and the staircase. "Maybe Suzan was in there."

Kirk shook his head. "Nope. Suzan's not allowed down here. No one is, unless I invite them."

Kat tried to lighten things up. "Now you've got my curiosity going. I'd love to see your secret man cave. But not right now. I've got to get back to Jace."

She tried to squeeze by him on the stairwell, but he blocked her. He clamped his hand around her forearm. Pain shot down through her fingertips. Was he intentionally trying to hurt her?

"I'll help you." Kirk squeezed even tighter.

"Ouch!" she shrieked. "You really don't know your own strength, big guy." Was Kirk threatening her? Maybe he had seen her after all.

Kirk froze as a thirty-something couple descended the stairs. They stopped abruptly when they spotted Kat and Kirk on the stairs.

"Is this a bathroom line-up too?" The woman stared at Kirk until he released his grip.

Kat yanked her arm away.

"Nope," Kirk said. "You mind? We're having a private conversation." He winked at the man.

"Got it," the man said, then turned to his companion. "Let's go, honey." The couple headed back up the stairs.

Kat brushed past Kirk and followed behind the couple, thankful for the opportunity to put as much distance between her and Kirk as possible.

She fingered the label in her pocket. It was like the Emperor's new clothes. Everyone wanted to believe, even in a terrible tasting wine. They would throw good money at it too, as long as it held the illusion of riches.

## Chapter 4

Kirk's heavy footsteps echoed behind her on the stairs. Just as she feared. He was coming after her. He figured she'd been at least near the room. She was still unsure whether he'd seen her emerge from the room downstairs. If he had, he wouldn't let her go that easy.

She needed to find Jace before Kirk did, so she could explain what she had found. Jace would know what to do to defuse Kirk. One thing she did know: she wasn't ready to confront Kirk on her own.

She glanced behind her only to meet Kirk's murderous glare.

He knew.

She spotted Jace engrossed in conversation with an older couple at the far end of the kitchen. He gestured wildly, then teetered on one leg before regaining his balance.

Great. Jace was drunk. Too much wine before dinner.

"Excuse us." Kat inserted herself in the circle. "Jace, I need to talk to you in private."

Jace looked over her shoulder. "Hey buddy, great party." He waved to Kirk, almost spilling his glass on the slender, gray-haired woman.

Kat turned to see a flushed and sweating Kirk. He looked furious.

"Now, Jace," Kat said under her breath. She steered him outside, away from Kirk and the others.

"You want to leave already?" Jace's words slurred together. "The party's just getting started."

"There's a problem. You need to sober up." She glanced back and was relieved to see Kirk now chatting with the couple. The man stood in front of Kirk, unintentionally blocking Kirk's exit. Kirk couldn't come after her without making a scene.

"Is Kirk mad at me? For drinking too much? He didn't look too happy."

"No, he's mad at someone else, not you." How much should she tell Jace in this condition? Was he too drunk to keep quiet about it?

"Sorry, Kat. I got a bit carried away."

"Let's walk." She steered Jace down the back stairs onto the expansive lawn. The stroll in the cool night air would be good, both to sober up Jace and to keep Kirk away for a few minutes. She steered Jace toward the far end of the property. Out of sight, out of mind for Kirk. She hoped so, anyway.

She had no choice but to tell Jace now, drunk or not.

"I can't believe it," Jace said. "On the other hand, it does explain a lot. Like his sudden generosity."

Kat nodded. "Too good to be true." She guided Jace to a bench at the edge of the lawn and sat down. They were just beyond the reach of the lighting set up on the lawn. Hopefully Kirk would only see an unrecognizable couple in the shadows and leave them alone.

She debated calling the police, but exactly what crime was she reporting? Fraud? If that was the case, she needed to secure proof of the fraud before Kirk could get rid of it.

She pulled the label from her pocket and showed it to Jace.

"You saved a label as a souvenir?"

"Not exactly, Jace. This label has never even been on a bottle of wine." She handed it to him. "It's brand new."

"How can that be?"

"It can't. Not if the wine is legit." Kat grabbed her cell phone from her purse and typed *Screaming Eagle* into the Internet browser. The wine was even rarer than she imagined. "Just as I thought."

"What?"

She showed him the search results. "Screaming Eagle only makes 600-700 cases a year. And there's a waiting list. People wait years for the chance to buy a single bottle. What are the odds of Kirk having hundreds of cases? Or having enough to serve it to hundreds of guests?" She briefed Jace on her discovery in Kirk's basement.

There was another problem. Barring assault or murder, the police were unlikely to arrive on a Saturday night, sirens blazing, for a suspected fraud, no matter how large. She couldn't expect outside help any time soon. That unfortunately gave Kirk plenty of time to hide the evidence and deny everything.

But she could use the number of guests to her advantage. Kirk had to keep up appearances, especially if his guests were also his customers. If she could plant the seed of doubt in their minds, her plan just might work.

Jace shone a penlight on the label. "How do you spell Sauvignon?"

Kat glanced at the label. "S-A-V—I don't believe it," she said. "There's a spelling error on the label!"

"Just like at *The Sentinel*," Jace said. "Kirk was never very good at spelling. Or even spell-checking his work, for that matter."

Indisputable proof. If she was right, that proof existed elsewhere at the party, not just on the label in her hand. Now she had a way to deal with Kirk. She stood up. "C'mon Jace, let's head back to the house."

# Chapter 5

Kat searched the party for Suzan, hoping to find her before Kirk. It didn't take long. Suzan stood at the large floor-to-ceiling fireplace, talking with a half dozen women who looked like they'd just stepped off the set of a *Real Housewives* reality show.

"Suzan!" Kat grabbed her elbow, stopping the conversation midstream.

"Kat?"

"I have a favor to ask. Can you get everybody's attention? Jace and I would like to propose a toast. To Kirk." She smiled at Jace, a few feet behind her. He returned her smile, not entirely sure what she was up to.

Kat scanned the room, looking for Kirk.

Suzan and her friends tapped their manicured nails on their wineglasses. Within a few moments they had the guests' rapt attention.

Kat stepped forward. "I have a special announcement to make." She glanced over at Suzan, who beamed from ear to ear. "We'll be giving away a case of *Screaming Eagle* to the first person that provides the correct answer to the question I'm about to ask."

"That's not a toast," Suzan whispered. "And we're *not* giving away a case of wine."

Suzan must be unaware of Kirk's scheme if she thought the case was worth tens of thousands. According to Kat's calculation, the case of counterfeit wine was worth a little over a hundred dollars at best.

"I'll explain in a minute," Kat said to her.

The room buzzed as the crowd moved closer. Then expectant silence as everyone put down their glasses and plates and waited for the question.

"What's all this about?" Kirk emerged from the back of the room.

"Bravo, Kirk!" A man yelled.

Kirk gave a weak wave. He marched up to Kat. "What the hell are you doing?"

Kat smiled sweetly. "You'll see." She looked at her audience. "Is everyone ready?"

A few murmurs told her they were.

"All right. There's actually two questions to answer. The first one is easy. Who can tell me the name and year of the featured wine tonight?"

Two women answered almost in unison. "Screaming Eagle Cabernet Sauvignon."

"1997," the second woman added. She was middle-aged and reed-thin. Her boney arms poked out of her red sheath dress like tree branches.

Kat pointed to the first woman, a slightly overweight blonde with too much makeup. "That's right, and you were first. Now for the money question. For a case of wine, spell *Sauvignon.*"

"Sure. *S-A-U-V-I-G-N-O-N.*"

"Correct!" Kat smiled at her. "You've just won yourself a case of very fine wine. Congratulations."

"Wait a minute," Kirk rushed forward and pushed Kat aside. "This ain't no spelling bee, and I'm not giving away a prize. Besides, you spelled it wrong."

"How is it spelled, Kirk?" Jace asked.

"*S-A-V-I-G-N-O-N.*" He held up a bottle. "See?"

A few people inched closer, squinting to read the bottle.

"See that?" Kat pointed to the bottle as she addressed the crowd. "A spelling mistake on a very expensive bottle of wine? What are the odds of that?"

Kirk grabbed Suzan's wrist. "Shut her up."

"Sweetheart, let go." Suzan yanked her wrist from Kirk's grasp as she realized all eyes were on them. "What's going on here?"

It was hard to believe Suzan was oblivious to the counterfeit equipment downstairs, but it was possible.

The woman who won the wine looked crestfallen. "I did win, right?"

Kat nodded. "You won a case of wine, all right. But it's not the wine you think it is." Kat held up her phone. "This is what I found downstairs in Kirk's so-called man cave. An elaborate wine counterfeiting operation."

Jace handed the bottle to Suzan, who deposited it on the fireplace mantle. Her mouth dropped open and she burst into tears. "Kirk, what's happening here?"

Silence.

"Kirk, what have you done?" Suzan's face was smeared with mascara. "Tell me."

Kirk scowled and lunged for Kat's phone.

The crowd gasped in unison.

Kat pulled her hand out of his reach just as Jace stepped between them. "No need, Kirk. I've already emailed the pictures to *The Sentinel.* They'll be banging on your door for an interview. You've finally gotten a headline-grabbing story that no one will ever forget."

"You're crazy." Kirk glared at Kat.

"No, but I'm a lot luckier than you right now." She held up the bottle. "This bottle doesn't merit the label that's on it."

She turned to Jace and winked. "You, on the other hand, owe me." She had practically written Jace's *Sentinel* story for him. Saved him hours of work, with pictures to boot.

Jace's eyes crinkled in amusement. "A second coat of paint on the veranda?"

"Good for a start." Hour for hour, attending the party had been totally worth a bit of fraud detective work on her day off.

And seeing Kirk caught and justice served, all before dinner? Priceless.

# Blue Moon

# Chapter 1

Katerina Carter peered out her living room window to next door neighbor Fiona Jackson's yard. She hid behind the curtain, careful not to blow her cover.

Roses and hydrangeas basked in the late afternoon sun. Blooms blanketed the front yard in an explosion of color. Even Fiona's grass grew greener than Kat's weed wasteland. But it wasn't Fiona's garden that concerned Kat. She stood transfixed by the stranger toiling in her neighbor's yard.

The man looked straight out of an FBI most-wanted poster, his dark shadow juxtaposed against the garden's brightness and light. His rolled-up sleeves exposed tattooed, stringy arms more suited to pushing drugs instead of a lawn mower. Fiona barely survived on a meager pension and certainly couldn't afford a handyman. Who was this guy and how did Fiona know him?

He abandoned the push mower in favor of a shovel and headed straight for Fiona's roses. Kat's mouth dropped open in horror as he stomped on the shovel and began digging up Fiona's showpiece roses.

No one ever set foot in Fiona's garden except the Gardens in Bloom contest judges. Fiona had won the city-wide contest for three years' running, and her whole garden strategy revolved around keeping her place as number one. Absolutely no one took a shovel to her prized plants. Fiona had mulched, weeded, and pruned her rare roses into submission months in advance of next week's judging. Yet the rough-looking man next door was digging them up.

"Spying on Fiona?" Jace halted mid-stride on his way to the front door.

Kat was focused so intently on the man next door that she almost jumped out of her skin. She banged her head against the window frame. "Ouch!"

Jace grinned and his blue eyes crinkled in amusement. "You okay?"

Kat nodded, embarrassed at being caught spying.

Jace wore a shirt, tie, and dress pants instead of his usual t-shirt and denim. Kat puzzled for a moment until she remembered their dinner plans. One year since they moved into their money-sucking Victorian house. One year, hundreds of hours in sweat equity, and tens of thousands in renovation expenses called for a celebration of their accomplishments to date.

"Must be a thrill-a-minute." Jace raised his brows.

Kat motioned Jace to the window. "See that guy outside? I think he's staying with Fiona." This was the third time she'd seen him since yesterday.

Kat encountered plenty of predators as a forensic accountant and fraud investigator. Far too often they targeted the elderly. The wiry man had a dangerous street look about him and certainly fit the profile. That he had materialized out of nowhere made him all the more suspicious.

"I'm worried about her, Jace. He can't possibly be up to any good." She felt protective of her elderly neighbor and this guy's appearance raised all kinds of red flags. "Why is he digging up Fiona's roses?"

Jace joined her at the window. "He does have that criminal look about him."

"So you see it too!" Or was Jace making fun of her?

"Not really," he admitted. "You're jumping to conclusions, as usual. If he's staying with her, he's probably a relative or friend. What's the big deal?"

"She doesn't have any relatives, remember?" Fiona had no siblings or children. Her husband had died about thirty years ago. Fiona didn't socialize much, either.

"I forgot about that. Maybe he's related to her late husband?"

"I doubt it." From what little she'd learned from Fiona, her late husband had no living relatives. He only had one brother, also deceased.

Suddenly everything made sense. "Fiona volunteers at the prison. I'll bet this guy was recently paroled." Fiona ran Weeds to Wonders, the prison's weekly gardening program.

"Paroled from prison? Or from her gardening program?" Jace raised his brows.

Fiona was a tough task master. She liked everything just so.

"Both," Kat laughed. Fiona never let anyone near her flowerbeds—not even to pull a weed. Something was very wrong with the scene outside.

"There's Fiona now." Their frail diminutive neighbor knelt in front of her flower bed and scooped a handful of loose dirt. "Why not go to the source? Ask her how she knows him?"

"I can't just come right out and ask." Not that she had to. She could spot a criminal a mile away. She just wished he wasn't next door. "Especially with him standing right there."

Jace shrugged as he walked towards the kitchen. "You'll think of something, you always do. Just don't jump to conclusions and assume something criminal is going on."

Business was finally booming at Carter & Associates, Kat's forensic accounting and fraud investigation business. She had wrapped up her latest case and today was her first day off in months. Jace had just submitted his latest writing assignment to *The Sentinel*, where he freelanced as an investigative journalist.

They had slept in and lazed around the house all day, both free from work for a few days. Tonight they planned to treat themselves to dinner at a swanky Michelin-starred restaurant downtown they had eyed for months.

Kat checked her watch. Plenty of time, although she wished she had noticed the stranger earlier. "This is different. It's my neighborly duty to find out why a strange man is tearing up Fiona's garden. She's a perfect target—a senior who lives alone."

Jace rolled his eyes. "You promised no work today, remember."

"I'll have a quick chat with Fiona and then we'll go." She turned away from the window just as something caught the corner of her eye. "Oh no!"

"Now what?" Jace paused in the doorway.

"He's chopping Fiona's roses!" The man wielded the pruners like a murder weapon, snipping relentlessly.

Jace shrugged. "So?"

"He's chopping them into pieces, Jace! He's destroying them right in front of Fiona." Digging up the fragrant tea roses right before the contest was shocking enough. Transplanting them was one thing, but to hack them into pieces?

Would Fiona actually destroy the roses just so no one else could have them? Maybe she would. Gardens in Bloom was known for its cutthroat competitors.

"What's wrong with pruning Fiona's roses?" Jace frowned. "Nice of him to help her."

"It's hardly pruning, Jace. More like a massacre. Besides, those are Fiona's Blue Moon roses. They've won her the Gardens in Bloom contest three years' running. She's gone crazy." Kat stared out the window, aghast at the carnage. All that remained were bare root balls and broken limbs, heaped on the sidewalk like a botanical funeral pyre.

"She's probably tired of them. She's allowed to change her mind."

"She raved about the contest just last week," Kat said. "She won't win without the roses or something equally spectacular. Besides, she can't afford to replace them on her small pension. She mentioned being a bit behind on her bills." Gardeners usually cherished life, nurturing every bud and bloom. Something was terribly wrong with the disturbing scene outside.

"That's probably where the new guy comes in. She's taken in a boarder to earn extra cash each month. He's also helping her with some yard work. No big deal." Jace yanked the curtain open.

Kat groaned and ducked out of view. "Don't make us so obvious."

It was too late. The man caught the movement and tilted his head in their direction. He squinted, the sun in his eyes.

Kat sighed. Since they had been discovered she might as well ask a few questions. "I'm going outside."

Jace sighed. "Don't stay out too long. I reserved a waterfront table. The restaurant won't hold it if we're late."

"I won't, I promise." Kat brushed past him and headed to the hall closet. She pulled on rubber boots and grabbed her basket of garden tools from the closet, thinking that a little weeding would serve as a good pretext to conversation. A few minutes left plenty of time to dress and change for dinner. "I intend to find out exactly how they know each other."

She stepped outside. The mystery man was down on his hands and knees, weeding between cracks in the front walkway. Fiona, clad in her gardening garb, directed him. The man glanced at Kat, then quickly averted his gaze.

Avoiding eye contact to make himself forgettable. Kat noted the crudely drawn dragon tattoo on his left forearm. From prison, no doubt.

She waved to Fiona and headed to her small garden strip that bordered Fiona's yard. She dropped her garden tools on the grass and selected a trowel. Fiona's flowerbeds were in full bloom, yet hers were overgrown, even the weeds parched and withered. No point in beating around the bush, so to speak. "I thought your roses were off limits?"

"Time for something new," Fiona turned to Kat, brandishing her pruners. "Maybe some yellow roses this time."

"Didn't you leave replanting a bit late for the Gardens in Bloom contest?" Fiona's garden was timed to bloom during contest judging week and her rare Blue Moon roses were the centerpiece. Yellow roses were so…ordinary. Why had Fiona deliberately sabotaged her contest entry?

"I didn't enter this year.' Her eyes widened as she checked her watch. "Sorry, Kat. I've got to go, I'm late for my appointment." She turned and trudged up her front stairs. She slammed the door behind her without a backward glance.

*Late for what? Fiona hadn't missed a single Gardens in Bloom contest in over twenty-five years.*

Kat turned to the man. If Fiona wouldn't talk, maybe he would. "I see Fiona's got you working."

"Yeah." He wiped his hands on the front of his torn jeans. "Least I can do."

"Huh?" Kat glanced up at Fiona's house to see the curtains drawn. She usually opened them at the crack of dawn.

"For letting me stay here. No one else willin' to take a chance on me." He wiped his brow. "Since I got out."

So it was true. He was actually *living* in Fiona's house. While she was kind to lend a helping hand, inviting him to move in was downright crazy. As crazy as digging up her prize-winning roses. "Out from where?" Kat dropped her trowel. Conversing with a man who avoided eye contact was unnerving.

"Prison."

Her worst fears confirmed. Rooming with an ex-con stretched the boundaries of Fiona's prison volunteer work. Teaching a gardening class was one thing, but room and board? Had Fiona lost her mind? "Why did Fiona go inside? She seemed in a hurry."

"Dunno. She's always busy with something." He shrugged. "She's probably getting her stuff ready for the insurance people later on."

"Insurance? What kind of insurance?" Life insurance? Fiona had to be at least seventy, an unusual age to buy insurance. The premiums would impact her very limited budget.

"I don't know. Maybe you should ask her direct."

She had plenty to ask Fiona if her neighbor wasn't so obviously avoiding her. Like why she had chosen an ex-con, possibly a thief or a murderer, as a roommate. She needed to talk to Fiona before she dug herself six feet under. It was nice to help people, but she needed some boundaries.

She yanked on a dandelion and almost lost her balance as the stem broke off in her hand. If Fiona wouldn't talk to her, she would go direct to the source of her worries. She stood and held out her hand. "I'm Kat. Katerina Carter."

The man stood also and walked towards her. He took her hand. "Declan Burke."

Enough to start a background check. He looked like an ex-con but his quiet and unassuming demeanor contrasted with what she had expected from a hardened criminal. Of course the most successful criminals used charm and distraction on their victims, so it didn't surprise her. Deception was particularly effective with seniors since they tended to be more trusting. Declan had been in prison for a reason. She wanted to ask what that reason was but didn't want to push her luck.

Declan's shirt was worn and outdated, like something from the eighties. She doubted the prison or even local thrift stores would carry clothing that old. Had Fiona also given Declan some of her late husband's clothing?

Declan read her mind. "Fiona got me these. In case you're wondering, I did twenty years, so I had nothin' but the clothes on my back. She took care of that for me."

He looked directly at her now, his uncertainty moments ago vanished with Fiona's departure. Fiona, tiny as she was, sometimes had that effect on people. Apparently Declan was no exception.

"That's very kind of her." While Declan seemed nice she took nothing he said at face value. A twenty-year sentence meant serious crime, murder, or something violent. Fiona was crazy to place herself in such a vulnerable position.

Declan shifted on his feet. "I can tell you're suspicious of me."

Kat shrugged, not knowing what to say. Declan was right.

"Don't blame you, really. But that's my old life. I'm on the straight and narrow now, thanks to Miss Fiona." He turned to the lawn mower beside him and grabbed the handle. "Speaking of which, I got to go now."

Declan pushed the lawn mower into Fiona's garage and closed the door behind him, abandoning the pile of dug up roses. Kat packed up her gardening tools and headed inside. She stole a backwards glance at the wilted heap of Fiona's Blue Moon roses. She had some dirt of her own to dig up.

# Chapter 2

By the time Kat showered and dressed, it was dusk. She resumed her stakeout at the living room window for one last look before heading out to the restaurant. Nothing had changed. The mutilated roses with their wilted blue blooms sat in a lifeless heap on the sidewalk. Abandoned. No sign of Fiona and Declan. Kat had hoped they would return to finish the job.

"Ready for dinner?" Jace peered in from the hallway. "Fiona isn't one of your fraud cases, remember?"

"This guy's trouble, Jace. I can't just abandon her." She had lost her appetite, knowing Fiona was about to be robbed blind by a criminal opportunist. Fiona's bizarre behavior was very concerning. "What if something happens while we're gone?"

"Nothing's going to happen." Jace held her shawl in his hands. "Let's go. There's nothing to see outside, and Fiona's problems—if that's what they are—will still be there tomorrow."

Maybe Jace was right. No one had come or gone during her surveillance. She had hoped to catch Fiona alone to speak to her, especially about the insurance business Declan had mentioned. What if she signed something she shouldn't? Then she could just tear it up, she reasoned. Tomorrow wouldn't be too late for that.

She crossed the floor and kissed him. "Five more minutes?" That gave them thirty minutes to reach the restaurant. Tight, but doable.

"Five minutes max. You're obsessed." Jace shook his head and retreated into the kitchen. His departure was followed by banging pots and pans and the fridge door slamming.

Kat caught sudden movement from the corner of her eye and slid across the floor in her socks. She stood at her vantage point behind the curtains. Declan staggered past their house, headed towards downtown. He was drunk or wasted on drugs. She didn't know which.

Fiona didn't drink or tolerate drunkenness. Had she finally come to her senses and kicked him out? Or had Declan simply left on an errand? There was just one way to find out.

She yelled towards the kitchen. "Okay, I'm ready. Let's go!"

No answer.

"Jace, let's go!" She ran to the hall. She hurriedly stepped into her shoes and grabbed her shawl. Was Declan's drunkenness to celebrate a new insurance policy on Fiona's life?

"A minute ago you wanted to wait." Jace bent to slip on his shoes. "I can't figure you out sometimes."

"Hurry." Kat already had the door ajar. "We'll be late."

"You change your mind just like that." Jace snapped his fingers. "Would be nice to have some advance warning."

But Kat was already down the front stairs, relieved to see Declan's shadowy figure a block and a half ahead. Far enough to avoid detection, yet close enough to track his movements.

Declan lurched from one side of the sidewalk to another, clearly inebriated. Getting wasted was sometimes a priority for newly released ex-cons. Was it that straightforward, or something more sinister going on? Whatever the reason, she intended to find out.

Jace headed for the driveway.

"It's a beautiful night," Kat said. "Let's walk to the bus instead of driving. Then we won't have to search for parking."

Jace shrugged. "Sure, if you want."

Kat settled into a brisk walk, wanting to get a closer look at Declan. Had he already taken out the life insurance on Fiona? If so, for how much?

"Hey, isn't that the guy from next door ahead of us?" Jace quickened his stride.

"Shhh, Jace. He'll hear us." Kat suddenly realized they had closed the gap to less than a block.

"Now I get it. You wanted to walk so we could follow him." Jace threw up his arms. "We are *not* spying on him, Kat. Can't we just enjoy ourselves for a few hours? Just for one night?"

"It's not like I planned it, Jace. But since he's here, we might as well see where he's headed. I can't just sit back and let Fiona endanger herself. She's taking a lot of risks, so the more I know the better. Especially now with the insurance. It's like a price on her head."

"What insurance?"

She repeated Declan's earlier comments about the insurance policy. "Fiona thinks she's helping an ex-con get back on his feet, but she's put herself in danger. She's a perfect target, with no relatives, no one that would question any insurance payout.

At best, he waits for her to die. At worst, he speeds up the process."

"Now you're really jumping to conclusions."

"I hope I'm wrong, but what if I'm right? Why else would Fiona get insurance? She has no family to provide for, so what's the purpose? It doesn't help her when she's dead. So why do it?"

"Whatever arrangement they've made is between the two of them. After all those years in prison, I'll bet no one will hire him. Fiona knows Declan will outlive her, so maybe it's her way of helping him. When she does pass away, the insurance payout provides him with a bit of a nest egg. Nothing wrong with that."

"Only that it makes her worth more dead than alive."

"You're being overly dramatic."

"I don't think so, and we're the only ones that can stop him." Was Fiona's appointment the last step in her insurance coverage? If the insurance was already in place, Declan could bump her off at any moment.

"I should have known you'd have an ulterior motive," Jace said. "But we really are headed to the restaurant, right? Because I'm starving."

Kat nodded. "Right after a little detour to see where Declan's headed." Could he take out an insurance policy on Fiona without her knowledge? Unlikely without a medical exam, since Fiona was at least seventy. But that only meant she had agreed to the insurance policy, not realizing the consequences.

"Can you go just ahead without me and hold the table? I'll be ten minutes behind you."

"Really, Kat?" Jace shook his head. "I'm not eating by myself."

"I promise I'll be right there. Fifteen minutes at the most." She made a mental note to talk to Fiona first thing tomorrow morning.

"All right. I'll walk with you as far as the bus stop," Jace sighed. "But make it quick. A romantic dinner alone is not what I had in mind."

# Chapter 3

Kat waved to Jace as he disappeared around the corner to the bus stop a half block away. He didn't wave back. She couldn't blame him for being a bit peeved at her. Stalking another man instead of paying attention to her own wasn't fair. But she felt compelled to follow Declan, given Fiona's precarious situation. Declan made a sharp right turn into the alley two hundred feet ahead. She quickened her pace, worried he could disappear into a back door. She rounded the corner, aware that he might easily spot her, even in his drunken state. She breathed a sigh of relief when she saw him in the center of the narrow alley. She slowed to widen the gap, worried he might hear her footsteps.

The deserted alley made her uneasy. Long shadows fell across the narrow passage. The eeriness was heightened with the approaching darkness and the fact that most of the neighborhood stores had either closed shop for the night or had moved downtown. The alley had been built in the early 1900's, long before the era of dumpsters and big trucks. Buildings jutted out to the property line, leaving no space for anything larger than a panel van.

Kat couldn't fathom where Declan was headed since the alley wasn't a shortcut to anywhere. His silhouette was momentarily visible as he passed under a lone light bulb that glowed over a back entrance halfway down the lane. Twenty feet past the light he disappeared into darkness once again.

The alley suddenly flooded with light as an engine revved behind her.

Kat jumped.

Tires squealed and headlights flashed on the ground ahead.

"Watch out!" Jace yelled from somewhere behind her.

Kat dove to the side of the alley and flattened herself against a brick wall. There was nowhere to escape. Air swooshed against her bare leg with enough force to lift her skirt hem. So close she thought the car had hit her.

Except it hadn't. The car had swerved at the last moment and narrowly missed her. Her hands shook when she realized how close it had been.

Jace must have followed her. Had the car hit him? She whirled around as his shadowy figure ran towards her.

Tires skidded before screeching to a hard stop ahead of her. The engine stalled momentarily, then whirred to life again as the car lurched forward.

Kat turned just in time to see Declan standing directly in the path of the oncoming car. He flew over the hood of the black sedan as the headlights caught him airborne in a split-second freeze-frame. Then he crashed down and shattered the windshield before bouncing off like a discarded rodeo rider.

The brake lights lit up and the car accelerated, then clunked to a stop as it hit Declan's body a second time.

Kat shuddered.

The sedan reversed and lurched forward a final time before driving right over Declan's body. There was no avoiding him in the narrow alley.

Kat's mouth dropped open. Her scream caught in her throat. "Declan!"

Ahead of her, silence. No sounds from Declan, immobile on the asphalt.

Kat pulled out her cell phone as she punched in 9-1-1. She breathed a sigh of relief as Jace ran past her. He must have had a change of heart and followed her into the alley. Thank goodness he was unhurt.

The engine revved as the sedan screeched around the corner. The alley went dark and the engine whine faded into the distance.

Kat raced towards Declan's crumpled body as she provided details to the 9-1-1 operator. Traffic through the alley was a rarity, even in broad daylight. The lane was a pedestrian shortcut, but vehicles usually avoided it due to the potholes and narrow clearance.

*Hit and run. What did she see?*

All she recalled were brake lights, skidding tires, and a black sedan. The accident had happened much too quickly to see anything other than the car's distinctive taillights. They were large and diamond-shaped, like a very old vintage car. Uncommon for sure. If she could describe them there was a chance of identifying the make and model.

Jace kneeled beside Declan and checked for a pulse. As Kat neared Declan's motionless body she noticed blood beneath his head on the asphalt and his leg contorted at an impossible angle.

He was still, except for a slight rise and fall of his chest. At least he was breathing.

The ambulance arrived within minutes, its flashing lights illuminating the dark alley. Two paramedics jumped out of the vehicle, a man and a woman. They shifted Declan onto a stretcher and slid him into the back of the ambulance. The female paramedic hopped into the back with him.

"Looks like a serious head injury. His leg's broken for sure." The male paramedic turned to Kat. "You know him?"

"Uh, yes." She gave the man Declan's name and address just as the female paramedic emerged from the ambulance.

Kat's hands trembled as she punched in Fiona's number on her cell phone. She suddenly realized that, if not for Jace's warning yell, she would have suffered the same fate as Declan.

"You riding with him?" The female paramedic held the rear of the ambulance open and waited for Jace.

Kat motioned to Jace. "Go with Declan. I'll go home and track down Fiona. She's not answering the phone." While they barely knew Declan, Jace could at least provide what little information they knew. And reassure Declan, if he ever regained consciousness.

She wished she had a better view of the car and driver. Without more information, it would be impossible to track. The vehicle was an older make and she wasn't exactly an automotive expert. There were probably hundreds or even thousands of similar black sedans around. Despite her misgivings about Declan, no one deserved to be struck down in a hit and run. Declan's hand up from Fiona had been quickly erased by a tragic accident.

Now that she thought of it, the car had almost come to a stop before swerving away from her. Yet the car had reversed only to hit Declan again. That meant the driver had control of the car. Was Declan's accident a targeted hit?

Kat's calls to Fiona went straight to voicemail. She toyed with leaving a message but what could she say? It seemed inappropriate to alarm her and only the hospital could provide details on his condition. She was in no position to speculate, but judging from the paramedics' reaction, Declan's prognosis appeared grim.

She waved goodbye as Jace stepped into the ambulance. Declan's first taste of freedom in decades had come to an abrupt and catastrophic end. Fiona would take the news very hard regardless of the extent of her feelings for Declan. Fiona measured her own self-worth through her achievements. Declan's successful rehabilitation was another one of her projects, just like her successful Weeds to Wonders prison gardening program or repeat wins of the Gardens in Bloom contest. That was how Fiona defined herself.

Was Fiona aware of Declan's drunken state or had he slipped out without her knowledge? Kat had so many unanswered questions as she turned to retrace her steps back home. The only thing she was certain of was that bad news was best delivered in person.

# Chapter 4

Kat half walked, half ran home after several unsuccessful attempts to reach Fiona. Fiona's landline went straight to voicemail and she didn't have a cell phone. While she needed to inform Fiona in person, it was best not to arrive unannounced. Face to face meant she could immediately drive Fiona to the hospital since her neighbor didn't drive.

The trees cast long shadows across the road ahead and she tripped on the uneven sidewalk, almost landing face first on the pavement. She regained her footing and trembled, still unnerved by the violent collision. She glanced backwards, half expecting the mystery driver to return and strike her down. After all, she had witnessed the accident. At the very least it was a hit-and-run or, If Declan didn't survive, vehicular homicide and a senseless and tragic death.

The driver had specifically targeted Declan, expecting to find him alone in the dark lane. Images of Declan hitting the windshield replayed continuously in her head. It was an endless loop of a disturbing movie she didn't want to watch.

Who would target Declan, and why? Imprisonment dramatically limited the number of people Declan interacted with. It also narrowed the field of who would want to harm him. Determining the motive could lead her to the suspect.

The motive puzzled her. Declan had no assets to speak of. Was the hit meant to silence Declan? If so, what secrets did he hold? She rounded the corner onto her street and found Fiona trudging up the sidewalk in the opposite direction. Kat waved her down, surprised her elusive neighbor was out after dark.

"Fiona! We need to talk."

They met in front of Fiona's house. Her neighbor looked exhausted, with dark shadows under her eyes.

"Uh, hello, Kat." Fiona's eyes widened in surprise. "Something wrong?"

"I'm afraid I've got bad news, Fiona. Declan was hit by a car. Jace and I saw the whole thing." Kat's voice broke as she described the hit-and-run accident. "I've been trying to call you—where have you been?"

Fiona seemed nonplussed. "I went for a walk. Oh, dear. Declan always had the worst luck. It's a shame things ended so badly."

"But, Declan's not—" Kat protested but Fiona waved her off. Fiona had referred to Declan in the past tense, like he was dead. "I've got to run, dear." Fiona scrounged in the pocket of her plaid McIntosh coat and fished out her keys. "I do wish Declan's final moments hadn't been so terrible."

Fiona brushed past Kat, keys in hand.

Kat trailed after her. "Declan's very much alive. But he is badly injured." Fiona, a pessimist, always jumped to conclusions.

Fiona froze mid-step. Her back was turned and Kat couldn't see her expression. "He's alive?"

"He is, but in rough shape." She recounted the accident in the alley.

Fiona coughed but didn't say a word.

"Lucky that you weren't with him," Kat added. "You might have been hit as well." Frail Fiona would not have fared as well as Declan, a man almost half her age.

Fiona turned towards Kat. She fished a tissue from her pocket and blew her nose. "How serious, exactly?"

"Only the hospital can answer that, but he didn't look good to me." Kat described the accident scene, omitting why they had been in the alley in the first place. Fiona would never forgive her if she found out she and Jace had tailed Declan.

Fiona swayed on her feet. She dropped her purse and it fell open as it hit the pavement. A sheaf of papers fell out.

Kat placed an arm under Fiona's elbow to steady her. "You're in shock. That's understandable, but don't worry, Fiona. He's in good hands at the hospital. I'm sure he'll be okay."

"Okay?" Fiona echoed her.

"Declan will recover, I'm sure of it." Kat was anything but sure, but it seemed like the right thing to say. She released Fiona's elbow and bent to retrieve a handful of the loose papers. "I'll walk you up the stairs."

"Don't bother." Fiona pulled her arm from Kat's and tugged at the papers. "Give me those."

"Sorry, just trying to help." Kat released her grip and handed Fiona the papers. She hadn't done anything wrong. Why was Fiona treating her like a criminal?

Fiona grabbed them and shoved them into her coat pocket. She winced in pain as she bent down to retrieve the rest.

"Let me get them for you."

"No need." Fiona snatched them off the sidewalk and tucked them underneath her coat. She stood slowly. "I can't lose these." Kat recalled her earlier conversation with Declan. Were these the insurance papers Declan mentioned? It wasn't the right time to ask Fiona about the logic of naming Declan the beneficiary of the policy. She could broach the subject after the hospital visit. The only fortunate thing about the accident was that it gave Kat time to talk Fiona out of her decision.

"Want me to drive you to the hospital?"

"Now?"

"Of course now. You must be anxious to see him. Want to run inside and grab some things? I'll start the car."

Fiona seemed momentarily confused.

"Some toiletries for Declan, maybe a change of clothes?"

"Oh, right." Fiona waved her off. "Let's go in the morning instead. I'm a bit tired to venture out again."

"Okay, tomorrow morning, first thing." Kat puzzled over Fiona's lack of urgency. If she were in Fiona's shoes she would have dropped everything to go. But stress did strange things to people, and she wasn't about to argue with her neighbor.

Fiona ascended her front steps and paused at the landing. "Nine is good."

Ten minutes later Kat sat at her kitchen table with freshly brewed coffee and her laptop. Fiona's arrangement with Declan was almost as odd as her reaction to his accident. Was there more she wasn't telling her? She just hoped whatever Fiona had done could be just as easily undone.

In the meantime she would see what she could dig up on Declan. A quick search of the online newspaper archives turned up a few decades-old articles on Declan Burke and his murder and robbery convictions. Details were sparse given the technology twenty years ago, but his sentence appeared to stem from a botched break-in. That made him a dangerous man.

Declan had been twenty-two at the time, which placed him in his early forties today. The article mentioned little else except that, even at that young age, he was a homeless alcoholic with no family and no fixed address. Declan had at least been truthful about that.

Even if Declan was sincere in turning his life around, it would only last as long as he had opportunity to do so. If job prospects evaporated, he would inevitably return to a life of crime. If his options were already exhausted, he might entertain illegal means to support himself. Maybe he was at that point already. If so, was Fiona next on his list?

Was Fiona aware of the seriousness of Declan's crimes? Prisoners rarely spoke of their convictions and it was taboo to ask. Had Fiona investigated his background before she opened her home to him? Kat was certain she would have. She could confirm this tomorrow when she drove Fiona to the hospital.

It seemed like hours since she had talked to Jace. She grabbed her phone and called him.

He answered in a hushed tone. "Things aren't looking good, Kat. When will Fiona get here?"

"She's not coming." Kat recounted her conversation with Fiona. "I think she's in shock. When I offered her a ride to the hospital, she snapped at me."

"I guess she's upset. You would be too."

"Yes. But I would have still rushed to the hospital." Kat sighed. "When are you coming home?"

"Soon, I hope." Jace exhaled. "It's bizarre that I'm holding vigil for a stranger. But there's no one else here. The only thing I know is his name and address, yet they're asking for input from me. Kind of scary and sad all at the same time."

"That's so good of you, Jace. At least someone's there for Declan, especially with Fiona refusing to go." Only then did it sink in that Jace hadn't actually met Declan. He had only seen him from their front window.

"I'd want someone to do the same for me. Especially if I were clinging to life like he is."

"He's that badly injured?"

"Yes." Jace's voice broke. "I feel for the guy. He's got no one to look out for him. The medical team keeps asking for a next of kin. I'll stay till he's out of surgery. I still need to give them my contact info—and Fiona's. There's no one here to give it to."

Kat checked her watch. It was after three a.m. "That doesn't sound good."

They talked a few minutes more, with Jace promising to call with any new developments. She headed upstairs, determined to get a few hours' sleep.

The only good thing about Declan's hospitalization was that he couldn't carry out the insurance scheme from a hospital bed. Whatever he had planned would be on hold indefinitely. Given his injuries, Kat figured she had at least a few days to convince Fiona to undo the arrangement.

She felt a twinge of guilt at her assessment, harsh but true. Yet one detail niggled at her. Declan didn't strike her as sophisticated enough to pull off an insurance fraud. At least not without help.

She tossed in bed, unable to sleep as the accident replayed in her head.

The car had hit so fast, she hadn't seen the driver and couldn't identify the car's make or model, other than it being an older black sedan. But she was certain it was at least fifteen or twenty years old. She might identify the make and model with pictures of older vehicles.

Each second freeze-framed in her mind, from the engine whine and whoosh of air as the car sped past until Declan's body thudded against the windshield. The red tail lights glowed across the rear and—a glimpse of license plate. She concentrated on that split second. Then she saw it. A license plate that began with an 'R'. The remaining digits on the plate were numbers, but they hadn't registered in her mind.

But she had an 'R', and that substantially narrowed the possibilities. 'R' license plates were issued only to automotive repair businesses and car dealers for temporary transport of unlicensed vehicles. While the license plates could be transferred amongst any number of cars, only a few businesses used them, making them easier to trace.

She would dig further first thing in the morning before heading to the hospital. An 'R'' plate was also likely to be a local business, narrowing the owner to hundreds rather than millions of potential sources. One of those shops harbored a dark sedan with a damaged windshield and hood, and she intended to find it.

# Chapter 5

Kat awoke just after seven a.m. to the aroma of brewed coffee and banging pots and pans. She followed her nose downstairs to find Jace making breakfast in the kitchen. She kissed him and poured a cup of coffee. "You must be exhausted. How did Declan's surgery go?"

"Okay, as far as I know. He had a blow to the head that hit a major artery," Jace explained. "The emergency surgery reduced the pressure on his brain, but it's too soon to tell anything. He's in a medically induced coma."

"Wow." Kat sipped her coffee as she flashed back to the black sedan in the alley. Declan's life had changed in an instant. She could have suffered the same fate if the driver had not swerved to avoid her. "He might not recover?"

Jace nodded. "He's still in pretty rough shape. Did you talk to Fiona this morning?"

"No. I'll give her the news on the ride to the hospital." Kat recalled Fiona's reaction last night. Hopefully Fiona would be more like her usual self today.

"Just as well. Now that he's made it through surgery, you'll have better news to share." Jace wrapped his arms around her waist and kissed her. "That could have been you instead of Declan. Thank goodness you're okay."

"The car went straight for Declan, Jace. The driver was gunning for him in the alley. They weren't after me." She shuddered as she remembered how the car had steered around her at the last minute. "Someone intentionally tried to kill him."

Jace shrugged. "That's what I told the police at the hospital last night. I thought it was personal too, but they don't. Said it's random, probably an impaired driver who fled the scene. They see it all too often."

If that were the case, she wouldn't be standing here. "That's crazy. A drunk wouldn't have swerved to miss me. Somebody wants him dead, Jace, but who?"

"Hard to say. Maybe some of his former cronies? As an ex-con, maybe he knows a secret or two. Whoever it is might want to silence him." Jace scooped scrambled eggs onto a plate for Kat and handed it to her.

Kat grabbed two slices of toast from the toaster and sat down at the kitchen table. "He had twenty years to speak up. Why wait till he's released from prison?"

"Maybe they aren't taking any chances. And they couldn't get to him in prison."

"People get hit in prison all the time."

Jace chuckled. "In the movies they do. I'll bet it's a lot harder to knock off an inmate in real life. It would definitely be harder to make a getaway."

Kat filled Jace in on her recollection of the car and 'R' license plates. "Did you see or remember anything else? Like the make of the car?"

"No." Jace shook his head as he joined her at the kitchen table. "I saw even less than you did. I was watching you, not the car."

"Do the police have any leads?"

"No, but they think it's a random hit and run. And since it involves an ex-con, I get the sense it's not high on their list. They gave me a case number though, for what it's worth."

Kat recalled Fiona's evening walk as they ate in silence. It was completely out of character for Fiona to be out after dark. Where had she been, and why had she acted so strangely? Kat intended to find out on the drive to the hospital.

## Chapter 6

The drive to the hospital with Fiona had been unpleasant. Fiona had snapped at her for even suggesting Declan's motives might be self-serving. Kat was no further ahead in deciphering Fiona's strange arrangement with the ex-con. In fact, she was worse off. Fiona had ceased speaking to her shortly after their arrival at the hospital. Awkward to say the least.

Kat stood at the foot of Declan's bed, staring at the myriad of tubes and machines connected to his still form. She was alone in his room while Fiona went to track down a nurse. A clear plastic bag lay on the floor by his bedside. It caught her eye and she walked over to pick it up.

The bag was marked with the hospital logo. Inside was a wallet, a set of keys, and an envelope, likely Declan's personal effects placed in the bag for safe-keeping. The bag must have fallen off his bedside table. Who would be so careless as to leave an unconscious person's valuables on a table top for anyone to see or grab? She opened the bag to verify that the contents belonged to Declan.

The outside of the envelope bore the imprint and logo *Alliance Insurance* but no addressee. Her suspicions were correct; Declan hadn't wasted any time getting insurance. She felt callous even thinking it, but Declan's accident and hospitalization had at least bought Fiona some time before he was discharged from hospital. Maybe enough time to talk some sense into her.

Technically, it was none of her business, she thought as she sat down in the bedside chair. On the other hand, her business or not, she wasn't about to stand idly by and let Fiona put herself in harm's way.

She pressed down on the plastic bag, flattening it against the envelope. She held it up to the light, trying to discern the contents though the envelope, but the paper was too thick.

It was difficult to talk Fiona out of the insurance arrangement without the underlying details. But that meant opening the envelope. The envelope was Declan's personal property. She would be crossing a line if she opened it. But what choice did she have? Clearly these were mitigating circumstances.

Kat took a deep breath and pulled the envelope out of the plastic bag. She extracted the letter. Her mouth dropped open when she read the first page. It was an insurance policy, except it was on Declan's life, not Fiona's. Someone named Richard Sandowski was listed as the sole beneficiary and stood to gain a million dollars if Declan died.

It was Declan who was in trouble, not Fiona. She had gotten it completely wrong. Well, not completely. Whoever Richard Sandowski was, he had a powerful motive to kill Declan. Was he the hit and run driver?

She felt eyes on her and looked up. Fiona stood over her.

"Give me those." Fiona snatched the insurance papers and the bag out of Kat's hand and shoved them in her purse. She snapped it shut and muttered something under her breath.

Kat gasped. "It was lying on the floor so I picked it up. I had to open it to make sure it did in fact belong to Declan."

Fiona's face reddened as she glared at Kat. "Sure you did."

"I'm just trying to—"

"Just trying to help? Well, you're no help at all, Kat."

That was all Kat could take. "I can't believe how ungrateful you're being, Fiona. We help your friend after a serious accident. Jace even kept vigil at the hospital all last night. I drive you here, and all you can say is that I'm no help?"

Fiona shook her head and turned away.

Kat stood. "You can blame me, but you have to take some responsibility, Fiona. Declan's in trouble. A good friend would help him instead of taking everything out on me."

"Maybe you had something to do with it." Fiona's face reddened. "You said you saw it happen. Maybe you pushed him."

"That's the most ridiculous thing I've ever heard. If you don't want my help, fine. But I think you owe me an apology. I'm going for a coffee to give you some time to think about it."

Fiona just stared into space, pointedly ignoring Kat as she stormed out of the room.

Kat's heart raced as she fumed over Fiona's words. Declan clinging to life wasn't exactly a normal situation, and it certainly begged a few questions. Maybe Fiona didn't want to answer those questions, but she didn't have to be so incredibly rude about it. The woman sitting at Declan's bedside contrasted sharply with the neighbor she thought she knew.

Kat headed down the hospital corridor thinking about Declan. Were the police aware of the million dollar policy? Probably not, or they would have made a connection to Richard Sandowski. She was more certain than ever that Declan's accident had been planned. The driver clearly had control of the car and had had not only swerved to avoid her, but had hit Declan twice. She flashed back to the mystery sedan with its triangular lights. Body shops and mechanics used 'R' plates. Just a little more information and she could connect the dots.

The cafeteria lineup was long and it was twenty minutes before she had paid for her coffee and returned upstairs. She walked slowly down the corridor, lost in thought. She wanted more details from Fiona before going to the police. But if Fiona refused to speak to her, she wasn't about to stand idly by.

The police didn't consider Declan's file a priority, but they might reconsider with this new information. But first she wanted to check out some local garages to see if they might be harboring a vintage sedan with 'R' plates.

She was jolted out of her thoughts as someone hit her arm from behind.

"Coming through—move!"

Kat cried out as the lid popped off her coffee cup and hot coffee spilled out. It scalded her arm as the cup flew from her hand and hit the wall. Kat turned as several nurses sprinted past her with a crash cart. They ignored her cries and turned into a room about fifty feet down the hall.

Declan's room. What the hell was going on?

She broke into a run and followed them as sparks of pain shot through her arm. She turned into the room behind the medical team with their crash cart. Declan's bedside chair had been pushed aside as the medical team worked on him.

"What's happening, Fiona?" Kat pressed her hand against her burned forearm to quash the pain.

No answer. Fiona stood by the window, a startled expression on her face.

"Fiona?"

Four nurses crowded around Declan's bed. Two of the four, a woman and a man, alternated as they delivered chest compressions. One nurse, who appeared barely out of her teens, connected the defibrillator before turning to adjust the ancillary equipment, wires, and drips at Declan's bedside. A heavyset woman, likely the charge nurse, barked orders. The instructions seemed hardly necessary. The precision in their movements indicated they were all well-practiced in their respective roles.

Fiona watched. Her eyes darted around the room but avoided Kat. She hugged her purse against her chest.

Kat turned to the charge nurse as the woman stepped back from the bed. "Is he going to be okay?"

"Too soon to tell, I'm afraid. But we got him back."

"Back from where?" She realized as soon as she spoke that Declan's heart must have stopped. "Never mind. I'm just glad you guys got here in time."

The nurse nodded and returned to the bedside, though the frantic panic of moments ago had subsided. A petite redhead entered the room and joined the team at the bed. A doctor or resident doctor, judging from her white coat.

"Fiona?" Kat put her arm around her neighbor's frail shoulders, argument forgotten.

A few feet away, the medical team's voices rose above the humming medical equipment and the air conditioner. "Everything will be okay."

"No, it won't." Fiona broke away from Kat's embrace and stepped towards the door. "Now what happens? When will he wake up?"

"I don't know." Kat shrugged. "You can ask the doctor once they're finished." One look at Fiona and she regretted her choice of words.

"Here we go again," said the charge nurse.

Declan's body jerked every few seconds as the defibrillator delivered a shock to his heart. He was unresponsive, but did he feel the pain?

"I can't watch this." Fiona bolted to the doorway.

Kat winced as she stole a glance at Declan, partially obscured by the medical team as they worked on him. She took a deep breath and followed Fiona out into the hallway. Fiona was twenty feet ahead, moving surprisingly fast. Kat caught up to her at the elevators. She wedged her hand between the doors and barely made it in before the doors closed.

They were alone in the elevator. Either it was an extremely fast door or Fiona had purposely pressed the button to close the door. Given it was a hospital, she guessed the latter. But why was Fiona trying to ditch her?

"What can I do, Fiona?"

"Leave us alone." Fiona stared straight ahead as the elevator headed down.

## Chapter 7

Kat stopped at a convenience store for snack food and a map, still furious with Fiona for both her outburst and refusal to ride home with Kat. Sympathy for her neighbor had been replaced by outrage, especially since Fiona now accused her of being involved. The woman was off her rocker.

Crazy or not, that didn't solve Declan's dilemma. No matter what the circumstances, no one deserved to be hunted down. Whether it was a gun or a car, it was still attempted murder in her books, and she intended to ensure the driver didn't return to finish the job. That meant she had to find him first.

She munched on her chocolate bar as she searched on her phone for a list of local automobile repair and body shops. She penciled them in on the map. There were twenty-six within a five mile radius, far more than she had expected. Auto body shops were especially plentiful, making her wonder about the driving abilities in her neighborhood. There were either a lot of bad drivers or just plain unlucky people.

Finding the car was key to ensuring the damaged vehicle wasn't repaired to obliterate the evidence. She still pursued the theory that an 'R' license plate almost certainly belonged to one of these shops. From there she could track down the driver.

Of course, the driver could simply hide their car and count on the passage of time to erase all memory of it before getting it repaired. But waiting months or years was impractical for most people, and concealing a car for long periods of time invited questions from friends and family.

Her first stop had only two bays, both empty. There were a few cars in the parking lot, but none even remotely resembled the dark sedan that hat hit Declan. She had entered the second, *AA Collision Repair*. It was much busier than the first and the gray-haired front desk attendant waved hello as he hung up the phone.

She described the car. "I'm afraid I can never remember the make and model. I want to surprise my boyfriend with new tail lights for the car he's restoring. Naturally I can't ask him or I'll ruin the surprise."

She had decided to ask about the tail lights for several reasons. One, because it was the only part of the car she felt she could accurately identify, and two, because she wanted to gauge the reaction of the shop employee. Lastly, if anyone else was looking for the same part, it could result in a lead.

"Sounds like 1960's, possibly a Chev? Can't really say without seeing the car though. Do you have a photo?"

Kat shook her head. "The tail lights are kind of like cat's eye glasses. Sort of triangular. Really fancy looking and old."

He pulled a grimy keyboard towards him and punched a few keys.

"Like this?" He swiveled the monitor so she could see.

The monitor displayed a powder blue sedan with tail lights identical to the car that had hit Declan.

"That's it exactly," Kat said. "Do you have them in stock?"

He shook his head. "This here's a 1959 Biscayne. Very rare. You can't special order them, got to find someone whose wrecking one of those babies for parts. Only one I know of in town is over at Craft Collision. Maybe Rick over there might have a line on some parts. If anyone knows, he would."

Kat thanked him and left. Now that she knew the make and model, things could go a lot quicker. That was good, since it was already noon and she'd checked out a grand total of four body shops and two auto mechanics. She had skipped the car dealers after scanning the Craigslist ads, figuring that any vintage cars for sale would be advertised.

# Chapter 8

Kat crossed the cracked concrete parking lot to the front entrance of Craft Collision. It was the most deserted of all the garages she had visited so far. It was just before noon. While the time of day might explain why no one greeted her, it was clearly not a thriving business.

The run-down exterior didn't inspire confidence either. Several rusted bumpers leaned against a crumbling brick and cement planter where, against all odds, bloomed a single delicate rose.

She pushed the jammed front door open and stepped into a grubby waiting area that sported signage from the 1940's. The walls probably hadn't been painted since then either. The unmanned front counter was almost buried under piles of soiled work orders and handwritten notes scrawled with part numbers, names, and phone numbers.

She couldn't locate a service bell but found a business card with the shop's name and address next to a half-dead potted cactus plant. She took one and stuck it in her pocket for later and walked over to the door that led to the shop. She peered through the open door. No one around.

"Hello?"

No answer.

She ventured inside. No activity that she could see, but the lights were on and a large toolbox sat open beside a cluttered workbench. She doubted anyone had heard her over the radio that blared from somewhere in the rear of the shop. The distorted 1980's heavy metal grated on her ears. Customer service clearly was not one of their strengths.

The open door meant someone was around though, so she waited a few more minutes.

She scanned the shop's four bays. They were all empty except for the last one which contained a red 1990's Honda. It looked forlorn without its passenger side fender and front bumper. Behind that bay was a paint booth that appeared to be the source of the radio distortion. She followed the sound and rounded the corner to the paint booth.

She froze.

It couldn't be.

But it was. Parked directly in front of her was the sedan. The front end had been repaired and primed, ready for paint. She didn't need to see the rear and the triangle-shaped tail lights to know it was the same car that had hit Declan.

She snapped a photograph with her cell phone and slipped her phone back into her pocket. She would get the police contact from Jace and pass on the picture. She was still annoyed that they hadn't contacted her as a witness to the accident. This gave her an excuse to talk to them and provide her eyewitness account.

She almost jumped as a man rose from a kneeling position beside the car. He was directly in front of her, but she had been so focused on the car that she hadn't noticed him.

"You can't be back here," he said, waving her away. "Insurance regulations."

"I tried waiting. But nobody came to the front. You need a bell on your door or something." By the looks of him and his shop, he didn't seem overly keen on dealing with customers at all. She wondered how much business he actually got.

He shooed her away and turned back to the car.

She studied the man. Was he the shop owner or just an employee? The rolled up sleeves on his white coveralls exposed poorly done tattoos. One forearm sported a snake but she couldn't quite make out the other one. A series of numbers or something. She noted with alarm the tattoo on his neck. It was a scorpion that bobbed up and down when he talked. Who gets a tattoo on their neck?

"I'm busy. Need to finish this job. Now go away." He didn't bother to turn around as he adjusted his paint sprayer.

"Speaking of which, when did this car come in?" She walked to the rear of the car and saw that the taillights were an exact match to the car that had hit Declan. "Do you know who owns it?"

While the front bumper and grill were missing, the cracked windshield clearly visible. Her pulse quickened. This was definitely the car that had hit Declan.

He dropped the paint sprayer and walked towards her. He didn't stop until he was a foot away.

She involuntarily stepped back, feeling violated by his intrusion into her personal space.

He twirled a toothpick between his thumb and forefinger. "What's it to you?"

"I'm just following up on a hit n' run." It had no plates, which made sense since it was about to be painted. Besides, 'R' plates were just temporarily affixed with a tie, only needed when the vehicle was actually driven on the streets.

His eyes narrowed as he pulled the toothpick from his mouth. He eyed her up and down. "You a cop?"

Her throat tickled from his stale coffee breath and she fought the urge to cough. She was getting a very bad vibe and was acutely aware that she was alone with this man. Not only was no one else in the shop, but no one would hear her scream. No one even knew she was here.

Stupid.

"Not a cop, exactly." She held her breath and turned her head. "A private investigator."

"Is that right."

It was more of a statement than a question. Her welcome, if it ever existed, was definitely worn out. "That's right. I'm working with the police."

His lips turned up into a slight smile. "I'm counting to ten. If you're not gone, I'll give the po-lice another case to in-vest-i-gate. You hear me?"

"What kind of case—"

He pulled a switchblade from his pocket and pointed it at her throat. "You have no business bein' here."

"Can't I just ask a few simple questions?"

He clamped a hand on her bicep and steered her to the front of the shop. The knife blade pressed sharp and precise between her shoulder blades.

"If you're smart, you'll go someplace else."

# Chapter 9

Kat hightailed it out of the parking lot without looking back. She pressed her back into her car seat to erase the tingle in the center of her back where the blade had scraped against her. She was still shocked that the guy had actually pulled a knife on her. She thought of calling the police, but it was her word against his. Her story sounded unbelievable and she had no evidence to back it up. She mulled it over in her head. Of course she should alert the police, but first she wanted to show the picture of the vehicle to both Declan and Jace.

She called Jace on her Bluetooth hands free as she drove to the hospital. She recounted her encounter at the body shop and asked Jace to alert police to the suspect car.

Ten minutes later, she faced Declan as he sat up in his hospital bed. He had made a seemingly miraculous recovery—a vast improvement from the situation this morning when his heart had stopped.

"You look a lot better than you did this morning," Kat said.

"Much better," Declan agreed. "The doc said I had a reaction to the meds in the saline drip. Probably an allergic reaction, but I don't think so. I remember feeling like this yesterday, too."

Kat sat down in the bedside chair. "I've got news. I think I found the car that hit you." Kat pulled the picture up on her phone and handed it to Declan. "The body damage has already been fixed, but I recognize it. Do you?"

"I don't know. It happened so fast. I never got a good look at the car or the driver." Declan's face darkened.

"Did you see anything at all?"

Declan shook his head but stopped. His eyes dropped to Kat's phone which he held in the palm of his hand. He paused like he was weighing his options.

"I know this guy." He handed the phone back to Kat. "That's Richard."

"Richard who?"

"Richard Sandowski. We did time together, but I don't really know him that well. We were both in Fiona's Weeds to Wonders gardening program."

"I saw an insurance policy in your personal items. You named him as a beneficiary." Kat lowered her cell phone into her lap and press the speed dial on her phone to call Jace. She muted the volume. Jace would hear her conversation with Declan, but Declan would not hear Jace on the other end.

Declan reached over to open the drawer of his bedside table.

Kat glanced down at her cell phone. The green indicator showed that Jace had answered and was on the line.

"Don't bother, the insurance policy is gone. Fiona took it. What's going on, Declan? If you hardly know Richard Sandowski, why name him as your insurance beneficiary?" She had repeated the details for Jace's benefit. Hopefully he would catch on and inform the police.

"It was Fiona's idea. The plan was to fake my death. Richard and Fiona would stage the accident. But they weren't supposed to hit me. They were supposed to find a homeless man, drug him, and plant my ID on him. Then we would split the proceeds. Fiona and I each got 45% and Richard 10% for his part in repairing the vehicle and funneling the insurance money through him. Only now I realize that all along Fiona had planned to hit me instead."

Kat was speechless. In hindsight it was obvious why Fiona was in such a state after Declan's accident. She hadn't been out for a walk, she had been behind the wheel. And might very well be on the run.

"I think she just tried to kill me again," Declan said. "She put something in my intravenous. It's the same way I felt last night, before the accident. Like I was drugged or something. That's why I left the house, to get away from her. Where is she?"

With Declan out of the picture, the pot dramatically sweetened for both Fiona and Richard. Fiona could net 90% of the insurance proceeds by getting Declan's share. Or Richard could take it all if he got rid of Fiona.

"I don't know. I've been trying to find her myself." If Declan was telling the truth, her next door neighbor was a cold, calculating killer. And although Declan was a victim, he was equally guilty. He only confessed once he realized he had been targeted. At least her instincts had been right about one of them. Given what Declan had just admitted to, he was also a flight risk.

"You need a lawyer, Declan. Aside from the fact that Fiona is trying to kill you, you're in a lot of trouble." No wonder Fiona had grabbed the papers. They connected Declan, Fiona, and Richard to the murder weapon, a 1959 Biscayne, and provided the motive. Following the money always led to the criminals. In this case, a highly unlikely group with an uncommon connection.

"I trusted her," Declan said. "I didn't even think we would really go through with it. We were still working out the details. At least that's what I thought."

Kat extracted the Craft Collision business card from her pocket. Sure enough, Richard Sandowski was listed as the owner. She flashed back to the auto body shop and realized that the single rose in the planter was a rare Blue Moon rose. That validated Declan's claims in her eyes, given the rarity of the rose and its connection to Fiona.

Declan's forehead glistened with sweat. "She said it was foolproof, that she was just using my name and knocking off a homeless guy. All I had to do was take out the policy and she would identify the body. No one would question a thing, as long as it looked like an accident."

And accidental death paid double, Kat thought. What were the odds of an elderly pensioner conspiring with a couple of ex-cons for a seven-figure fraud?

Miniscule, especially when the crime involved murder.

Kat's thoughts flashed to Fiona's late husband. Fiona had done this before.

# Chapter 10

Kat and Jace relaxed at their waterfront table, finally enjoying the dinner they had missed two nights earlier. The views from the terrace were spectacular, trumped only by the mouthwatering salmon dinner they had just finished.

A soft breeze blew off the Pacific Ocean as the sun sank slowly behind the mountains. A west coast sunset, a sumptuous seafood dinner, and another case behind her. Technically not a case, since no one had hired her, but righting a wrong amounted to the same thing in her books. All in all, a perfect day.

Kat was so stuffed she could barely finish her dessert. But she wasn't about to leave even a crumb of the delicious concoction behind.

"Was dinner worth the wait, Jace?" Kat savored her last mouthful of lemon cheesecake. "Waiting makes it taste even better, don't you think?"

Jace laughed. "I don't know about that. One thing I do know, though. Next time we could just skip all the drama and just drive to the restaurant. Then we wouldn't have had to wait in the first place."

"Then we would have missed Declan's accident."

"I know," Jace said. "And Fiona would have gotten away with murder. I can never quite figure out how you manage to get involved in these things."

"My inquisitive nature?"

"Suspicious nature is more like it. I'm not complaining though. I might have been her next victim once the money ran out." Jace speared a strawberry and popped it into his mouth.

"I can't help it, I just notice when people act out of character. Like Fiona and her Blue Moon roses. She would never dig them up and let them die unless she could afford to replace them with something even better. Not only would that be pricey, but it seemed strange after she had confided in me about her money troubles just a couple of weeks ago. I figured her finances had suddenly improved, but how? She had no other means of income besides her fixed pension. It planted the seeds of suspicion in the back of my mind."

"Because everything's driven by money." Jace rested his hand on hers.

Kat leaned across the table to kiss him. "Not quite everything. But close. When people's finances suddenly improve for no apparent reason, there's always an explanation. I just never expected it to be murder."

"She almost got away with it, too. If you hadn't insisted on following Declan, we never would have connected Fiona and Richard Sandowski."

"It was a hunch," admitted Kat. "Good thing you taped the conversation I had with Declan. I wouldn't have believed Fiona was capable of that myself without the details from Declan. The police didn't at first either. It not only convinced them, but it provided enough evidence to charge all three of them."

"Fiona had me fooled too," Jace said. "Now she can make even more friends in prison."

The police had located Fiona at Custom Collision, arguing with Richard Sandowski after he demanded a bigger cut of the proceeds. Now both were behind bars.

Fiona would need all the help she could get, since Richard had threatened to tell all. Not just about plotting Declan's murder, but also how he had helped Fiona with prior murders. First they killed her husband and then her brother-in-law.

"Why her brother-in-law?" Jace asked. "He would hardly name Fiona as a beneficiary. He had no dependents, so he didn't even need life insurance."

"Exactly. Except Fiona had obtained insurance on him with a forged signature and used Richard to impersonate him for both the medical exam and the meeting with the insurance company. Funny thing about insurance, at least in those days. They insisted on a medical exam, but they never asked for identification of the insured person. It relied on the honor system. Once the insurance was in place, Richard killed the brother-in-law in exchange for a cut of the insurance money."

The police were reexamining the deaths of both Fiona's late husband and her brother-in-law. Her late husband's official cause of death was a heart attack, although investigators now suspected he had been poisoned. They planned to exhume his body.

"After the payout from her husband's death, Fiona realized that accidental death paid double. A few years later when she plotted

the demise of her brother-in-law, she ensured that his death was accidental. He plunged down a cliff after his car's brakes failed."
It finally caught up with her in the end, Kat thought. Declan was cooperating with the investigation. While he also faced a stiff prison term, he hoped his testimony might result in a lighter sentence. Richard and Fiona both faced charges for Fiona's brother-in-law's death, and Fiona would likely be brought to trial for her husband's death as well.
Just desserts for a woman who had almost gotten away with a third murder.

COLOR OF MONEY
GREEN
WASH
COLLEEN
CROSS

# Chapter 1

Katerina Carter glanced over at her boyfriend, Jace Burton. He ran his hand absently through his dark curly hair, head bowed, as he concentrated on his notes.

Dennis Batchelor had sent his private airplane to Vancouver to collect them. The billionaire environmentalist had handpicked journalist Jace to write his biography. He had insisted on meeting him at his remote mountain lodge in Southeastern British Columbia's Selkirk Mountains.

Neither Kat nor Jace had flown on a private plane before. Kat couldn't take her eyes off the view as the twin engine Cessna gained altitude and left Vancouver's glass and concrete cityscape behind. Jace, on the other hand, remained completely oblivious to their luxurious surroundings. They were the only passengers on board.

The plane's cavernous interior was opulent compared to a commercial airplane. Kat stretched her legs out and was surprised they didn't hit the seat in front of her. In fact, there wasn't a seat in front of her. The plush furniture was more like something you'd see in an executive office or a living room than a typical airplane interior. The cabin furnishings included a rectangular oak table and chairs, similar to a pared-down boardroom. Kat and Jace sat in two of the half dozen reclining leather armchairs with a table between them. It sure beat flying economy.

Kat looked forward to the weekend adventure. She was between cases in her forensic accounting and fraud investigation practice and business had slowed with Christmas approaching. She couldn't wait for her mini vacation in the mountains. With just two weeks before Christmas, she was getting in the festive spirit. In less than two hours they would be Batchelor's guests at his wintry mountaintop lodge. The time of year, coupled with the remoteness of Batchelor's mountain lodge, made air the only feasible mode of transport. She was along for the ride—and the weekend.

The area had an interesting history and she looked forward to exploring it. They would land in Sinclair Junction, the only town of any size near Batchelor's lodge. It was founded on a gold strike and prospered when the railway extended west. But it had fallen on a century of hard times until its recent resurrection as the informal marijuana grow op capital of Canada. It was an odd locale for the billionaire to establish his home.

Maybe it wasn't as strange as it seemed. The environmentalist and founder of Earthstream Technologies had made his fortune from being green.

None of this had even been on the radar until Batchelor called Jace out of the blue to write his biography. It was an offer he couldn't refuse. Not only for the six-figure paycheck, but also the exposure he would get as Batchelor's biographer.

Writing a biography memoir was a far cry from Jace's freelance journalism work at *The Sentinel*. But it was still writing, and diversification was a good thing considering the declining state of the newspaper industry. Writing a billionaire's biography paid well, and it just might help Jace transition his writing talents into a new career.

Only twenty minutes into their flight from Vancouver and they had already left the Coast Mountains behind. The sky was clear and below was a vast expanse of forest broken only by blue lake water that glistened like a jewel in the bright winter sunshine. Ahead loomed the snow-covered peaks of the rugged Selkirk and Purcell mountain ranges, and beyond that, the Rocky Mountains. Once they landed in Sinclair Junction they would be met by a driver to take them into the mountains and to Dennis Batchelor's lodge.

The environmentalist had parlayed his environmental activism into a billion dollar business. He put his money where his mouth was with environmental consulting, solar and wind energy companies, and generally "investing in green", as he liked to refer to it.

"What will I do with myself, Jace?" All weekend with nothing to do, a huge change from her normal 24/7 work practices. As the sole employee of her burgeoning forensic accounting and fraud investigation practice, she was unaccustomed to downtime. "I should have brought some work."

Jace shook his head. "This is your perfect opportunity to relax. While I'm working you can kick back and have fun for a change."

"I plan to, but I'm not sure I can do it for an entire weekend." She patted her duffel bag as a measure of security. Inside were guides and maps of the area. She could snowshoe or hike, depending on the amount of snow on the ground. She had also packed a half dozen mystery novels in case she was stranded indoors. The one thing she had a hard time with was doing nothing at all.

"It's not that hard once you get used to it. Think of this as your intervention. For once the tables are turned. I'll be working all weekend." Jace would complete a first draft for Batchelor's review and approval by their departure on Sunday, then finalize the book once they returned to Vancouver.

Nothing wrong with leisure time, Kat decided. She just wasn't used to it. At any rate, she had brought her laptop as a backup plan in case any issues arose at the office.

A severe winter storm had blasted the area the last few days, so their travel plans had been up in the air until this morning, when the weather had temporarily lifted. "I hope we don't get snowed in," Kat said. "I have a client meeting at the office first thing Monday morning."

"I'm sure the weather will hold." Jace looked up from his notepad. He was an avid outdoorsman and search and rescue volunteer. He practically idolized Batchelor for his environmental work. "I still can't believe he chose me of all people to write his biography. He could have hired anyone."

"He didn't choose just anyone." She placed her hand on top of his. "He chose you."

"I'm kind of nervous. What if I screw up?" Jace's usual self-confidence was absent because he was so in awe of Batchelor.

Kat squeezed his hand. "Don't be ridiculous. You've been writing for *The Sentinel* for more than ten years. He chose you because you're a great writer."

"I've never written an entire book before, let alone an autobiography for a famous billionaire."

"You can do it. It could open up new opportunities for you."

"I know." Jace sighed. "Somehow I thought my first book wouldn't be a biography. I thought it would be an action novel or something."

"Doesn't matter. You know how to write, and Batchelor trusts you. Your outdoor experience gives you both a lot of common ground." In addition to being a search and rescue volunteer, Jace was an avid hiker and skier. If it involved the outdoors, it involved Jace. Both men loved the outdoors and respected the environment.

"I hope you won't be bored by yourself, since I'll be busy day and night with this guy. I've got to complete a first draft by the end of the weekend. What will you do with yourself?"

Kat laughed. "I'll think of something." Although it would be nice to just relax for a change, maybe she could lend a hand. Jace often helped with her fraud investigation cases; maybe she could return the favor. "I'm sure we'll catch a few stolen moments."

"Can't promise anything. You know how these tycoon types are. I have a hunch I'll be with him every waking hour."

"That's okay. I can always go into town and explore."

Kat eyed Jace's notes. "Is anything in his biography off limits? I'll bet he has some secrets to tell."

"I wouldn't have accepted the job if it was." Jace stretched out his long legs. "Or put my name on it. A bit of controversy is a good thing. That's the kind of stuff people want to read about."

"It makes it objective and balanced. If that's the case, you'll do just fine." Dennis Batchelor was revered for his environmental work but had plenty of enemies with his no-holds-barred approach. Some accused him of self-interest, putting his personal goals ahead of his environmental causes with media-grabbing tactics. But that same ruthlessness separated the billionaires and the also-rans.

Kat scanned the lavish cabin. The plane had less than half the number of seats as a commercial plane and the atmosphere was much more informal. No security and boarding line-ups, no crammed luggage in the overhead bins and no unruly passengers. It was the first, and probably the last, time she had flown in a private airplane.

They had snacked on smoked salmon, bruschetta and exotic cheeses, washed down with sparkling mineral water. She could definitely get used to this rock star treatment. But she'd better not, because the flight was only an hour long. She was acutely aware that this was likely the only time she would experience such luxury. It was a far cry from the cramped, bring your own food economy flights she was accustomed to.

Batchelor had founded GreenThink, the environmental lobby group famous for its stance against clear-cut logging, fish farms, and pretty much anything that combined big business with nature. Since its inception thirty years ago, it had lobbied governments and inspired environmental protection and conservation.

In an ironic twist, the tenacious environmental crusader had himself become the face of big business. Earthstream Technologies, his own wildly successful company, had sprung out of his environmental work and launched his multi-billion dollar business empire. Earthstream's patented decontamination technology remediated contaminated sites at a fraction of the time and cost of competitor's products.

Earthstream's motto of *'Green Makes Good'* was true in more ways than one. Batchelor's companies employed technologies that improved or conserved the environment. In addition to environmental remediation and clean up, the company had developed a patented technology that dissolved toxins without harsh chemicals. Earthstream was a textbook case of how doing good could also be profitable.

Kat jolted in her seat as the Cessna hit a pocket of turbulence. She glanced out the window to see that the once bright and cloudless sky had darkened with cumulus clouds.

The Cessna began its descent. It broke through the clouds, exposing steep snow-capped mountains and the vivid turquoise blue of a glacier-fed lake nestled in a large rift valley. The plane circled the water before touching down on the lakeside airstrip. They stepped off the plane to blinding sunlight and a cold breeze that blew in off the lake. Snow dusted the surrounding hillside. Kat shivered in her heavy down jacket as she contemplated the next leg of their journey to Batchelor's mountaintop lodge.

They were greeted by a tall, bearded man in his late thirties. He held out his hand and smiled. "Ranger. I'll be taking you to the lodge."

Kat wondered whether that was his first or last name but never got the chance to ask. Within seconds he and Jace were engrossed in animated discussion about ski equipment.

She glanced around the tarmac and noted little activity at the small airport. Theirs was the only flight, though a half dozen other planes were parked in or outside their hangars. Aside from

Ranger's Land Cruiser, there were no other vehicles around to meet the flights.

She knew the town had fallen on hard times but had expected more signs of life. She slung her pack over her shoulder and followed Ranger and Jace off the tarmac towards the truck.

Soon they were headed up a steep road to the main part of town. She stole glimpses of the historic downtown as they passed through and was already enamoured with the late nineteenth-century stone and brick buildings. A gold and silver boom had erupted a hundred years ago, followed by mere decades as a railroad transportation hub. The architecture stood as proof of its short-lived prosperity.

After almost a century of slow decline, the town reinvented itself as the unofficial marijuana capital of British Columbia, but even that commerce had dried up. Whatever fortunes had been made in the hills had disappeared along with the people, and the town seemed shabby and worn.

She wanted to stay and explore, but their final destination was still an hour away. After a few blocks of closed cafes and tired-looking storefronts, the town gave way to a two-lane highway surrounded by dense forest. Only a few cars passed in the opposite direction during the entire trip, so she was surprised when they suddenly skidded to a stop after three quarters of an hour.

A dozen vehicles, mostly trucks and SUV's, were parked haphazardly on the shoulder. Ranger slowed and turned onto the gravel road directly in front of the cars. One of the vehicles blocked the road.

They were in the middle of nowhere. Where had the cars come from?

A few dozen men and women stood across the road fifty feet in from the highway junction. They brandished protest signs. An older woman in the center broke from the group and began walking towards them. It was a blockade.

Kat squirmed in her seat. "Who are those people?"

Ranger slowed the truck to a crawl. "Just a bunch of radicals. There's a lot of them around here."

"What do they want?" Jace asked.

The men and women who blocked the road all carried signs. One read *Protect our drinking water.* Another said: *We live here. No toxic water.*

Several feet down the road another group huddled around a makeshift fire in an oil can. A semi-permanent plywood structure provided shelter. A few plastic chairs were scattered underneath.

"Anything and everything," Ranger said. "They're totally against development of any kind. As if their houses and farms aren't the same sort of thing."

Kat stole a glance at Jace. "Do you live around here?"

Ranger nodded. "I live on the lodge property in a separate cabin."

Kat assumed that meant he didn't own any land in the area. It explained his nonchalant attitude towards development. He didn't care one way or the other since he had no property at stake.

"What's wrong with the drinking water?" Kat asked.

"Nothing, really. They're overreacting and making trouble with their scare tactics."

"Why would they do that?"

"There's an old mine nearby. It's been shut down for a couple of years, so there's no activity. Anyways, a small section of the tailings pond—that's where the waste rock, water, and solvents end up—broke and they think that it's contaminating the water."

"Isn't it?" Jace asked.

"Technically, yes, but it's pretty minor. The tailings pond water did over flow, but it never reached Prospector's Creek. The groundwater tested positive for contaminants, but that was three years ago. The site was completely cleaned up and nothing ever reached the water supply or anybody's property. But that's not how they see it. They claim they've suffered losses, but I say they're just looking for an excuse to fight." Ranger slowed the truck as he neared the group.

"If this area is so remote, why are they even here?" Kat asked.

Ranger met her gaze in the rear view mirror. His brows furrowed. "What do you mean?"

"Well, they can stand here for days without another vehicle going by."

"They saw me leave and knew I'd be back, so they mustered the troops," he said.

"But the protest has no impact on you, does it? Is the demonstration for our benefit—your guests?"

"Partly. But even if you weren't here they would have blocked the road. They like to harass us. But like I said, it's pointless. The water's clean—always has been—and it's tested regularly." Ranger slowed the car as a slender woman in her sixties approached the truck. "It's got nothing to do with Dennis anyways."

Ranger rolled down his window. "Elke."

"You can't pass."

"You can't stop me. I live here."

Elke peered into the truck "Who are these people?"

"None of your business. But I'll tell you anyways. They're friends of Dennis's. Now be a good neighbor and let us pass."

Elke scowled but backed away from the truck. Ranger drove slowly past the group as they shouted obscenities.

Once they had passed the crowd, Kat turned to look back. "Quite the welcome wagon you have here."

The protesters dropped their signs and headed back to their makeshift plywood shelter. "It's awfully cold to be standing around out here."

"The smart ones packed up a long time ago," Ranger said. "But there are always a few diehards."

"And Elke is one of them?"

"Yep. She and her husband want a financial settlement. Ridiculous, since they haven't been harmed in any way. They say their property value has dropped, but property values have always been low around here. They're just looking for an excuse to make money."

"Why bother Dennis? Where are the mine's owners?" Jace asked.

"Offshore," Ranger said. "Since the mine's owners aren't around, they figure they'll get attention if they harass Dennis. We try to ignore them."

"Where is this mine?" Kat hadn't seen any type of business activity since leaving Sinclair Junction.

"The Regal Gold Mine is just up the road. It borders Dennis's property. If an environmental activist like Dennis isn't worried about it, they shouldn't either. They're making a mountain out of a molehill, just looking for a fight."

"Who exactly owns the mine?" Jace asked.

"Regal Gold Mines is owned by a Chinese company who likes to keep a low profile. There's no way to reach the absentee owner. The protestors have complained to the government who says it's not their responsibility either. So they figure the next best thing is to go after Dennis, since he's an environmentalist. They think they can shame him into taking it on as a cause." He shook his head. "They're wrong. He doesn't like being told what to do."

Kat laughed. "Kind of ironic, don't you think? Dennis Batchelor being targeted by protestors?"

Ranger remained silent. He didn't meet her gaze in the rear view mirror this time.

She thought it was funny, but maybe she should have kept her mouth shut.

They drove up the steep gravel road as it climbed higher up the mountain. Every few minutes there was a break in the trees and Kat caught a glimpse of a valley below. It was breathtaking. Huge mountains surrounded a turquoise lake bordered by snow. "It's very beautiful here, so pristine and wild." She understood why Batchelor had chosen the area for his home. It was a quick jaunt to Vancouver by plane, yet remote and not easily accessible to the media and the general public.

Minutes later the road levelled out and they emerged onto a large plateau atop the mountain. Dennis Batchelor's lodge was visible from a mile away at the edge of the plateau. The massive stone and wood structure was built on a stone outcropping that jutted out of the otherwise flat landscape. It resembled a log cabin on very expensive steroids. It was surrounded by smaller buildings and forest on two sides. The main façade was glass and faced the valley below.

They enjoyed hot cappuccinos in the great room while their room was readied. It was a self-contained cabin built on the cliff edge. Kat was getting to like this more and more.

The lodge's great room was bigger than her entire house. Floor to ceiling glass was interspersed with massive wood beams and stone, giving it a feeling of casual grandeur. The lone wall featured a massive rock fireplace with a roaring fire. The hearth was flanked with pictures of Batchelor over the years. The photographs were in chronological order, a pictorial timeline of Batchelor's life and the environmental movement he had inspired.

The first photograph was the one that had gained Batchelor an international following. Several protestors blocked a logging road, among them a defiant twenty-something Dennis Batchelor, the focal point of the image. He had chained himself to an old growth Sitka Spruce tree. He grinned defiantly at the camera. A dozen loggers faced him, their passage blocked. Police stood behind the loggers, reluctant to take any action that might provoke a fight.

A moment frozen by the camera lens had been the catalyst to sway public opinion on the plight of the Carmanah Valley and its fabled spirit bears. Protests had been ongoing for years, but that day was the tipping point. Protestors mobilized en masse to join the fight. It marked the beginning of Batchelor's environmental crusade.

While Batchelor was far from the first of the protestors, his charisma and outrageous attention-getting antics attracted a critical mass of followers. His daredevil stunts made great video footage, and he took on an almost mythical action hero status. Many stunts were downright dangerous, but he got the attention he sought. He thought nothing of skydiving from an airplane right into a logging operation.

His idealism coupled with his youthful good looks won him many followers, especially female ones. Public opinion forced the government to preserve and protect the remaining old growth forest.

He was still in his early twenties when he had founded GreenThink, the grassroots environmental movement that inspired a generation of young people. A few years later he combined his passion for the environment with a string of profitable businesses. The most recent, Earthstream Technologies, was a billion-dollar success story. Kat wondered if the hippie chained to the tree had ever imagined that he would be a famous billionaire one day.

"You made it." A deep male voice boomed from somewhere behind them.

Kat turned to see Dennis Batchelor standing in the doorway. He was thirty years older, forty pounds heavier, his once handsome face replaced with jowls and dark shadows under his eyes. While he still bore a slight resemblance to the youthful protestor in the photograph, the billions hadn't come without a cost.

He wore a flannel shirt, faded jeans, and worn cowboy boots. He caught her assessment. "Nobody wears suits here. It's come as you are."

"Makes sense." Kat sipped her cappuccino and pointed to the largest of the photos. In it, Batchelor stared down a logging truck in the middle of an otherwise deserted logging skid road flanked by centuries old Sitka spruce trees. "I remember seeing that picture when I was just a kid. I had never really thought about the environment until I saw you."

"No one did. That's why I had to stand my ground." Batchelor laughed. "Though I feared they would drive right over me.  It was pretty extreme back then."

"You saved the forest that day," Jace said.

"Somebody had to do it," Batchelor said. "While we still could. Building that road would have brought all sorts of problems. People, vehicles, polluting businesses. Once the habitat's destroyed, it's pretty hard to get it back."

"You inspired a generation, including me," Jace said. "Getting the truth out there, no matter how controversial. That's why I became a journalist."

Batchelor smiled. "That's very flattering.  It's also why I called you for my biography. I need to work with someone who understands what I'm all about."

Writing Dennis Batchelor's biography was a huge opportunity, a chance of a lifetime that could make—or break—Jace's career. Rumors abounded that the tycoon was notoriously difficult to work with, but Kat saw no evidence of that. At least not yet.

Batchelor strode over to the large hearth. "You appreciate the outdoors like I do." He nodded at Kat. "I thought you both might enjoy a weekend here. Isn't it breathtaking?"

"Pristine wilderness," Jace agreed. "This is a beautiful place."

"Took me ten years to build it," Dennis said. "After all that, I rarely get home to enjoy it.".

# Chapter 2

Kat and Jace's so-called cabin was three thousand square feet of luxury, an authentic log cabin with a twenty-foot ceiling and a second floor loft.  The main floor was an open plan with the exception of two bedrooms and a bathroom.

"I can't believe we have this place all to ourselves," Kat said.

Jace nodded. "At least you'll have a chance to enjoy it. I'll be busy all weekend working with Dennis."

"We'll get some time together, won't we?" Kat envisioned skiing or snowshoeing in the spectacular surroundings. "Maybe later this afternoon?"

"I wouldn't count on it. People like Dennis seem to work twenty-four hours a day, always looking for ways to make even more money. That's what this book is about too—a way to capitalize on his name. He wants to see a rough draft by Sunday."

"That's insanely fast. It's probably worth it in the end, though. Working with a billionaire should make a name for you in the process." A book on Dennis Batchelor was practically guaranteed to be a bestseller. People idolized the renowned environmentalist.

Kat unzipped her bag and pulled out her laptop. She plugged it in. "If I have to do nothing at all, I couldn't find a better place to do it in."

"All you need to do is relax," Jace agreed. "Turn off your phone and unplug the world."

She looked forward to some down time but wanted to check her messages first. She cursed as she realized she had no cell phone signal. "It doesn't seem to work here. Too remote for cell service, I guess." It hadn't occurred to her that there might not be cell towers in the mountains. How did Batchelor manage without it?

She focused on her computer instead. "Uh-oh. The Internet's down, too. I can't get a connection." Batchelor must at least have a satellite connection. They were notoriously slow and unreliable.

"You don't need one." It was a constant battle between them. Jace left his work at the office, while Kat blurred the lines between work and home. Or as Jace would say, she had no life. The tables were turned though. This time Kat would be the one with more leisure time.

Jace had already unpacked most of his clothes and put them away in one of the two matching hand- carved bureaus that flanked the king-sized bed in the master bedroom. Kat's belongings remained in her suitcase. She'd deal with her stuff later, once she had her laptop set up.

"I thought you left that thing at home." Jace frowned. "What's the point in being here if you can't enjoy the surroundings?"

"It's too hard, Jace. I can't unwind until I confirm everything's okay back home. I'll just check my email once in a while." Her happiness actually depended on a Wi-Fi connection. She knew how stupid that sounded, but at least she was honest with herself.

"I'm the one working, not you." Jace rolled his eyes. "I should have inspected your bags before we left. You need an intervention or something. Just forget about work for one weekend, okay?"

Jace was probably right, but as an investigative journalist, he got a steady paycheck from *The Sentinel*. She, on the other hand, was in business for herself. No work meant no pay. He was probably right, though. With Christmas approaching, her work had slowed to a trickle anyways. All her fraud investigation cases had wrapped up and she was free till January. Most people had already wound down for the holidays. She should do the same. Technically she was on vacation, with a completely free weekend at a luxurious wilderness lodge, albeit one with lousy Internet. Her only task was to enjoy herself. How hard could that be?

But what if someone needed her help? A new client?

Unlikely at this time of year. "I guess you're right." She closed her laptop. She was cut off from the outside world for the moment anyways. She'd try again once Jace started to work.

It was a bit foolish to spend time looking at a screen when she was surrounded by pristine wilderness. The only downside was that Jace would be busy, but she could entertain herself just fine. She could snowshoe, hike, or just lounge around in this wonderful cabin.

She sprawled out on the king sized bed and sunk into the down comforter's luxurious softness. She rolled onto her side to enjoy the scenery through the floor-to-ceiling windows. French doors opened out onto a large deck with a 180-degree vista of the valley below.

"Come see the view. It's amazing." She propped herself up amongst the half-dozen pillows and surveyed the room. The best thing about their cabin was that it was self-contained, with a fully stocked kitchen that included a well-appointed wine cooler.

"Just a sec." Jace appeared in the doorway, briefcase in hand. "I'll look at it later once I've got my stuff organized."

"Don't wait too long."

Their accommodations were a few hundred feet from the main lodge and Batchelor's private residence, but a small stand of evergreens hid the lodge completely. All amenities were within reach, yet they were completely alone. The sense of solitude in the wilderness was one she had only experienced once before on a week-long Alaskan wilderness trek. They'd flown in for that trip as well. But that's where the similarities ended. While they were in the bush for both trips, this experience was decidedly more upscale.

The snow had begun falling moments after their arrival at the cabin, but already the thick flakes coated the ground in a thin layer of white. Her eyes followed the flight path of a golden eagle as it circled for a landing on the pine tree that bordered their deck.

"Look, Jace. There's a nest right outside." She pointed to the top of the tree where the eagle perched on the edge of a massive nest. She could watch all the activity through the windows without even getting out of bed. How was she ever going to leave this place?

Jace dropped his stuff and joined her on the bed. "Lucky you. Too bad I have to go to work."

Kat pouted and snuggled up to him. "Poor thing."

The eagle disappeared into the giant nest, oblivious to their stares. Probably hunkering down to wait out the snowfall.

Their cabin was built right into the cliff. The entire south side was glass, affording a breathtaking view of the valley hundreds of feet below. The architect's design followed the contours of the cliff and used the natural geography to provide shelter from the wind. The deck jutted out from the cliff, suspended out another thirty feet or so, providing a bird's eye view of the landscape.

It was enough to take your breath away.

Few came here since Batchelor's property was nestled in a hard to reach corner of the Selkirk Mountains. The rural road they had come in on was easy to miss; the only other access was by helicopter or snowmobile.

She gazed at the view. How had Batchelor discovered such a remote place? "I can definitely get used to this." The forest on the east side of the cabin was visible at the corner of the window. The trees sported a light sugar coating of snow from the flurries that had started an hour ago. Quite a change from the brilliant sunshine when their plane had landed a few hours ago.

Jace rolled towards Kat and wrapped his arms around her. "Me too. "

"When do you have to meet Batchelor?"

"An hour from now." Jace sat up and pulled a radio from his pocket. Dennis's voice crackled over the air. The men talked for less than a minute. "Change of plans. He wants to start now."

"I guess you don't keep a billionaire waiting." Kat smiled but she was disappointed. Jace was already tethered to Dennis with a radio. So much for a little time together before he began work. "You'd better go."

Jace kissed her. "I'll be back soon. We're just discussing the outline I sent him earlier." Jace had sent it last week after signing the contract.

Kat sighed. "I'll be here. Doing nothing, of course."

She gazed out the window. Sunset was still hours away, though the sky was gray as the low clouds closed in. Maybe it was a good day to stay in and simply enjoy the cabin.

A fire in the hearth crackled and warmed the suite. The fire was already burning brightly upon their arrival, a nice touch. The fire was both relaxing and warming. Jace was right. Relaxation was good for the soul. Unfortunately she was a restless soul.

Kat got up and knelt by the hearth. She grabbed a log from the woodpile beside the fireplace and added it to the fire. She stoked the fire, mesmerized by the flames. Who was she kidding? She wasn't mesmerized, she was bored. She wanted to sit around and do nothing, but found it impossible.

But going outside wasn't an option right now with the fire burning. She might as well do some stretching. She inhaled a deep yoga breath as she knelt by the hearth. Then she coughed from the smoke from the hearth.

Forget that.

How could she invoke Zen-like calm while Jace worked his butt off nearby?

She doused the fire and decided to go for a walk around the grounds while it was still daylight. The fresh air would be invigorating. Besides, she had plenty of time to relax by the fire with Jace later.

She pulled on her boots and jacket and headed outdoors along the stone pathway that led to the lodge a few hundred meters away. She had noticed several side trails that branched off from the main walkway between her cabin and the lodge and now was as good a time as any to explore. She had ventured less than ten feet when she ran into Jace.

He stomped down the path, his face flushed and angry. He didn't even acknowledge her.

"That was quick," she said as Jace brushed past her. "Forget something?"

"Only my common sense."

She reversed course and fell in behind him. He had been gone less than thirty minutes. "What's going on?"

"I'll tell you inside." He stormed past her and ascended the cabin stairs. He stamped his feet on the doormat a little harder than necessary to remove the snow caked on his soles. He unlaced his boots and kicked them off. "I knew Batchelor's deal was too good to be true."

Kat removed her boots and followed Jace inside. She grabbed their footwear and brought them inside just as a cold wind blew snowflakes into the entryway. It was so unlike Jace to be angry, especially when it came to work.

Jace pulled off his jacket and threw it on the dining room chair. He marched over to the closet and grabbed his duffel bag and tossed it onto the bed. "Batchelor lied to me. He doesn't want a biographer. He wants me to ghostwrite his memoir. This is not what I signed up for."

Just what she had been afraid of. The mutual admiration had seemed over the top, and this sudden reversal had Jace soured on his childhood idol. "That's too bad. But he's paying you a lot. Is it that big of a deal?"

"Of course it is. We agreed on a biography 'by Jace Burton'. Not an autobiography where I'm just an anonymous ghostwriter."

Kat sighed. She'd swallow her pride for a hundred grand. Within reason, of course. "It is different from what he told you, but he's still paying you a hundred grand."

"It might be a lot of money, but it's a lot of work for me too. This contract would have established me as an author. Now, as a ghostwriter I'll do all the work, yet be invisible."

"He tells you that now, after we came all the way here?" She had thought it too good to be true, but hadn't wanted to burst his bubble that last week when Batchelor had first broached the subject. And it had all been arranged so fast, leaving no time to ruminate.

"He planned it that way. He probably knew I'd turn down a ghostwriting assignment."

"You believe he purposely tricked you to come up here?" While she had expected a catch to Jace's six-figure deal, she doubted Batchelor had purposely misled him. Jace probably hadn't read the fine print.

"Yep," Jace sighed. "How could I be so stupid?"

"It's not the end of the world, Jace." She grabbed a bottle of merlot off the kitchen counter and searched for a corkscrew. It was apparent Jace wasn't returning to work today, and if anyone needed to relax and mellow out, it was him.

"It's insulting. You know what ghostwriting means."

Kat felt guilty about enjoying herself when Jace clearly was not. She didn't want the weekend to end just as she was starting to relax.

"I realize it's not what you expected, but what's wrong with his name on the cover instead of yours? He obviously thinks highly of your writing." Not great, but she'd do it for a hundred grand. She located a couple of wineglasses in the cupboard and filled them. She handed one to Jace, who placed it on the table.

"That's not the biggest issue." Jace walked over to the bureau and scooped out a handful of his clothes. He dropped them into his duffel bag. "It means I write the story as he tells it. Whether it's the truth or not. No independent verification. No objective viewpoint. I'm merely a scribe to him. It's insulting."

"You're letting your emotions rule. Stop and think it over." Jace tended to be a bit rash when wronged or upset. This assignment was worth a lot of money. Money they could use to pay for the endless renovations on their money pit Victorian house.

"Nothing to think about. I'm done."

"But you already know so much about him. You can easily write that book, even without talking much with him." Kat sipped her wine. It was velvety smooth. "Don't take it so personally."

"How can I not? I'll do it only if it's on my terms—what we originally agreed to." Jace unfolded the contract. "The contract makes no mention of ghostwriting."

"But you already have an outline done. It should be easy for you to write. So what if your name's not on it? Maybe it's better that way." Kat wandered over to the window and admired the view. A light cloud cover hid the sun, casting eerie shadows on the landscape. "Why not make the best of a bad situation?"

"Better in what way? So I can compromise myself?" He walked back to the table and sipped from his wineglass. "Hmmm. This is pretty good."

She didn't mention that she hadn't brought the wine; it was straight from the fully stocked wine cooler, compliments of Batchelor. "Let me see that."

Jace handed her the contract.

"You're not compromising yourself. You're completing an assignment, just like anything you do at *The Sentinel.* Do you get to choose what you write about at the newspaper?"

He sighed. "No, I guess not."

"This is the same. You're doing a vanity piece to make Batchelor happy, and you're being very well paid for it. You signed a contract, but he can't exactly force you to write anything you don't want to. If and when that happens, you discuss the specific instances at that time. I'm guessing there won't be much, other than a few exaggerations."

Jace frowned.

"Besides," she added, "We're stuck here until Sunday. We have no way of leaving on our own."

"No doubt part of his plan," Jace muttered.

But he had calmed down. The wine was working.

Kat scanned the contract. It was clear from the contract language that Jace's name wouldn't appear. However, the clause was buried near the bottom of page eight, so it wasn't obvious. She wasn't about to point it out and anger him further.

"Maybe you're right." Jace paused. "I guess I don't even know if there's anything I *would* object to until it comes up. I can push back if and when the time comes. It's a bit early to assume the worst. I just feel like he tricked me with the contract language."

"I'll bet his lawyers make him put clauses like that in everything. He is a billionaire, after all." She omitted the fact that Jace could have avoided the confusion if he had carefully read the contract prior to the trip.

"I still doubt he'll be objective. He's not going to say anything bad about himself."

"The ghostwriting thing is a blessing. You no longer need to worry about content, since your name's not on the book. I know it's not ideal, but why not give it a shot? You can quit any time you feel compromised or uncomfortable. But don't assume the worst. Not yet, anyway." Regardless of whether Jace cooperated with Batchelor, their chartered plane didn't return until Sunday afternoon. And they needed transport off the mountain to meet it at the Sinclair Junction airport.

"I suppose you're right." Jace placed his wineglass on the mantle as he added some logs to the fireplace.

"The fact Batchelor chose you is a compliment in itself. He's got the money to hire anyone he wants." Too bad that he'd shattered Jace's view of his onetime idol.

"I guess." Jace joined her at the window. "At least you're enjoying yourself."

"How couldn't I? Just look at this place." Their luxurious cabin would cost thousands per night at a mountaintop resort. The spacious post-and-beam log cabin was larger than their house, and its heated slate floors and lush throw rugs were much more opulent. The spectacular cliff side views took her breath away.

Kat opened the sliding door and stepped out onto the deck. In less than an hour, the snow had blanketed the rocks and transformed them into large white mounds. The clouds hung low over the valley, giving it a mystical, eerie feeling. Everything was still and silent, the birds now burrowed in their nests as the snow intensified.

She shivered and returned inside. "We've still got a few hours before dinner. Let's go for a hike in the snow. You can blow off some steam."

"First things first," Jace pulled Kat onto the bed. "Let's relax here instead."

That wasn't quite what she had in mind, but it was definitely a lot warmer inside. "Isn't it peaceful? I could watch the snow fall for hours."

Kat snuggled into Jace's chest. The scenery was a nice contrast from rainy Vancouver. The wintry landscape put her in the Christmas spirit. Best of all, it was visible from the comfort of their king-sized bed. The snowflakes were bigger now, and the valley view obscured. Maybe staying inside wasn't so bad after all.

Jace suddenly bolted upright. "Wait, isn't that Ranger?" He pointed to the kitchen window. "What's he doing out there?"

Maybe their cabin wasn't as secluded as she had first thought. Thirty feet away just beyond the screen of trees, she saw Ranger's large form and that of another, smaller man. They stood beside a snowmobile on what appeared to be an access road, probably part of the road they had arrived on.

"They look like they're arguing about something," Kat said. The smaller man gesticulated angrily as he mounted the snowmobile. Jace walked to the window to get a better look. Kat followed. From their vantage point they observed unseen. They couldn't hear any of the conversation, but it was obvious that Ranger was ordering the stranger to do something. But it wasn't going over well. The man hopped off the snowmobile and stomped towards Ranger in the snow. He gesticulated wildly as he yelled at Ranger.

Ranger grabbed the man's arms and yanked them down. He pushed the man backwards.

The stranger teetered before stepping forward to regain his balance. Ranger shoved him again and he fell onto his back in the snow beside the snowmobile.

The snowmobile had a small trailer attached. Both were heavily laden with cardboard boxes. The boxes had large red lettering, but it was too distant to be legible.

The man pushed himself up, one arm on the boxes. He said something to Ranger, but he appeared more subdued this time. Ranger threw his hands up and stormed off towards the lodge. Within minutes he reappeared on a second snowmobile. The two men sped off on their vehicles, Ranger in front. They left a trail of snow spray in their wake.

Kat now had second thoughts about a snowmobile excursion with Ranger. His mood swings didn't exactly make for good company.

"Jace?"

"Hmm?"

"Isn't it ironic that our environmentalist friend has a huge lodge that consumes tons of power? And all these vehicles? How many environmental crusaders have their own private plane?"

"You've got a point there."

"Ask him about it."

Jace snorted. "I can't do that."

"Why not? Just because you're ghostwriting doesn't mean you're muzzled. Why not force the issue?"

Jace cast a doubtful look.

"He has to address it in his book, or other people will do it for him. That's how you can convince him to tell the real story. Even if your name's not on the book, you can still be proud of how it's written."

"I suppose I could ask. Worst thing he could do is kick me out of here. And to do that, he'd have to fly us home." He smiled. "That's exactly what I want anyways."

"Just ask nicely." She hugged him. "I want to enjoy this place a bit before you wear out our welcome."

"I'll try, but no guarantees if it means compromising my values. Better get in your fun now, before it's too late."

She intended to do exactly that.

## Chapter 3

Saturday morning dawned clear and bright. Kat's stomach rumbled, but she was apprehensive about breakfast at the lodge with Batchelor. Jace had ruminated over Batchelor's contract trickery all night, and she was a little worried he might lose his cool.

He only had to cooperate with Batchelor for a weekend to earn a cool hundred grand for his efforts. It wasn't quite as simple as that, of course. The two men would complete the first draft this weekend. Jace would revise and polish the draft into a finished manuscript over the coming months. He only had to keep his temper in check for the weekend.

Jace had counted on not just the lucrative payment, but also the name recognition and exposure that came with his name listed as author. That was his sticking point. As a ghostwriter, only Batchelor's name showed on the book cover. Jace's contribution was anonymous.

While she didn't blame Jace for feeling misled about the biography, it was a done deal and unfortunately he hadn't read the fine print. A contract was a contract and he had to honor his commitment. He had to endure Batchelor for only a day until they returned to Vancouver tomorrow night.

Batchelor was already seated in the dining hall when Kat and Jace arrived for breakfast at the lodge. He nodded in acknowledgement while he talked on a headset. Like most tycoons, he worked constantly. Kat's worries about awkwardness were unnecessary. Batchelor, at least, showed no animosity.

Kat glanced over at Jace but he wore a blank expression. His emotions remained in check but just barely. His calm demeanour from moments ago had vanished, but tension simmered just below the surface. Was it because she knew him so well, or could Batchelor feel it too? How long until Jace erupted? He would have a hard time maintaining his cool as he worked with Dennis all day.

Dennis Batchelor had either already eaten or else had decided not to. A glass of ice water and a stack of manila files sat before him. He finished his call and downed his glass of water before turning towards them. He studiously avoided eye contact with Jace but smiled at Kat. "Good morning."

"Morning," she replied. The unspoken tension was awkward to say the least. Apparently Dennis had picked up on Jace's mood after all. Luxury digs or not, this was shaping up to be one long weekend.

The uncomfortable silence grew as she sat across the table from Jace. Dennis rose and walked over to the refrigerator. His heels clicked on the marble floor, accentuating the lack of conversation. He placed his glass under the ice dispenser and ice clinked as it tumbled into his glass. He returned to his seat and twisted the cap off a bottle of water, all without saying a word.

The silence was unbearable and she scanned the room for a conversation starter.

She was surprised to see bottled water at each place setting. "You don't have tap water?"

"Not since the water pipe burst yesterday. It's from the cold weather we've been having lately. This is a temporary fix until the repairs are completed."

Kat opened a bottle and filled her glass. Bottled water seemed such a shame when they were surrounded by glaciers and snowpack. She glanced out the window to the three-foot high snowdrifts that surrounded the lodge. Plenty of fresh water in that. Melting snow was hardly efficient, but trucking in—or flying in—bottled water had to be even less so.

Batchelor must have guessed her thoughts. "Our tap water comes from a glacier-fed lake. It's a shame you can't try it."

"I'll just try it in town."

He shook his head. "You can't. The burst water pipe is at the reservoir, not here at the lodge. I'm afraid you can't get the water anywhere right now."

"I guess it can't be repaired in the wintertime." The weather was too cold, and with the highway closed, it would probably be difficult to find a contractor willing to visit the remote area in the dead of winter.

Batchelor didn't respond.

The chef prepared cooked to order eggs while they filled their plates from the sumptuous buffet. There was an assortment of cheeses, breads, and even fresh salmon. There was so much food that Kat wondered if there were other guests. She wished there were, since her current tablemates weren't exactly talkative.

Kat changed the subject. "I think I'll go for a hike today. Any good trails nearby?" While Jace and Dennis worked all day, she would make the most of her visit. Once the two men were alone they would be forced to talk to each other.

"Not really. There's not much to do around here, but Ranger can take you to the village if you like."

"That would be great." Kat perked up at the thought of returning to the little town with its quaint little shops and cafes along the main street. There might even be an outdoors store of some sort. She would browse the shops for an hour or two and finish up with a walk or hike on the outskirts of town. Batchelor's reference to a village surprised her, since Sinclair Junction appeared to have at least several thousand people.

"Ranger will have to take you by snowmobile, now that the highway's closed from the snow last night."

Even better. She had never been on a snowmobile before.

As if by magic Ranger appeared in the doorway. No doubt he had eavesdropped on their conversation, which unnerved her. She had a mixed impression of him after witnessing his altercation with the stranger yesterday.

"I didn't know there was another way to get up here."

"It's really just a trail. We don't depend on the highway, especially in winter when it's often closed from avalanches and rock slides. Closures sometimes last for days or even weeks. When the road is open during the winter, with the snow and ice, it's treacherous at best. That's why we flew you in. Even in the summer the trip takes at least nine hours of driving."

"I thought Sinclair Junction was bigger than that. It looks more like a town."

"I'm not talking about Sinclair Junction. There's a village nearby, called Paradise Peaks. That's where the trail goes."

"I didn't see a village on the way in." Kat hadn't seen any indications of a nearby settlement. Except, of course, for the protestors.

"The village is in the opposite direction from the road you arrived on. It's not much of a destination, but there is a small general store. It's just a few miles from here."

Her heart sank as she realized she wouldn't get to explore the historic town after all. No shopping, either. "That close? Maybe I'll walk instead." She looked forward to breathing the clear mountain air and getting a little exercise.

"You can't walk. There's no road and the snow's too deep. You'll have to go on the backcountry trail by snowmobile. You'd never find it on your own."

"That sounds great, Dennis. I'll take you up on your offer." She stole a sideways glance at Jace, who pretended to be absorbed in a magazine as he ate. She remained flexible, even if it wasn't quite what she had expected.

"I think you'll like the village. The general store has operated since the late 1800's," Dennis said. "It's got everything you could possibly imagine, from hardware to hunting gear to honey. People come from miles around."

"It seems so remote here, like there's hardly anyone around. Where are they all hiding?" She hoped the village population included more than just the protestors.

"It's deceiving. There are hundreds of people within a few miles, but they're scattered amongst ranches and homesteads. Invisible from view, but nearby nonetheless."

Kat wondered how all the hidden people earned a livelihood. Rumor had it that the hills harbored a number of illegal marijuana grow operations. She wasn't aware of any other industry nearby. Mining had been big but had collapsed mid-last century. Maybe pot had replaced it. She decided against asking about the rumored grow-ops and made small talk instead. "I can see why you like it here. It's so quiet and peaceful."

"We like it that way," Dennis said. "Most people come here to get away from the rat race."

"Ready?" Ranger smiled at Kat.

She grinned. "I'll grab my jacket and stuff."

"Great, I'll meet you outside in ten minutes."

Kat said goodbye to the men, glad to escape the awkward silence.

Minutes later Kat sat behind Ranger on the snowmobile. They glided through the fresh powder, the sunlight sparkling off the snow spray left in the snowmobile's wake. The loud engine prevented conversation, which suited Kat just fine. She admired the winter scenery as they crossed the rolling terrain.

The route took them across an open plateau that seemed to go on for miles. Snow covered trees lined one side of the plateau, while rocky cliffs abruptly dropped off about a kilometer away on the opposite side of the plateau. They traversed along the edge of the forest until it gradually filled in around them and the cliff edge disappeared from view.

An hour into their ride they screeched to a halt. Fallen trees across the trail several feet away blocked the path. Ranger cut the engine and turned to her.

"Almost didn't see it in time. They're at it again." He hopped off the snowmobile and walked over to the fallen trees. He tried to move one as he swore under his breath. It didn't budge.

"Who's they?" Kat asked.

"The activists don't like people coming through here. Not that they have any say in the matter. This is government land and they have no right to block public lands."

"What are they protesting? Same as the others?"

Ranger ignored her question. "I'll have to take you back. We'll take the truck into town."

"You sure have a lot of angry people around here. Something in the air?" Ranger's comments dispelled the laid-back pot growing hippies she had imagined.

"Something like that." He turned the snowmobile around and they headed back to the lodge. Soon they had reached the fence at Batchelor's property boundary. Ranger stepped off the snowmobile and opened the gate.

Kat was momentarily tempted to check in on Jace and Dennis, but decided against it. Besides, she was enjoying the fresh air of the wintry morning, and it was a waste not to look around a little. "Maybe I'll just explore around here, get some fresh air."

"If you want. Just don't wander off the property." He pointed towards a gentle slope that veered away from the mountains and the direction of the protestors. "See the edge of that clearing?"

Kat nodded. The trees were sparser, and light streamed through them.

"There's a trail over there. Follow it and you'll reach the road. Instead of following the road, cross it and continue along the trail. It's a circle route, so you can follow it back to the clearing. There's a nice little lake at the end of the loop."

"Okay." Why hadn't Ranger or Dennis mentioned the trail before? After all, she had originally wanted to go for a walk.

"We'll meet back here and I'll drive you back." Ranger looked past her just as the sound of approaching snowmobiles grew louder. "Right now I've got some business to take care of."

"All right. I'll be back here in—"

"Make it an hour." Ranger abruptly turned away and revved the engine. He sped off in the direction of the other vehicles without another word.

The snowmobile motors faded into the distance as Kat set out on her trek. The snow reflected the bright sunlight and all was silent except for her footsteps. The snow was fresh, light, and fluffy from last night's snowfall. Her tracks were the only break in the otherwise endless expanse of white.

She reached the trailhead ten minutes later. The tree canopy protected the trail from snow so walking was easier going. She glimpsed the road through the trees five minutes later and reached the lake a few minutes after that. Very anticlimactic. Ranger had obviously underestimated either the length of the trail, her fitness level, or both.

Now what? She still had forty-five minutes until Ranger returned—a lot of time to kill. She doubled back and walked the trail again, noticing the deep snowdrifts that welled around the trees. Rabbit and other small animal tracks paralleled the trail. Anywhere with small game likely had predators, too. What kinds inhabited a high alpine plateau? Wolves, maybe bobcats? Were they watching her now?

She shivered as she realized predators were silent by design. Their continued existence depended upon it. But if any predators hid nearby, they remained invisible.

Kat was now acutely aware of the silence. No songbirds, since it was too cold for most birds to winter in the area. But she saw no hawks or other birds either. She relaxed a little as she realized that all but the raptors would have migrated south for the winter. Any diehards would congregate at lower elevations where the temperature was warmer. The heavy snow dramatically lessened food sources for both predators and their prey. Animals in the area either hibernated or spent most of their time burrowed deep in their dens.

Her rationalization didn't make the silence any less eerie. She reversed course and repeated the trail several more times. The only interesting sight was the lake, though it wasn't much to look at in winter. It was completely frozen over, encircled by snowy hills. No birds or wildflowers, just a silent wintry forest. She returned to her starting point. By now almost an hour had elapsed. Still no sign of Ranger.

No sound of his snowmobile approaching either. Despite the silence, she got the eerie feeling that something—or someone— was watching her. She remembered Dennis's comment that hundreds of people lived nearby. Where were they all hiding?

She jumped as something crashed through the underbrush. Probably just a deer.

Maybe she was just being paranoid. Ranger wouldn't have directed her here if it were dangerous. There was no harm in exploring further while she waited, as long as she kept her sense of direction. She still had ten minutes before she was due at their appointed meeting place.

She spotted another trail opening on a nearby incline and wished she had noticed it sooner. Ranger's assumption that she wasn't up to the task annoyed her. The steep incline was exactly what she needed: a bit of cardio exercise and a possible viewpoint.

She trudged uphill, noting that the trail had at least a ten percent incline. The steepness provided a benefit, though, since the elevation likely provided a bird's eye view of their meeting spot. She could quickly scramble down once she caught sight of Ranger.

Her day hikers weren't meant for snow and ice and she slipped a few times as she struggled to gain purchase on the icy hill. Snow seeped into her boots and she regretted not bringing gaiters to keep her ankles dry. She hadn't really thought things through when she dressed for the outing. Then again, she had expected to explore a town, not hike up a mountainside. Not that it mattered, since she was in no danger of freezing. She would be back at the lodge warming by the fire in less than an hour.

She scrambled up the last section of incline, sweating inside her heavy jacket. Ranger was crazy to think she needed an hour on the other trail.

She exited the trail and emerged onto the plateau just as a gunshot rang out. She froze in fear. Ranger hadn't mentioned hunting nearby, and she hadn't seen any evidence of deer or other game. What other reason was there for gunshots in the wilderness?

While Ranger wouldn't have dropped her off in the middle of a hunting range, she had deviated from his instructions. She was at least half a mile away from their meeting place. She shouldn't have taken the trail. Her jacket blended in to her surroundings. What if the hunter mistook her movements for game?

She froze, unsure what to do. Instincts told her to return to the trail for cover, but she was unsure about the gunshot direction. She needed to distance herself from the shooter, but sudden movements might engage the shooter's trigger finger.

Should she forget about Ranger and just return to the lodge on her own? She decided to wait a bit longer, hoping Ranger had heard the shot and would return quickly. Where the hell was he anyways? According to her watch, he was now ten minutes overdue.

A branch snapped behind her.

"Don't move or I'll shoot." The woman pressed her rifle into Kat's back.

# Chapter 4

The woman's voice was soft but firm. "Hands up where I can see 'em."

An armed holdup was the last thing Kat had expected in the backcountry.

Kat slowly raised her arms. "Don't shoot. I'll leave now."

"You'll do as I say. Now turn around. Slowly."

Kat complied only to face the rifle barrel inches from her chest. Her eyes travelled up the barrel and met the steely blue eyes of a very fit looking gray-haired woman. She was about six inches shorter than Kat, but given the gun she wasn't about to challenge her.

The woman shifted on her cross-country skis and glared at Kat. She recognized Elke, the woman they had encountered at the road blockade. "I didn't mean to—"

"I'll do the talking." She kept her gun trained on Kat. "Tell me who you are and why you're here."

"I'm Dennis Batchelor's guest. I think we met at your blockade—"

"Hands up, I said."

Kat obeyed. "I think I'm still on his land." She hadn't passed a fence or other boundary marker to make her think otherwise. Maybe there weren't any markers or property line. In any event, acting confident might defuse the situation. Where the heck was Ranger when she needed him?

"That's open for debate." Elke's rifle was disproportionate to her tiny frame. So was her huge pack. A collapsible shovel was attached with bungee cords and a pair of ski poles lay on the snow by her feet. She appeared prepared for anything.

"Okay, my mistake." Ranger hadn't indicated exactly where the lodge property ended. She regretted deviating from the original route.

"You got that right." Elke tilted her head in the direction of the lodge. "Now turn around and make yourself scarce."

"Lower your gun first." If Elke's heavy pack threw her off balance, she might accidentally pull the trigger.

Elke snorted. "Why should I?"

"Look, I'm sorry if I startled you. Your disagreements with Dennis Batchelor are none of my business and I'd like to keep it that way. I'll leave immediately if you'll just lower your gun. I'm not turning my back with that thing pointed at me." She didn't want to agitate Elke further, but that trigger finger scared her.

Elke didn't budge. "You a part of this too? Driving us out so Batchelor can profit?"

"I have no idea what you're talking about. I'm just here for the weekend while my boyfriend works on a project with Dennis." She should have left when she had the chance. "I think I'd better go now."

"Hold on—what kind of work?" Elke's eyes narrowed.

"He's a journalist," she said. "He's writing Dennis's biography." Gun or not, it was no business of Elke's. She regretted giving further details.

"Full of lies, no doubt. If that's what your boyfriend is really doing." But Elke lowered the gun slightly. It now pointed at Kat's feet.

"Of course it is." Kat's heart raced. She risked angering Elke further, since saying nothing could be worse. Things could deteriorate very quickly with a gun-wielding crackpot in the wilderness. "Why else would we be here?"

"Don't spin doctor things. You're as bad as Batchelor." Elke shifted her balance slightly. "Everything's about money for you people."

"What people?" Kat resented being lumped in with Batchelor. She refocused on the gun. Was the safety on? Would it go off? "For the last time, can you please stop pointing your gun at me?"

Elke complied this time and dropped the rifle to her side. "How can Batchelor call himself an environmentalist? He's let them ruin our drinking water all in the name of profits?"

"How is a broken water pipe his fault?" How could Elke blame him for the reservoir problem?

"Is that what he told you?" Elke shook her head. "I hope you're not drinking it."

"I'm drinking bottled water. At least temporarily, till the problem gets fixed."

"Don't hold your breath. That water's been bad for three years, ever since the tailings pond overflowed and contaminated our water. The mine won't fix it. Matter of fact, they won't do anything now that it's shut down." Her fingers formed quote marks in the air. "They say it's un-economical."

Elke's accusation differed significantly from Batchelor's version. Three years was a long time to forgo tap water. "Dennis told me about the mine, but said the tailings pond had been remediated."

"Of course he says that." Elke scoffed. "The company did some half-assed repair to the breached wall. Technically they repaired it, but not in time to stop poisoning our groundwater."

"Can't it be fixed?" Surrounding waterways and soil had to be remediated and restored after an environmental accident. It was the law.

Elke shook her head. "It takes years. Nature has to take its course. Over time the contaminants dissolve. Meantime, we can't drink the water or grow crops."

Crops that might include marijuana. Which explained Elke's gun.

"I remember hearing about the accident now. It was all over the news when it happened. I kind of forgot about it when the media coverage died down."

"Everyone did. The politicians made their promises and the company agreed to fix things as long as the cameras were on them. In the meantime our cattle were poisoned and our crops died. People got sick."

"But that was a few years ago. Are you sure it's the water?" Canada wasn't exactly a developing country. There were laws in place to hold companies accountable. "The mine couldn't operate unless the tailings pond was fixed."

"Well, you catch on quick." Elke's eyes narrowed. "The mine isn't operating. They say gold prices are too low, and they're broke. Truth is, they struck a deal with government for a clean bill of health as long as they mothballed the mine. Walk away and they wouldn't be prosecuted. Where does that leave us?"

"Can't you take the company to court?" Mining extraction used many chemicals including cyanide. The purpose of tailings ponds was to keep the contaminants contained. If the company had left the pond unrepaired, they were liable for damages.

Elke shook her head. "Regal Gold is owned by a Chinese company. They're untouchable legally. That's one reason they've abandoned the mine. The other reason is depressed prices. Gold prices would have to double from current prices for the mine to break even. The owners have no incentive to operate it, let alone spend money to fix things. So they just walk away—abandon their investment."

"I see." Absolutely nothing to do with Batchelor.

"Do you? Did Batchelor tell you about his plans to drive us all out? He thinks he can outlast us by ruining our water, taking away our jobs."

Back to Batchelor again. Elke's rant jumped all over the place, blaming everyone.

"Wait a sec," Kat said. "Batchelor didn't ruin the water. He doesn't have safe drinking water either."

"He can afford to truck in drinking water. We can't."

"The water is a huge inconvenience to him, too. Even if what you're saying is true, he doesn't operate the mine. Blame the mine for not fixing things."

"He's in on it."

"Why would he be in on it? Do you have proof?" Batchelor had no reason to lie about the water.

"Not directly," Elke said. "He knows how to cover his tracks. I know what I'm talking about."

Kat seriously doubted that. "Have you contacted the government? They have regulations to ensure companies follow the rules."

"They're all involved. They cover for each other." Elke shifted her weight. Her gun, which was propped up against her leg, fell to the ground.

Kat jumped.

Elke bent and retrieved her gun. "Us ordinary people always get shafted."

"Well, I probably should be getting back to the lodge." Forget Ranger, wherever he was. She'd run as soon as she was beyond firing range from this crackpot conspiracy theorist.

"If I were you, I'd steer clear of that man. You know the saying, guilt by association?"

Kat nodded. "Where exactly is Batchelor's guilt in all this? He's impacted just as you are."

"He calls himself an environmentalist, yet he's silent on contaminated water in his own backyard. All he had to do was alert the media that this was never fixed properly. He could get the right people's attention and get it all fixed. Why hasn't he?"

Kat shrugged. Elke had a point. Batchelor had built his lodge several years ago, prior to the accident. Now his sanctuary was compromised with undrinkable water. "You think he's somehow involved with the mine?"

"All I know is that he has the power to do something but won't. Kind of suspicious for an environmental activist, if you ask me."

Kat scanned the horizon but saw no sign of Ranger or the snowmobile. She had better things to do than to argue with an armed stranger. She struggled to hold her tongue, though it was a stretch to blame Batchelor. It was a local problem, not hers, she reminded herself. "I really have to go."

Elke blocked her way. "They can silence the media and the government, too."

"Not the government." Kat wasn't sure who 'they' referred to. "There are regulations for this type of thing. No one's above the law."

"You're naïve."

"No I'm not. It's easy to measure contamination. Test results don't lie, and if they exist, someone should report them." The woman was a crackpot. A crackpot with a gun.

"They can be manipulated. Batchelor kept his mouth shut because there's something in it for him."

*He kept his mouth shut because there's no problem.* Kat didn't dare say it aloud. "I guess anything's possible."

Elke glared at her.

Kat tried to steer the discussion back on track. "Why can't you report them yourself? What's stopping you from going to the press? If what you just said is true, you'd expose a huge conspiracy with big business and the government."

Elke's face darkened. "You'd think so, but it always ends badly."

Kat glanced at her watch. She had already wasted twenty minutes over a dispute that was really none of her business. "I've really got to go." If she retraced her steps she would hopefully run into Ranger.

Elke was a nutcase, but some of her claims rang true. Wealthy people like Batchelor rarely tolerated major inconveniences for days, let alone years. How many environmentalists trucked or flew in bottled water for years on end?

Environmentalists also tended not to locate their wilderness retreats near mining operations. The Regal Gold Mine was active long before Batchelor's lodge was built. She flashed back to the news reports from the accident three years ago. She didn't recall any mention of Batchelor. Odd, given his penchant for publicity.

Elke had a point that environmentalists normally objected to environmental disasters in their own backyards. Kat peered over the woman's shoulder. Ranger was overdue by more than an hour now, and she had no way to contact him or anyone else without a cell phone signal.

"Ask Batchelor what he thinks of the Regal Gold Mine," Elke said. "Bet you won't get a straight answer."

"You really think he's somehow involved in the mine?" Maybe there was more to the story. If so, Jace might have gleaned some information as part of the biography.

"Of course he is. He lied to you about the mine being remediated, or else he wouldn't be drinking bottled water."

"But it's a broken pipe—"

"That's a flat out lie. First the tailings pond, then the mine shut down to avoid paying the environmental fines and remediation costs. The company just abandoned it, because it was too expensive to fix the tailings pond. People lost their jobs and left. The few of us remaining have a right to clean water. The only thing broken is our dreams."

They both started at the crunch of boots in the snow. Kat's hopes were dashed when she realized the man wasn't Ranger.

"Elke? I wondered where you were." The man came over and introduced himself. "I'm Fritz." He held out his hand as he spoke in accented English. Kat surmised they were husband and wife.

"Katerina Carter. Call me Kat." She shook his hand.

Fritz was much friendlier than Elke. He also had a calming effect on his wife, for which she was grateful. "We were just talking about the Regal Gold mine."

"Ah," he smiled. "Her favorite subject. She's told you about the contaminated drinking water?"

Kat nodded.

"It's not just our drinking water. The groundwater leaches into the grass our animals graze on and into our milk and meat. The offshore owners don't care."

"That's terrible," Kat agreed. It was also a shame that Dennis Batchelor couldn't or wouldn't use his influence to make things right. She decided to ask him directly when she returned to the lodge.

"But the water and the mine aren't your problem. You'll have to excuse Elke. She's very passionate about the subject." He sighed. "Me, I've moved on. There's nothing I can do against such powerful people. What brings you here?"

"Just visiting while my boyfriend does some work for Batchelor."

Fritz's face darkened. "Is that right?"

Kat immediately regretted her choice of words, which made Jace appear to be Batchelor's employee. "He's writing Batchelor's biography." Technically a ghostwritten autobiography, but that was irrelevant to the couple. "Batchelor said his mission was to protect this pristine wilderness."

"He probably didn't mention the road he's building."

"What road?" Kat flashed back to the photos on Batchelor's wall. If Fritz's claim was true, what had happened to the environmental champion who had chained himself to a tree? His comments echoed Elke's. Yet Batchelor hadn't mentioned a road. In fact, he seemed dead against development of any kind. "That's enough, Fritz. Let's go." Elke grabbed her husband's arm and steered him away just as a snowmobile motor grew louder.

Ranger came into view.

Kat breathed a sigh of relief as the snowmobile approached. She turned to say goodbye to the couple, but they were already a dozen feet away, skiing in the opposite direction.

She turned and walked towards the snowmobile, thinking about the mine and the couple's claims. She had halfway closed the gap when a loud bang stopped her in her tracks.

# Chapter 5

The crack was impossible to miss from Kat's vantage point. A massive snow slab had broken from the mountain directly above them. The snow ledge above it formed a deep 'V' fault line where the snow collapsed inwards. It held in suspended animation for a brief moment before gravity took hold, like a nature film in slow motion.

Then all hell broke loose.

One side collapsed and hurtled down the slope, an arrow seeking its target. The bull's eye was a few feet from where she and the Kimmels had stood less than a minute ago.

The split second of silence seemed eternal as faces and places, memories and her future flashed before her. Armed with perfect insight of what would unfold, yet powerless to stop it.

Another loud boom sounded as the second slab sheared off the mountain. The ground shook, almost knocking her off her feet. The vibration was accompanied by a low rumble. It grew in crescendo, almost but not quite drowning the Kimmels' screams. It was as if the entire top of the mountain had been chiseled off and dropped down the slope. It grew as it gathered snow in its wake, widening as it plummeted down the slope.

Kat spun in the direction Elke and Fritz had taken. The slide fanned out to a hundred feet across as it snowballed and raced down the mountainside. It was less than fifty feet above her, yet she stood paralyzed by fear. She could never outrun an avalanche.

Her eyes followed the trajectory only to see Elke and Fritz dead center in the middle of the slide zone. Fritz stumbled and fell as they frantically tried to reverse course.

"Help!" Elke screamed as she tugged on Fritz's arm, struggling to pull him upright. It was too late.

The snowball gained velocity and pummeled down the slope. It widened as it closed in twenty feet above the couple. The freeze frame bore into Kat's consciousness, the couple microscopic against the massive surf wave of snow just above them.

Then it swallowed them.

And there was nothing she could do.

Nothing at all.

It was coming for her, too. She screamed and ran in the opposite direction.

The trees.

Their thick trunks were all that would save her from burial in an icy grave. They might withstand the force of thousands of pounds of snow. Or they might not. The trees stood at the periphery of the otherwise bare slide zone, clear evidence of the carnage from earlier slides.

The trees were her last hope—but only if she reached them in time.

The closest stand of trees was just thirty feet away but her feet barely moved in the deep snow. Walking hadn't been a problem, but running was a herculean effort. Every footstep sunk in the snow like quicksand.

The rumble intensified as the sky darkened. The snow loomed above her like a Hawaiian surf wave.

She had to run, or die.

The copse of fir trees stood just ten feet away now, dwarfed by the avalanche. Even the trees might collapse under the barrage of snow, but it was her only chance of survival.

The vibration shook her to the core. Her heart exploded in her chest as she pushed herself forward. One step, two steps...

Could she make it?

She focussed on the treetops as they swayed under the first wave of snow.

Snowflakes tingled her cheeks as the snow barreled towards her. She reached the trees and collapsed in a tree well, exhausted. She pressed her back against the trunk and braced herself for the barrage to come.

A microsecond later the wall of snow hit with a forceful whoosh. The trees disappeared as the snow surrounded her. All she saw was white as icy flakes stung her exposed face. She instinctively reached upwards and waved her arms to push the snow away. The mountain reverberated as she fought to stay upright.

Just as quickly the slide was gone.

So was everything else.

She lay on the ground in the two-foot well at the base of the fir tree. She struggled to her feet, bruised and battered.

She brushed the snow off her jacket and surveyed her surroundings. Even here on the avalanche periphery, the damage was severe. Just her tree and one other still stood. The remaining dozen or so trees had snapped like twigs into pieces. Dumb luck that she had chosen a tree strong enough to withstand the force of the avalanche.

A close call.

Too close.

She looked up at the mountain peak and saw that at least a third of it had vanished. The avalanche slab had been even larger than she suspected. Her eyes followed the slide trajectory down the mountain. Everything in its path was obliterated, the landscape completely transformed.

Gone was the stand of the trees that Elke and Fritz had traversed before they reached the open slope. Most of the other trees lining the slope had also disappeared, buried under thirty feet or more of snowpack. The spot she had stood on moments earlier had taken a direct hit. If she hadn't run, she would have been buried.

The trees above her would have been hit too, except for the simple fact that they were just a few feet beyond the avalanche's direct path. The snow cloud that enveloped her had merely been peripheral spray, not the slide itself.

She had been lucky. In the right place at the right time when it counted.

A cry stuck in her throat as her eye caught movement. A pair of ski poles slid a dozen feet down the slope before they snagged on a small branch that poked from the snow. Five minutes earlier that branch had been the top of a forty-foot evergreen.

Except for the poles, the pristine snow betrayed nothing. No footsteps, path or trail. No movement.

All signs of human life erased.

Except for the poles.

When the couple left her minutes earlier, Elke had carried her rifle in one hand and poles in the other. Her ski poles rested atop the snow only because she hadn't used the wrist straps. Now she was gone.

Fritz had been ten feet ahead of his wife, but there was no sign of him either.

She had talked to them less than five minutes ago. Yet in a flash, they were encased in an icy prison.

Kat raced towards the last place she had seen them. She had to dig them out before they suffocated. Next to impossible, without a shovel to dig or a transceiver to locate them under the snow. In fact she had no avalanche or rescue equipment whatsoever. Without a cell phone signal, she couldn't even call for help.

All she could do was dig with her hands.

She yelled out, hoping for a response.

Silence.

She dug her hands into the snow, expecting the fresh soft powder she had been walking in. But this snow was hard and icy, older layers of freeze and melt as the weather changed. It was like cement. Soon her gloves were soaked through and her hands raw from the ice.

She had progressed less than a foot down in five minutes.

They could be dead by now. There had been no response from the couple, no sign that they were even in the spot she last saw them.

She realized in horror that this wasn't even necessarily where they had been buried. The snow might have carried them ten feet, or even a hundred feet further, before burying them. They could be anywhere.

They might not even be together, depending on the angle and velocity of how the snow had hit each of them. Had they been wearing avalanche transceivers? That only helped if someone with a receiver was here.

"Hey! Get over here, now."

It was Ranger, waving from the snowmobile. He stopped beside the two remaining fir trees.

"No. You come here. There's people buried. Get help." Kat resumed digging.

"I just radioed for help." Ranger yelled back. "You have to get out of there. Now, before another slide hits. That slope is extremely unstable."

"I have to get them out. Have you got a shovel?" Time was of the essence before it was too late. She couldn't stop now.

"There's nothing we can do without getting killed ourselves. Get over here, quick. " Ranger spoke into his radio and waved Kat over.

Seconds later a male voice crackled a reply. The radio static was so bad she couldn't discern the words. Nor did she care. Her sole focus was finding the Kimmels.

"We've got to save them." She had never experienced an avalanche firsthand but knew that no one extricated themselves without help. Victims were buried in concrete-like snow, unable to move their arms and legs. Even inches away, they were invisible and undetected by would-be rescuers.

The few who escaped alive usually had location transponders and a quick-thinking rescuer nearby. Even if shovels and probes were immediately put into action they were only effective some of the time. Time was not on the victims' side. Anyone not located and dug out within minutes suffocated.

Elke and Fritz lay somewhere under the snow, trapped. Did they hear her voice, unable to respond? Or was it already too late?

"I heard the avalanche." Ranger looked up from his radio. "I called Search and Rescue, but I can tell you, it's already too late for them. You might still make it, but you've got to get the hell over here, now."

She remained immobile.

"Kat, it's been almost thirty minutes. Nobody could last that long."

Thirty minutes? It seemed like under ten, but with all that had happened she had likely underestimated the elapsed time. It seemed like only minutes. Ranger was right, but that didn't make it any easier. Kat stood and trudged over to Ranger and the snowmobile, exhausted and saddened.

"What triggered the slide?" Kat scanned the mountainside, looking for evidence of skiers or snowmobilers above, but there was no sign of human activity.

Avalanches were rare in December. They were more common in the spring, when the temperatures were more likely to fluctuate, creating a cycle of freeze and thaw. She knew that much from Jace's work as a search and rescue volunteer. The weather here might be different than in the coastal mountains near Vancouver, but all avalanches operated under the same principles.

"Don't know. Sometimes it's the skiers themselves. They're tempted by the wide-open expanses and ski right across them. That's where it's most dangerous. It's also where the best powder lies."

But the couple had barely trudged through the trees when it started. And the slide had started far above them. No way could they have triggered it.

"Shouldn't Search and Rescue be here by now?" Ranger's comments troubled her. Fritz and Elke were experienced locals, so they would have known the terrain. Something didn't add up. Ranger looked up at the sky. "Help should be coming by helicopter. I thought they'd be here by now."

Kat still held a faint glimmer of hope for the couple, but the clock was ticking. "Can't we go a bit closer? Just to get a sense of where we might start to look? It might take some time. We could at least help the rescuers pinpoint where they disappeared."

"Maybe a little." Ranger nodded. "As long as we stay close to the trees and away from the avalanche path."

She followed him as he cut a wide circular path around where she had stood moments earlier. They walked slowly along the perimeter of brush and trees, looking for any sign of the couple or their equipment. Other than the ski poles, there was no sign of where the mountain had swallowed them.

Avalanches, like tornados, often dropped victims far from their original locations. They could be anywhere at or below their original location, and many feet under the snow. Rescue was against the odds.

"What's that?" Kat pointed to a dark object a hundred feet below them. She knew the answer before Ranger spoke. It was Elke's rifle. Elke was still nowhere to be seen.

"Doesn't mean she's anywhere near. It stayed atop the snow because it's lighter."

They stood at the same altitude the couple had last been, just a few feet away. She scanned the snow but saw no evidence of the couple's tracks before they disappeared under the slide. They had been directly in the line of fire. The impact itself might have killed them or at least knock them unconscious.

She was about to turn away when she noticed the tracks.

"See that?" She pointed at the snowmobile tracks, thirty feet above them. Odd, since she hadn't heard another snowmobile. And Ranger had come from the opposite direction. "Do you think that triggered it?"

Ranger shook his head. "That slab broke off yesterday, probably caused the slide today. Those skiers should have known better, too."

An odd thing to say.

Kat flashed back to Ranger's earlier comment. He had referred to the person carrying the rifle as 'she'. Ranger had arrived after the avalanche. How had he known that one was a woman and that she had been the one carrying the rifle?

"Yesterday?"

"Like I told you, it's dangerous to stay here." Ranger gazed up at the sky. "No idea why the chopper's not here yet, but the longer we stay, the more we risk our own lives. Whoever they were, there's no hope of survival."

"I recognized one of them—Elke from the blockade yesterday. She was with her husband. I even talked to them for a few minutes right before the…tragedy." A sob caught in her throat.

"A tragedy." Ranger's voice was devoid of emotion.

Kat recounted her discussion about the mine. "These people, they mentioned a road Batchelor wanted built. Do you know anything about it?"

"They don't want it to go through, even though it's for everyone's benefit. They pretend to be environmentalists, but they're not. They're pot growers, and a road increases the possibility of getting busted." He glanced over at the avalanche. "Guess that won't happen now."

Kat shivered. Still no sign of the rescuers. "Can't you radio again? Where are they?"

Even in the unlikely event Elke or Fritz had the foresight to wave their arms in front of their faces to create an air pocket, their survival chances were nonexistent now. Not that they had a chance to start with. She felt responsible since she was unable to rescue them.

Ranger spoke into his radio again then turned to her. "They're still ten minutes away on another call."

Kat's heart sank. The irony of the road struck her. "I suppose a road would have helped them in this case. They just didn't know it."

Ranger nodded. "You can't stand in the way of progress."

That wasn't quite what Kat had meant, but in a way Ranger was right.

# Chapter 6

Kat sat opposite the hearth in the lodge great room, her trembling hands warmed by a steaming cup of freshly brewed coffee. She sunk into an overstuffed armchair, still shaken from the avalanche.

Pure luck had saved her from being buried under two tons of snow.

But Elke or Fritz had suffered a much worse fate. Would they have lived if help had arrived on time? She would never know, and she felt sick about it. Search and Rescue did eventually arrive, but more than an hour after the avalanche.

"You shouldn't have gone off on your own like that." Jace sat on the edge of Kat's chair, his arm resting on her shoulder. "You're lucky the avalanche missed you."

She didn't feel lucky.

Ranger stood at the edge of the fireplace, water rivulets beading down his waterproof pants. A small puddle pooled on the black slate beneath his feet. Dennis looked up from the table, where he sat surrounded by notebooks, papers, and two laptops. The two men had abandoned their work since Kat and Ranger's return.

A look passed between Dennis and Ranger. Then they both focussed on Kat.

"It was too close for comfort." She shivered and wondered why Ranger hadn't warned her of the unstable snowpack. True, she had wandered a few hundred feet from his prescribed route. But still…

"A few more steps and you wouldn't be here talking about it." Ranger turned to Dennis. "Maybe it's not such a good idea for her to be out this time of year."

Ranger and Kat had returned to the lodge once the search and rescue crew halted rescue operations at the avalanche scene. They hadn't done much other than note the trajectory of Elke's poles and rifle. They too had questioned the snowmobile tracks, but neither Ranger nor she could explain them.

The operation was now classified as a recovery effort rather than an active search, since it was apparent no one could have survived. The search and rescue lead cited the elapsed time since the slide occurrence and the risk to the team's safety.

Dennis nodded. "With multiple avalanches, it's probably best for you to stick around the lodge."

So much for exploring the great outdoors. They were only here for the weekend anyway.

In the safety of the lodge, Kat finally had time to think about the accident. What if she had met Elke just a hundred feet further along the trail? She would have been buried right along with them. She shivered at the thought.

"It's such a shame they traversed across the slope the way they did." Dennis shook his head. "Reckless, especially with the snowpack conditions around here. They knew better."

Ranger nodded. "The avalanche risk is pretty high right now. What were they thinking?"

Kat flashed back to the accident. She had only been on the very periphery of the slide, yet the blast of snow had hit her like a brick wall. "Elke and Fritz never stood a chance."

"So often there's no warning," Dennis agreed. "Even locals like the Kimmels make mistakes."

Kat turned to Ranger. "You never mentioned any danger." If Ranger was so concerned, why hadn't he mentioned the avalanche danger when he dropped her off? Although he had directed her in the opposite direction, she could have easily traversed the same slope as Elke and Fritz and met a similar fate.

"You didn't stay where I told you to go. Besides, there wasn't any danger, until now," Ranger scratched his chin. "Then two slides in one day. I never expected that."

Three slides, Kat thought. Surely yesterday's slide should have been a predictor. The unsettled weather was likely a factor. Last night's snowstorm compounded the risk by depositing a heavy layer of new snow atop the existing snowpack.

Today's avalanche had killed two people. It had occurred in exactly the same spot as yesterday. Ranger feigned surprise, but his lack of emotion contradicted his statement. He reacted as if the accident was an everyday occurrence. At the very least, the earlier slide should have triggered a warning when he dropped her off.

So many questions raced through her mind, questions that lacked satisfactory answers. Ranger's behaviour was very odd.

"Will the police interview us?"

Ranger stared at her like she was crazy. "It was an accident."

"But two people died." Surely that warranted an investigation, even somewhere as remote as this place.

"I've taken care of things already," Ranger said. "I've briefed the police about the accident and so has Search and Rescue. They can't recover the bodies until the spring snow melt anyways. Too dangerous."

Except for a few minutes after their return to the lodge, Ranger had barely left her sight. She hadn't seen him make a call. "But what about the accident scene? Surely they should look at that?"

"Too dangerous at the moment. Could trigger another slide. They've already got our account of the accident and it's not going to bring them back."

"Our account?" She was a first-hand witness whereas Ranger hadn't been close enough to see anything but the aftermath. "Don't they need to talk to me directly?"

"I recounted your details." Ranger paused for a moment, then added, "They'll get in touch with you later."

"But I want to talk to them now, while things are fresh in my mind." No investigation while the evidence was present? Danger or not, that just seemed like shoddy investigative practice.

She glanced at Dennis to gauge his reaction, but his head was buried again in his notes. She realized that the tragic accident had an upside for him, since it conveniently extinguished his most vocal protestor. A coincidence, or something more?

"They're locals?" Jace frowned. "I'm surprised they were caught in the slide. In my ten years of search and rescue I've never seen that. It's usually tourists and inexperienced hikers, people unfamiliar with the area."

"The Kimmels were getting on in years," Dennis said. "They made a poor decision. They were complacent, or maybe they've just forgotten how dangerous the mountains can be."

The couple were in their late sixties, but fitter than people twenty years their junior. Kat thought Elke was fitter than she was. Age didn't appear to be an issue for either of them, physically or mentally. "They seemed pretty together to me."

"Have they always lived in the area?" Jace asked.

Dennis nodded. "The Kimmels emigrated from Germany forty years ago and have been here ever since. Fritz worked at the local mine until he retired a few years back."

"The Regal Gold Mine?" Fritz hadn't mentioned he had worked at, let alone retired, from the mine. But why would he? Theirs was nothing more than a five-minute conversation between strangers.

"That's the one," Dennis said. "Let me guess. He told you about a conspiracy to poison local residents."

Kat hesitated. "Not quite, though he did accuse the mine of negligence. He also thought you should play a more active role."

A flicker of expression passed over Dennis's face. A second later it was gone. He turned to Ranger. "See if we can help the family with the funeral arrangements."

"Are you absolutely sure there's nothing Search and Rescue can do? To at least recover their bodies?" Kat couldn't imagine what it would be like for their family.

Ranger shook his head. "Too risky."

"They've just been left for dead?" Kat knew of the risks from Jace's search and rescue volunteer work, but the quickness of the assessment surprised her. "I want to go back there. Someone should."

Dennis shook his head. "It won't make a difference. They're gone and we can't help them anymore. You're suffering from survivor's guilt. Let it go."

"How can I? We can't just leave them there."

"We won't," Dennis said. "Once the weather cools again and the snow layers stabilize, we'll look for them. Could be a few days or a few weeks."

Or longer, Kat thought. He just wanted her to stop talking about it.

"It sounds harsh, Kat, but it's too dangerous for the searchers." Jace stood and strode over to the table. "If they're not out within minutes, it's no longer a search and rescue. There's no hope of survival. It's too dangerous to risk other peoples' lives for that."

"Jace is right," Ranger said. "We'll risk triggering another slide."

"I get that, but it's still terrible." She turned to Ranger. "How well did you know them?"

"Fairly well, I guess. That's not to say I liked them much. It's a tragedy and all, but I have to say it: they were troublemakers."

"Why do you say that?" They seemed nice. Other than Elke holding her up at gunpoint, that is.

"I agree with Ranger. They wouldn't give an inch," Dennis said. "Their land adjoins mine, and we've had numerous run-ins with them in the past. They tended to take action first and ask questions later. All the same, I'm sorry they were caught in the avalanche. I wouldn't wish that on anyone."

"What kind of run-ins?" Kat wanted to know more.

"Just neighbor disputes. Not that it matters anymore." Dennis turned to Jace. "Time to get back to work. We've got a story to write."

The fire roared in the hearth, but Kat felt a chill in the air.

# Chapter 7

An hour later and back in her cabin, Kat stripped off her wet clothes and stepped into the shower. The hot water washed away the physical chill, but it couldn't erase her thoughts of the tragedy. The Kimmels' lives had been extinguished in less than a minute. Their protests were instantly silenced, their voices no longer heard. She shivered at the thought.

Elke and Fritz were practically strangers, yet she felt a connection after witnessing their tragic deaths. She fought back tears, yet felt irrational to be so upset about people she didn't even know. Her reaction likely stemmed from her own close call. The accident hadn't bothered Dennis or Ranger much. Both chalked it up to a force of nature and then got on with their day. While they obviously disliked the couple, Kat had expected more emotion over neighbors they had known for decades. Had they been in the area, they could have been victims too.

How could they be so callous?

She stepped from the shower onto the heated stone floor, the warmth comforting under her feet. She towelled off and wondered how Dennis and Jace could just carry on working. Of course, Jace hadn't been there, he didn't know the couple, and he had no choice but to follow Dennis's lead. Dennis was another story. Like it or not, the Kimmels were his neighbors, and the accident had occurred nearby. His nonchalance troubled her.

Kat changed into jeans and a sweatshirt and built a fire from the stack of logs beside the hearth. She was probably overreacting, traumatized by her own close call. After all, she barely knew the couple. But something felt wrong. Although she couldn't pinpoint it, she couldn't shake the feeling that she had missed something important.

Her suspicions grew while she stoked the fire. The Kimmels' fatal accident seemed a serendipitous outcome for their enemies. Judging by Dennis and Ranger's comments, the Kimmels' were the driving force behind the mine protests, and Elke Kimmel, the de facto leader. Maybe it wasn't an accident at all.

Assuming it wasn't an accident, who wanted the couple dead? The mine's owners certainly benefitted from their deaths. However, as absentee owners, they weren't in the vicinity. Could they be indirectly involved?

Dennis's dislike for the couple was obvious, though he hadn't come right out and said it. It struck Kat as odd given their shared background as wilderness lovers and protestors that gave them plenty of common ground. It should at least have elicited a bit of sympathy. Ranger's behavior was also strange, especially his insistence that the search be scaled back.

Was she imagining a conspiracy where none existed? Maybe, but conspiracy theories often contained elements of truth. Maybe that was the case here.

Her latest theory had come to her in the shower. The more she thought about it, the more convinced she became that today's avalanche was something more sinister than an accident. Ranger had the means, motive, and opportunity. He intensely disliked the Kimmels, and his time and whereabouts immediately prior to the accident were unaccounted for. He had a snowmobile, which could have made the tracks high up on the mountain slope.

It also explained why he hadn't been keen on answering her questions.

To hell with Ranger, search and rescue, and the police. If they were unwilling to step up and investigate, she would. This wasn't one of her usual fraud investigation cases, but it shared the same basic elements: means, motive, and opportunity.

That is, if it even was a crime. But given all the inconsistencies, how could it not be?

She replayed the events over in her mind. Where to begin? She rifled through her bag and extracted a notepad and pencil. Since she was stuck in the cabin with nothing better to do, she might as well jot down a few notes while the details were fresh in her mind. They would come in handy if and when the police eventually got around to talking to her.

First, she noted Dennis's earlier comments and his reaction to the news. She put a question mark beside his relationship with the Kimmels. She would explore that in more detail later.

Certainly Ranger and Dennis held no great affection for them. Were there others? The remaining protestors would be a good source of information. She needed to reach them without letting on to Ranger or Dennis.

She refocused on the snowmobile tracks, since they had likely triggered the avalanche by destabilizing the weaker snow layers. The unstable weather patterns over the last few weeks were a factor. The constant freeze and thaw from snow and freezing rain coupled with warmer temperatures over the last few days had weakened the snow pack.

Even she knew that from snowshoeing in the backcountry. It was Avalanche 101.

Snow layers accumulated with each snowfall, and some were heavier than others. The thickness and density depended on the humidity and duration of the snowfall. Temperature changes set off a cycle of warming and cooling, melting and refreezing. On warmer days like today, some layers thawed more than others. How much depended on the location, like whether they were in the direct sun. A warm day and thaw was often enough to weaken the layers' adhesion and start a slide. Newer layers that hadn't yet bonded with older layers were particularly prone to slides.

It was obvious from looking at the hillside that it was prone to avalanches, given its sharp angles down from the two mountain peaks above that formed a natural bowl in the slope's middle. Earlier avalanches had removed trees from this part of the mountain, the telltale scar now the path of least resistance for future slides.

Search and Rescue, Ranger, and Dennis knew the weather impacts and the avalanche history of this particular area. Presumably the Kimmels and all the other local residents did too. While the risk was common knowledge, only Mother

Nature knew the exact time or place of a future avalanche. Where the slide would happen could be predicted but never the exact timing.

All of that pointed to a tragic accident instead of a sinister crime. Except that the avalanche had occurred in the morning, before the sun had warmed the slope. The snow hadn't thawed since the temperature was cold and the slope was still in shadow. Avalanches almost always occurred in the afternoon, after the sun warmed the unstable snow.

Maybe Mother Nature had some help.

She flashed back to the snowmobile tracks she had noticed just prior to the slide. Had a snowmobile triggered nature's natural forces? Knowing the instability of the snowpack, could someone have purposely triggered the slide?

She penciled in 'snowmobile' and made a note to check who else had one. In such a sparsely populated area there were probably only a few snowmobiles. However, every local likely had access, whether owned or borrowed. It hardly narrowed the field of suspects.

Not everyone had the opportunity to trigger the slide, though. Only those already on the mountain and in the vicinity had the means to do it. Who else was nearby on the mountain?

Ranger, for one.

But she hadn't seen or heard a snowmobile prior to the slide. She would have certainly heard the motor if he had driven across the slope above her.

Unless the tracks were made earlier. She recalled Ranger's comment of a slide the day before. The snowmobile tracks could have been made yesterday. While they were easily spotted from below, the danger after today's slide meant that no one had inspected them up close. The tracks might not be fresh. The snowmobile might have triggered yesterday's first, smaller slide instead. The now weakened snowpack had been ripe for a second slide. It seemed far-fetched for a chain reaction to be set in motion after a twenty-four hour delay, but it happened all the time.

Temperature changes and the resulting freeze and thaw cycle created unstable snow layers. A melted ice layer was much heavier than a powder snow layer. It became top heavy and didn't have enough time overnight to bond or re-bond to the layer underneath. Add in an unstable slope from a recent slide, and you had a recipe for disaster.

Except the weather had been very cold lately, and another storm was expected tonight.

One of the other protestors might have had a motive to harm the Kimmels. She could easily determine that by stopping by the blockade and questioning them. Most would have alibis, since they could vouch for each other's presence at the blockade.

One of the group might know the reason Elke and Fritz had even been on the slope in the first place. According to Ranger, they normally spent their days at the protest blockade. Yet today was different. They had been heading home from the protest site even though it was still morning. It was far too early for them to call it a day. Was it an unlucky coincidence, or had someone or something caused them to deviate from their regular routine?

That raised another question. Given the Kimmels knowledge of the terrain, why had they chosen that route in the first place? Why hadn't they taken the road or a safer trail?

On the other hand, if the slide was intentionally set, it was almost impossible to precisely time the slide at the exact minute the Kimmels were on the slope. The culprit had to be present at the exact moment of the disaster.

Most avalanches were triggered by something or someone. The Kimmels were too far down the mountain to set it off themselves. It had started far above them at the slope's peak. Yet she hadn't noticed any other people nearby nor seen any tracks. That didn't mean there weren't any, since she hadn't walked through the entire area. There were probably other trails leading to the ridge that she wasn't aware of. She scribbled a note to check all access points.

No matter what, somebody had been there. They couldn't avoid leaving tracks in the snow, whether snowmobile tracks or footprints. The snow would preserve those tracks, at least temporarily until the next snowfall. It was imperative to look for them now.

She disagreed completely with Ranger's comment about it being too dangerous to return. A third of the slope had collapsed. There simply wasn't enough snow left to form a new avalanche. Now was actually the perfect time, before the next snowfall obliterated the tracks.

Her thoughts flashed back to the out-of-town protestors Ranger had accused of blocking the trail with fallen trees. Who were they, and what exactly did they want? He had been vague on details.

The only way to find out was to locate and talk to them. But she wasn't supposed to leave the property due to the avalanche area. She didn't know their names or contact info, so she had no other way to reach them. Another reason to head outside on an exploratory mission.

One thing was certain. She couldn't wait any longer and risk a fresh snowfall obliterating the evidence. Dennis and Ranger could recommend that she not return to the hill, but they couldn't tell her what to do. They also couldn't interfere if she kept her plans secret.

Dennis and Jace were busy writing, and if Ranger questioned her she'd say she was just out for a walk around the property. She had the perfect opportunity to check things out for herself. As long as she was very careful she would be fine.

She checked her watch. Two o'clock. At least a couple of hours prior to nightfall, plenty of time to reach the slope if she left now. She put the camera in her pack and pulled on her boots. Maybe no one else thought it warranted follow-up, but she did. In fact, she had every right to demand an investigation, since it had been a close call for her, too. Clearly Ranger and Dennis felt the case was closed. And—if she believed Ranger—search and rescue felt the same way. She did not know if or when the police would investigate, but she had a hunch it would be never. The only way not to leave things to chance was to follow up herself.

If no one else would investigate, she would.

# Chapter 8

Kat walked quickly along the trail leading to the lodge but skirted across the driveway to avoid detection from anyone inside. Her path was directly in the line of sight from Dennis's study window. As long as no one looked out the window in the next minute or so, she could remain undetected. She breathed a sigh of relief when she reached the opposite side of the driveway.

Ranger's Landcruiser was absent from its parking spot beside the main entrance. An unexpected stroke of luck. In the unlikely event anyone spotted her, she would claim to be out for a walk along the property's fenced perimeter. The walk part was true, but her route led off the property to the avalanche site instead. She was now beyond the line of sight from Dennis's study but still visible from the lodge's other windows if anyone happened to look outside. In less than a hundred feet the elevation drop would make her invisible from any of the lodge's ground floor windows. As long as Ranger didn't return before she was safely out of view, no one would see her leave.

That thought gave her pause. She probably shouldn't return to the avalanche slide area alone without at least telling someone, Jace in particular. On the other hand, she couldn't interrupt him just because she had decided to go for a walk. Telling him in person also meant Dennis or Ranger would know about her fact-finding mission, awkward to say the least. Without cell coverage she couldn't even call him. Even the cabin didn't have a phone.

Even if she told Jace privately, he would insist she stay on site for safety reasons. That wouldn't do, because she was certain the avalanche was no accident. Trouble was, she had no proof of that. Proof she could only find by visiting the site.

She debated leaving a note, but decided it was best not to. Jace would just worry, though she could take care of herself just fine. She would tell him later, once safely back in the cabin and armed with whatever evidence she uncovered.

Jace had relied on Dennis and Ranger's assessment of the conditions, which she felt were exaggerated. She was the only one with first-hand knowledge, since she had been there. Dennis hadn't seen it, and Ranger had only shown up after the fact. She was perfectly capable of assessing the danger areas and remaining out of harm's way. She had done so once already today.

She planned to photograph the slope and the snowmobile tracks, preserving the evidence before it disappeared forever. Search and Rescue, Ranger, and the others considered the Kimmels' deaths a tragic accident, but she felt otherwise. Their lack of motivation to investigate further struck her as odd at best and suspicious at worst. Knowing the cause prevented future tragedies, so why wouldn't they follow up? Either they were lazy, negligent, or had other reasons not to research further. She suspected the latter. At any rate, she remained unconvinced it was a random accident. That meant she had to preserve the evidence before it was erased by tonight's snowfall. The snowmobile tracks weren't enough to trace the driver, but they certainly narrowed the field. The tracks might even point to a particular make and model. She didn't know enough about snowmobiles to be sure, but experts could identify a make or model from a photograph. There was probably other evidence on scene that was only visible from on top of the slope. She'd rather not be the one who did that, but someone had to. It was too late to help the Kimmels, but not too late to determine what happened and prevent another tragedy.

She glanced up at the sky. The sun had disappeared behind the dark clouds that moved in from the north. The clouds were low and close, the nimbostratus kind that brought snow. The storm might hit earlier than predicted.

The weather forecast called for heavy snow, up to a foot at the lower elevations. The accumulation could be double that at this elevation in the mountains. It was her last chance to view the tracks before they were completely obliterated with new snow.

She probably had an hour or so before the snowfall started, coincidentally the same amount of time she needed to reach the top of the slope. The peak was a shorter walk than the roundabout snowmobile tour Ranger had taken her on, and she wondered why he hadn't taken her to that spot in the first place. Aside from being safer atop the ridge, it probably had a fabulous view. She now had her bearings, helped by her off-route trek this morning and her current route. Several nearby trails led in the same direction. She opted for the one closest to the road they had come in on yesterday.

She patted her camera, determined to get as many photographs of the tracks as she could. She planned to take pictures of the ridge and the slope beneath it post-slide. Then she would send the photographs to nonlocal, unbiased avalanche experts for a second opinion. Jace, with his search and rescue background, might even have initial insights. They both had plenty of contacts back in Vancouver and elsewhere to draw upon.

At any rate, she had no time to waste. She checked her watch. Already two o'clock and a return trip on foot brought her dangerously close to dusk. She hoped the snow held off until then. She increased her pace to a brisk walk and stayed near the trees to avoid detection.

She regretted not leaving Jace a note, but it was too late for that now. Retracing her steps not only delayed her trek but also risked discovery. If Ranger or Dennis became aware of her quest they would undoubtedly stop her. Time was of the essence if she was to return before the storm hit.

She reached the fence line, a wood post and barbed-wire barrier that stretched the length of the property. She bent over and stepped through two of the wires, careful not to snag her clothing on the barbs. She paused on the other side, still doubtful about going solo. She was unfamiliar with the area and was still shaken from the avalanche. What if there was a repeat slide and she was caught alone? No one would even know she was there.

If it had been an accident, there was nothing to see and no reason to return. The odds of the avalanche being intentionally triggered were infinitesimally small and not worth risking her safety.

But still.

If the slide was premeditated, it provided an almost fail-safe way to get away with murder. She replayed the accident in her mind. The Kimmels' had been vocal members of the community, yet everyone seemed to have already moved on. Not everyone, she realized. She had only spoken with Dennis, Ranger, and a handful of locals from Search and Rescue. No one from the protest group. The protestors were exactly the people she needed to talk to. They knew the Kimmels and were also better equipped to preserve any evidence.

She debated back and forth as she trudged through the snow. The road was just a few meters away from the trail, close to the junction where the protestors had set up their blockade. They might have already checked out the avalanche site themselves. If that was the case, her trip was completely unnecessary. She was tired of second-guessing herself. A talk with the protestors might be a better start.

The blockade was located in the general direction as the slope but much closer, a twenty-minute walk at most. She could be back at the cabin in an hour instead of two, while still daylight and before Jace finished with Dennis. It was much easier to tell him about her adventure after the fact. That way he wouldn't worry about her safety.

The protestors might share her suspicions. Their views undoubtedly differed from Dennis and Ranger's, two men that were hardly representative of the locals. They could provide background information about the Kimmels as well as the slope's avalanche history. The couple's friends would probably appreciate her first-hand account as a witness and survivor. Talking to the protestors provided both further information and closure.

She trudged along until she reached an adjoining path. Within minutes, she was stopped in her tracks by fallen trees. She recognized it as the same path she had been on with Ranger earlier in the day. She paused to take a closer look at the barrier Ranger had attributed to the out-of-town protestor group. At least two dozen logs were stacked about five feet high and the trail had a steep drop off, surrounded with dense bush. Whoever had placed them there had required machinery to cut the trees down. Each tree was at least three feet in diameter and had fresh chainsaw cut marks. The out-of-town protestors came well-equipped.

She retraced her steps back to the original trail. The Kimmels were forced to traverse the avalanche slope as a direct result of this barrier. Their only other choice was the circuitous route by trail and road, at least twice as long.

According to Ranger, the Kimmels were a permanent fixture most days at the blockade, leaving at the same time each afternoon. Anyone who wanted them dead simply needed to lie in wait for them at the appointed time.

She froze mid-step. She had encountered the Kimmels mid-morning, rather than their normal afternoon departure time. Why had they deviated from their schedule? They would still be here if they had gone home at their usual time. The other protestors might know the reason behind their sudden departure.

Kat worked her way along the trail and twenty minutes later stepped onto the road, less than fifty feet from the blockade.

Flames shot up from an oil barrel but there were no protestors in sight. Her heart sank. It hadn't occurred to her that they would disband early after hearing about the fatalities.

As she approached, she noticed a dozen protest signs leaned neatly against a pickup truck. Somebody was here after all.

A grizzled, bearded man in his seventies approached her. He wore an ancient-looking ski jacket with Regal Gold Mines insignia and a crest that read 'Ed'.

"You're from the lodge."

Kat nodded. In a place this small everyone probably knew she was Dennis's guest, even if she didn't know about them. She introduced herself anyways. "My name's Kat. Can I talk to you about the Kimmels? I was there when it happened."

He narrowed his eyes. "You seemed to come out of it okay."

She noted with relief that he was unarmed. "I was just lucky. Though I don't feel very lucky. I'm here and they're not, though." She felt a catch in her throat. "It seemed more than just an accident, though. I saw snowmobile tracks at the top of the ridge."

The man said nothing.

"Why did the Kimmels leave the blockade mid-morning? Don't they normally stay all day?"

"You seem to know an awful lot about them. Did Ranger tell you?"

She shook her head. "No. As a matter of fact, he won't even talk to me about them. I'm guessing they're not exactly on friendly terms."

"You got that right." He glanced back towards the barrel fire. "I'd head back to the lodge if I were you. There's a storm blowing in. You wouldn't want to be caught in it."

Ed was polite but obviously distrusted her.

"About those snowmobile tracks. I'm certain that they triggered the slide. Maybe it was set on purpose, and Elke and Fritz were the intended victims. Did they have any enemies, anyone that wanted to harm them?"

"You'd be best to mind your own business. It's not any of your concern."

"Whose business is it, exactly? Nobody seems to care." The couple's death was practically a non-event to Dennis and Ranger, but surely it mattered to Ed and the other protestors. They could be targeted too.

"And you do?"

"I saw them right before they were buried in the slide. I could have died too. Whoever did this has to be stopped."

"You spoke to them?"

That struck a chord, finally.

"Elke and Fritz told me about the other protestor group." She recounted the blocked trail. "I can't help but think someone forced them onto that route. They were there because their regular route was blocked."

"I believe in peaceful protests. Elke and Fritz did too. The other protest group disagreed, said things weren't moving fast enough. They're big money, press coverage types, professional protestors selling a story to the six o'clock news. They're a crowd-pleasing flavor of the moment type of operation. They don't live here; they don't even talk to us. They even renamed some of our local places."

"They can't just do that."

"But they do, with made up names in their glossy marketing brochures. The mountain's getting reinvented, with names like

Raven Spirit Ridge and Great Bear Forest. More people hear those names now than the real ones. They drown us out, till everyone's forgotten the real names, our real history.

"They want to drive us out, too. Me, I've been here all my life. My great-grandfather homesteaded here. We cleared the valley, founded Paradise Peaks. Now they say we're ruining the wilderness. We're not doing a damn thing different than we've always done. We live here, and we were here first.

"They're the problem, making publicity we don't want and attracting all these do-gooder granola bottled water types, with their hemp clothing and hybrid cars."

Kat nodded and let him talk.

"There's nothing we can do about it. There aren't that many of us anymore, and we're tired of fighting for years on end. Some folk moved to find jobs after the mine closure, and everyone's fed up with the bad water."

Ed and the protestors were the victims, not the bullies. "Yet they want to build a new road?"

"Yeah. Dennis said he'd foot the bill since a new road makes things safer. He says the only way to finance cleaning up this mess is to bring in tourist dollars, make it like a wilderness mecca. Well, we don't agree. We're not getting bullied into accepting his damn asphalt when a dirt road's just fine. We don't want to see any more 'save the forest' do-gooders. We just want to live out our days in peace."

No wonder they despised Batchelor. He had some sort of alliance with the out-of-town protestors to achieve his own aims. He was a bully, trying to shove commerce down their throats in a take it or leave it proposition. It had worked for the most part. Most everyone had been driven out, except for a few stubborn retirees.

"Would you ever leave?"

Ed shook his head. "They'll have to carry me out. Most of us grew up here, raised our families and retired here. Elke and Fritz felt the same way."

Somebody knew they'd only leave in a coffin, not a moving truck. And they'd made it happen. "This road—where will it go?"

"From the base of the mountain right up to the top."

"By the top, you mean to the plateau, where Dennis Batchelor's lodge is located?"

He nodded.

What did an abandoned mine, bad water, and fatal avalanches have in common? They got rid of people, one way or another. A new road brought more people in, but they were different people than the current residents. She understood the protestors' frustration, since their only alternatives were to put up or leave. Who could live without clean water?

Batchelor was most certainly involved and she intended to uncover exactly how.

"You still didn't tell me why the Kimmels left the protest this morning."

"An emergency at home involving their daughter. She lives with them."

"What was the emergency?" Kat shifted her balance.

"Didn't say. They left in a hurry," Ed replied. "It was Ranger that brought the message. We don't have cell phones up here."

It seemed unlikely that Ranger had received an emergency message. He had been with her on the snowmobile until an hour before the accident, and during that time there had been no radio communications. The protestors also had radio communication, so why weren't they notified instead of Ranger? A legitimate message surely would have been delivered to them directly. Ranger seemed an unusual choice to relay a personal message to people who despised him.

Ranger knew the reason for the Kimmel's trip, yet he hadn't mentioned it at the accident scene or afterwards. More importantly, the message he delivered was the only reason the couple had even been on the slope at that time. It was a telling omission, and one that made her suspect he was somehow involved. The tragedy appeared to be less and less an accident.

# Chapter 9

Ed Lavine had lived all his fifty-seven years in Paradise Peaks. He couldn't remember an avalanche of the size and scale Kat described. Or so many avalanches within such a short period of time.

"We've seen smaller slides on that slope, but nothing like this." He frowned. "Elke and Fritz's regular route never crossed that ridge. But with the tail blocked and their daughter's emergency, they had no choice."

Kat felt vindicated. Finally someone else agreed that the circumstances surrounding the Kimmels deaths were suspicious. It had been worthwhile to stop by the blockade after all.

"When did Ranger give them the message about their daughter?"

Ed frowned. "Maybe mid-morning, sometime between ten and eleven? I never checked the time." He placed a metal lid over the barrel and smothered the remaining fire. "Now that I think of it, he could have given Elke and Fritz a ride, since he was headed in their direction. Instead he just tore out of here like a man on fire."

"You'd expect a ride in an emergency." Ranger had dropped her off around ten a.m. If Ed's memory was accurate, Ranger would have headed to the blockade almost immediately after dropping her off. He likely arrived ten minutes or so later. That left a very small window of time for him to both receive and deliver news of the Kimmels' emergency.

She was bothered by the fact that the Kimmels were ahead of her on the trail. True, she had walked the lake detour several times, but that accounted for maybe twenty minutes at most. The blockade was at least a half hour walk from the avalanche site. Somehow the timing seemed off.

"What kind of emergency?"

"An altercation in the woods, on the edge of the Kimmels' property. Shots fired at Helen, their daughter."

"You mean, on purpose?" Snipers in addition to avalanches? Paradise Peaks was much more dangerous than its name implied.

Ed nodded. "Ranger thought at first it was a careless hunter, but Helen told him it was two guys from the other protest group. They were headed to the house, guns drawn."

"You've talked to Helen about this?"

"I haven't, but a couple of Elke's friends are with her now. Their property's kind of remote; you have to access it on foot. Ranger must have heard it on the radio."

No wonder the Kimmels took the shortcut. It also explained why Elke had drawn her gun. "You don't have a radio up here?"

"Most of us do, but nobody heard a thing."

Not the gunshots or the radio. "But Ranger heard both. There sure are a lot of guns up here."

"It's remote here. You can't be too careful." Ed's eyes narrowed. "Good thing Helen was armed. She shot back."

"Yet you didn't hear any gunshots?" The blockade, the Kimmels' property and the slope were all contained within a radius of a couple of square miles. It was quiet, with nothing other than trees to diffuse the gunshots. Why hadn't he heard them?

"You're right. I should have heard them. The sound travels for miles up here."

"There's one thing I still don't understand. You and the other group are both protesting the tailings pond, yet you're enemies. Aren't they environmentalists, just like you?"

Ed shook his head. "That's a city word."

"Huh?"

"What you call environmentalists. Protecting the landscape comes natural for us. We don't need a special word for it. When city folks came and gave it a name, we knew we had trouble on our hands. They talk about protecting the environment while they drive their gas guzzling SUV's and live their throwaway lifestyles.

"We live here and they don't, for one thing. We just want our drinking water fixed. They claim they save the environment, but they're just using us as a photo op for donations and publicity. They've even renamed things. The Great Bear Forest came straight out of their marketing machine. Pretty soon they'll be changing maps too."

Ed lifted the barrel lid. The fire was completely extinguished. "They were around a lot in the summer, but not so much now. They do stuff at night, but we don't see them."

"Like the blocked trail?" The trail that had stopped her and Ranger earlier also prevented the Kimmels from taking their regular route home. There only choice was to traverse the slope. Ed nodded. "Things are getting out of hand."

"What happened to Helen?"

"Huh? Oh, nothing. The men disappeared as soon as she fired her gun." Ed pulled his keys from his pocket and headed towards the truck. Kat hadn't noticed the snowmobile in the truck bed until now. "Think I'll head up to that ridge and have a look myself."

"Can you take pictures?"

He looked puzzled.

"We can get experts to reconstruct the slide and figure out what triggered it." She fished in her pocket and handed him a business card. "Take lots of photos and send them to me." This was a stroke of luck, though she wasn't entirely sure she had won his trust.

He turned to his truck and opened the door of the truck bed.

"Wait—how do I get to the mine?" Large wet snowflakes fell and coated her shoulders. She brushed them off as she listened to Ed's directions.

"Why do you want to go there? It's closed." Ed's eyes narrowed.

"I want to see it for myself, especially the tailings pond." Since Ed was checking out the slope and the snowmobile tracks, she had extra time. Even with a detour to the Regal Gold mine site, she would still be back at the cabin long before Jace returned.

The mine was somewhere nearby; she didn't know exactly where. "How do I get there?"

"Head straight up about a mile till you get to the fork in the road." He pointed up the road in the direction of the lodge. "Instead of going left to Batchelor's, take the right fork. I'm surprised you haven't seen it. It's right next door to his land. Just a slight detour on your way back."

Dennis obviously hadn't wanted her to see it. That explained the hour-long snowmobile ride Ranger had taken her on, when she would have reached the same destination with an hour's walk. It was a roundabout way to prevent her from seeing the mine. Otherwise she might want to check it out. That realization just increased her desire to explore the site. Now she had a perfect opportunity to check out the mine without anyone bothering her.

She thanked Ed and set off. The afternoon light had waned to a dull gray. Trees lining the road cast ominous shadows across the snow-covered surface. She shivered, wondering where the other protestors were right now.

Ten minutes later, she reached the fork, further confirmed by Batchelor's fence on the property line.

Batchelor's desire to build a road was almost certainly fueled by something other than goodwill. Building a road meant he intended to stick around. Yet he was content to indefinitely sip bottled water? Billionaires weren't exactly the compromising type and Batchelor was no different. Something just didn't add up.

# Chapter 10

Kat trudged up the road as the snow swirled around her. Flakes blanketed the road like icing on a cake, the treetops sugar-coated with a dusting of snow. She was surrounded by a magical winter wonderland. It seemed impossible that this scene coexisted with a toxic mine just minutes up the road. Christmas never looked like this in Vancouver.

The road wound around the mountain as she ascended. The low cloud obscured the plateau, limiting her visibility as the road spiralled up the slope. She stopped to remove the wet powder snow caked on her boot soles. She stomped her feet as she realized that Ranger hadn't explained why the protestors held Batchelor accountable for the mining disaster. Elke had also been short on specifics. Surely Batchelor wasn't considered responsible simply because of who he was. There had to be more to the story, and Batchelor's proposed road likely had something to do with it.

Fritz had mentioned the road. Ranger's insinuation that the Kimmels grew pot and worried about the road interfering with their criminal activities seemed ridiculous. While anyone could grow pot, she highly doubted the elderly couple were involved in drugs. Grow-ops were typically a young person's game.

She refocused on the mine as she reached the turnoff. She chose the right fork as Ed had instructed. The trail paralleled a waterway. Probably Prospector's Creek, the source of the local drinking water and the unfortunate recipient of contamination from the tailings pond breach.

Prospector's Creek was more like a river than a creek. Like everything else in this rugged region, it was oversized. The creek was too large to freeze over. Even in winter it remained fast flowing, impassable to even the most determined trespassers.

A fence bordered the creek on the opposite bank. It was hardly necessary, since the creek itself formed a natural border. Batchelor's fence, she realized. She continued uphill along the creek bank but saw no sign of the mine. The dense tree cover provided shelter and the snowy ground gave way to dirt and roots. No possibility of avalanche here.

The darkness in the forest made for slow going. The winter wonderland of moments ago had morphed into a spooky scene straight out of a Grimm's fairy tale. She imagined unseen eyes watching her, though that was ridiculous. She just wasn't used to such quiet and solitude to appreciate the natural beauty around her. A rather sad state from her always plugged-in, multi-tasking world. It had taken an environmental disaster for her to even think twice about it.

She hiked for another thirty minutes and was about to turn back when she saw it. Another fence ran perpendicular to the river, cutting right across it. A small, faded no trespassing sign nailed to the fence indicated the lower boundary of the mine property.

Kat climbed over the fence and followed the creek. A few minutes later she emerged from the forest to an open expanse of land.  A dozen feet or so away stood a decrepit wooden building and beside it a parking lot. A battered older model white Ford F150 truck was parked in the lot. She surveyed the site and spotted the mine shaft entrance on the far side of the property. A washed-out sign above the building entrance read *Regal Gold Mines*. Fresh tire tracks in the snow indicated the truck's recent arrival.

Other than the F150, the mine site was devoid of activity. It confirmed Fritz's claim that the mine had shut down. The truck probably belonged to a security guard.

In the fading light it was impossible to see anyone inside the truck cab, so she remained in the forest and watched for any signs of life. Once she was certain no one was near, she inched towards the rear of the building, out of view from the parking lot.

She watched the lot for several minutes before she approached the building, eager for a closer look. The tailings pond must be somewhere nearby. She trudged towards the building just as a second vehicle pulled into the parking lot. She ducked back behind the building.

The second vehicle's door opened and slammed shut. It was impossible to see anything from her hiding place behind the building, so she had to rely upon her ears. Footsteps crunched on snow as they approached.

"We solved the problem."

Kat drew in her breath as she recognized Ranger's voice.

"Apparently," replied the unidentified man. "You made it kind of obvious. They're all talkin'."

Who were they? Was the avalanche the 'problem'? She wasn't aware of anything else the locals had a problem with. She inched forward and peered around the corner of the building to identify of the second man, but she only saw his back as he disappeared into the building. He must have been in the parked truck? Had he spotted her?  Probably not, or he would have mentioned it to Ranger.

The building appeared to be a large shed or workshop, probably where equipment was maintained and stored. Either it was an outbuilding or the entire operation was fairly small.  She had expected something more substantial.

Her split second glimpse of the stranger's backside wasn't enough to gauge his height, since the large doorway was at least fifteen feet high. His bulky winter jacket also made it hard to guess his size. In short, she couldn't identify him without a better look. Presumably Ranger was already inside since he was nowhere in sight.

Damn.

She couldn't hear a word outside the building. She debated sneaking inside or at least closer to hear their conversation. No. That would be too risky. What was she doing here anyway? More importantly, what was Ranger doing here?

On the other hand, whatever they were talking about was no concern of hers.

Unless it was.

Fritz and Elke had expressed concern about the mine just before their untimely deaths, blaming it for their contaminated drinking water.

Batchelor had mentioned a broken water pipe as the reason for the lodge's bottled water. Surely Batchelor's lodge drew its water supply from the same contaminated source as the Kimmels' water. If so, Batchelor had lied. Lying about why the water was undrinkable hardly made him responsible for it, however. It was understandable why he wouldn't tell his guests that the local water was toxic. The optics weren't good for a famous environmentalist and it invited all sorts of questions. Questions he would rather avoid entirely.

She inched forward, hugging the side of the building. She remained hidden but had a view of the parking lot. She would see the men's backsides when they exited. That was as long as the men returned to their vehicles parked on the opposite side of the lot.

Assuming the mine was the problem, why had the Kimmels directed their anger at Batchelor in addition to Regal Gold? Did they know something she didn't?

Kat jumped as gunshots rang out. They came from somewhere to the west, towards the opposite end of the property. Her heart raced. She never should have come here.

She scurried back behind the building and held her breath, expecting the men to burst from the building at any moment.

They didn't. Either gunshots were commonplace or they had expected them. There were likely hunters nearby, and Ranger and his companion's lack of concern corroborated that theory. Regardless, she had no business being here and should probably leave now while she could.

She turned to leave just as the men's voices grew louder. She remained in her hiding place and took a deep breath.

The door flew open and banged against the siding. Their footsteps crunched on the snow as they walked across the parking lot. They argued about something, but they were too distant now to be audible. She tiptoed closer, careful not to make a noise. Just a snippet of conversation could help her figure out what they were doing.

Their voices rose.

"Shutting them up's temporary, Burt. You have to fix the problem once and for all. If Boss gets wind of this, he'll have my head." Ranger stormed towards his Landcruiser.

*Shut up who? Ed and the other protestors?* Whatever or whoever needed fixing was a mystery.

Ranger opened the door of his SUV and then turned back to the stranger named Burt. "Fix the damn water or you'll be next."

It really was about the water. Did the mysterious Burt have something to do with the Kimmels' demise? If Burt was next as Ranger implied, who was first? The Kimmels?

"I'll see what I can do." The man called Burt finally came into view.

He was in his mid-forties, short but heavy-set, with a ruddy complexion and a scraggly red beard. His head was covered with a toque. He held a cigarette in one hand and a gun in the other. What was it with these people and firearms?

It was the same man who had argued with Ranger earlier.

Both men finally left. Kat lingered for another ten minutes after the sound of their vehicles faded to silence. Once satisfied no one was around, she ventured into the yard.

The mine was obviously abandoned. Weeds, now dead from frost, had sprouted amongst the equipment. Assuming the weeds had grown during the summer, their presence indicated many months of inactivity. She could validate the facts later at the lodge. For now she focused on exploring the property. It might be her only opportunity to be alone and undisturbed.

The garage door was secured by a latch, but the padlock was unlocked. She removed it and pushed the door open. She entered the building to see rusty conveying equipment and not much else. It surprised her that the mine had operated until recently, since the equipment appeared to be from a bygone era, old, decrepit, and rusted.

Yet Regal Gold Mines had operated right up until the tailings pond breach a couple of years ago. No surprise that a company that polluted drinking water and refused to clean it up wouldn't spend money on decent equipment. Any money saved on capital expenditures went straight to the company's profit line.

Nothing to see in here.

She turned to leave and stopped in her tracks. Dozens of wooden boxes were stacked on pallets against the wall by the entry door. She had walked right by them without even noticing. The boxes seemed a recent addition since they were free of dust and dirt. She walked closer. Red lettering on the box read *Powershot Explosives, providing quality mining, quarrying, and construction supplies since 1959.*

Dynamite.

While dynamite was used in mining operations, this mine had been mothballed years ago. Yet the packaging appeared new. The boxes listed the weight and manufacturing date. Most of the dates were less than a year old, odd for a defunct mine with rusted, idle equipment. Either the shed was used for storage, or someone had new plans for the mine. She somehow doubted the latter. Surely dynamite and other supplies would be among the last things to buy before restarting the decrepit mine.

Since there was no shortage of storage in a rural area like this, someone had intentionally hid their cache here. Remote or not, storing hundreds of pounds of dynamite in an unlocked building seemed downright negligent. A carelessly discarded match or cigarette could blow the place up in minutes. Kids, teenagers, anyone could enter the unlocked building. She shuddered at the thought as she snapped a few pictures with her camera.

Kat exited the building and walked to the edge of the parking lot in search of the tailings pond. Soon she saw the source of the problem. Given the name, she had expected the tailings pond to be an actual pond. It was more accurately a small lake, at least a kilometer in diameter. A high artificial bank encircled the water, but one large section had collapsed. It wasn't hard to see why, given the high water level and sheer volume of water that threatened to breach what remained of the wall.

The Kimmels property was located directly below the mine site and would suffer a direct hit if the whole thing collapsed. Prospectors Creek would easily overflow with that volume of water all at once. Batchelor's property was at risk too, but to a lesser extent.

Tailings ponds contained the contaminated residue from the mining extraction process. Among other things, it included the chemicals used and the ore remaining after the gold and copper had been extracted. Properly designed, the pond would have contained the residue for years beyond the mine's life, unless it was physically compromised. This one had failed miserably.

It would have taken years of operation for the tailings to rise to the current level. That gave management plenty of time to increase the size or build another tailings pond before the current one reached capacity. Yet they decided to keep costs low and maximize profits instead. Had the pond's water level been addressed, the environmental disaster before her would have been completely avoided.

A half frozen stream of water trickled over the breached pond retaining wall in a dark meandering scar that ran directly into Prospector's Creek.  She walked towards it to get a closer look. Heaps of half rotted dead fish were piled on the creek bank, preserved in their frozen state. She gagged and turned away.

Even with expensive remediation, it would take years before the water was drinkable again. Yet the cleanup hadn't even started. Was there another reason it hadn't been addressed? Frustrate people long enough and they would sell their properties and move away. Whatever the reason, it was a very long time to do without drinking water.

It seemed a fight made to order for the aging environmentalist. It was close to home, involved water and the environment in a pristine wilderness. Why hadn't Batchelor raised the alarm? If anything, he should have been aligned with the Kimmels. Yet he was pitted against them. It didn't make sense.

Kat pulled out her camera and snapped pictures to show Jace.

"Hold up." The man's voice was soft but firm. Twigs cracked under his footfalls as he emerged from the brush. "Put that thing away. You can't take pictures here."

Kat swirled around to see an elderly man, his clear blue eyes focused on her. So was his gun sight.

He wore a faded baseball cap with a four-leaf clover emblem on the front. A decades-old blue ski jacket hung loosely on his lanky frame, the worn sleeves several inches too short for his arms. He was old, at least seventy. His arm trembled as he pointed his rifle barrel squarely in her direction. The slightest movement might discharge the firearm.

She slowly raised her hands. "Don't shoot. I'm just a tourist, looking around." Her heart pounded. Other than Ed, who was basically a stranger, no one even knew she was here.

"No, you're not. We don't have tourists in these parts. Who are you really?"

Kat gave her name. "I'm staying at Dennis Batchelor's lodge." Where had the man come from? The only vehicles in the clearing had been Ranger's and Burt's, and they were both gone. She was alone with the gun wielding man.

"Is that right?" He eyed her suspiciously.

Kat returned his stare. It wasn't any of his business. If she held firm, he would surely let her go. What reason did he have not to?

He made no move to lower the gun and their eyes locked, each challenging the other.

Kat grew impatient. People around here weren't very welcoming. "Yes, that's right. Call him, he'll confirm it. Can you put that thing down, please?"

"You delete the pictures you took, maybe I'll consider it."

"Why should I? They're just of the scenery." It wasn't exactly true, since she had taken some photographs of the building's interior. "I'm not doing anything illegal."

He looked a bit unsure and lowered the gun. "Say I give you the benefit of the doubt. What are you really doing here?"

"Just out for a hike. I heard there was an old gold mine up here, so I came to see for myself. It's very interesting. I love this old stuff."

The man's shoulders seemed to relax a bit. "Well, you'd best be moving on. I'm the watchman for the property, and no one's allowed up here. It's trespassing."

"That's odd, because I wasn't the only one here. Two men just left. They were in that building over there." Kat pointed to the building. The man seemed too geriatric to put up much of a fight. Then again, he had a gun. Where had he been when Ranger and the other man were here?

"Oh?" His expression was unreadable.

"Ranger and another man I don't recognize." She watched for his reaction.

"Ranger?" The man's face darkened. "He's got no right to be up here. I better have a talk with Batchelor about that. Want to keep things peaceful tomorrow."

"What's tomorrow?"

"The protestors are staging a sit-in up here at the mine."

Ed hadn't mentioned that. Would it still go ahead without Elke and Fritz? "And you're letting them?"

The corners of the man's mouth turned up in a slight smile. Or a smirk. She couldn't be sure.

Just because the security guard patrolled the property didn't mean he shared the company's views. Small town jobs were hard to come by. It suddenly occurred to her that he was likely one of the protestors too. Pretty clear what side to take when it involved your own drinking water.

Did he know about the Kimmels' accident this morning? She debated asking but decided against it. Of course he knew them. Everybody knew everybody up here. If he hadn't heard about the accident yet, she wasn't the right person to tell him. He would know soon enough.

"Do me a favor?" Kat asked. "Don't mention you saw me up here. People are kind of sensitive about this place."

"Don't I know it," the man said.

"I didn't catch your name," Kat said. Maybe he could provide some background on the water dispute.

"That's right. You didn't." He tilted his head in the direction of the trail. "Now you'd best be goin' if you want your pictures, before I change my mind."

Kat didn't need to be told twice. She had seen enough guns today.

# Chapter 11

Kat walked as fast as she dared without running. A target burned on her back as she retreated, though she probably imagined it. She made a beeline for the trail and safe cover of the forest. She doubted the gun-wielding security guard would actually shoot, but she wasn't about to test her luck. She'd done that once already today.

She breathed a sigh of relief once she reached the clearing edge. He probably wouldn't have shot her, since gunfire attracted unwanted attention. On the other hand, guns were so ubiquitous here that no one even paid attention.

To complicate things, no one other than Ed knew she was at the mine. With no witnesses, the guard could have gotten away with murder. That was obviously a worst-case scenario, but she had trespassed on the property and given him a reason to pull his gun. Had he fired the unexplained gunshots moments earlier? More critically, had the bullets found their mark?

Ten feet into the trail, the brush closed in around her. She glanced back and was relieved to no longer see the parking lot. The guard couldn't see her either. She broke into a half-run, traveling as fast as the slippery roots and branches beneath her feet allowed. She crashed through the brush, anxious to put as much distance as possible between herself and the security guard.

If that's what he actually was.

He hadn't identified himself as such; she had simply assumed that because he guarded the mine. He wore no uniform. While it was possible that security guards in remote parts dressed casually, guards anywhere normally had identifying insignia, even something as minor as a company logo baseball cap. Security guards most certainly didn't wear shabby ill-fitting clothing.  And they were usually younger than seventy.

None of that mattered now that she was safely away from the mine. In less than an hour, she would be back at the cabin. That was good, because dusk was approaching.  The forest was eerily silent and it was difficult to see the trail in places. She had forgotten how quickly nightfall came in winter.

Several minutes later, she emerged onto another trail that led off at a ninety-degree angle from the one she was on.  Based on the direction, it seemed a more direct route back to the lodge. She debated whether to choose the longer, certain route, or take her chances with the shortcut.

In the end she chose the shortcut. The snow fell harder now that the temperature had dropped. It was already darker than moments ago, with probably only fifteen minutes or so of daylight left. Whatever light remained didn't penetrate the tree canopy and she had difficulty seeing more than a few feet in front of her. Running was no longer an option; even a brisk walk was difficult. It made sense to find the fastest route to the road since she was unfamiliar with the area. The second trail almost certainly went there, given the direction. She could always revert to the original trail once she crossed the road.

Despite the dense brush, a few inches of snow had already accumulated on the path. She walked quickly, the silence broken only by fresh powder that crunched under her footfalls. Another time she would have enjoyed the tranquility, but right now it was damn spooky.

In less than ten minutes she saw an opening. The detour had been a smart move and had shortened her trek to the road considerably. She bounded up the path onto the road, relieved. While the road had accumulated a few more inches of snow than the trail, it was much easier to walk on an asphalt road instead of an uneven trail of rocks and tangled roots.

She had been on the road less than a minute when she froze in her tracks.

Stopped a hundred feet in front of her were Ranger and Burt, the man with Ranger at the mine. They were transferring boxes from the rear of Ranger's Land Cruiser to Burt's F150.

She scrambled back into the bush, afraid she had been spotted. She needn't have worried since the men carried on with their task, oblivious to her presence. She inched closer, ready to duck out of sight at a moment's notice.

Her breath caught in her throat when she realized that they were the explosives boxes from the mine building. Explosives were good for one thing, and one thing only: blowing stuff up. Burt must have loaded his truck in the mine's parking lot just before her arrival. She shivered as she realized how close she had come to discovery.

The security guard had expressed surprise at Ranger and Burt's presence at the mine, but he could have lied. After all, he had spotted her quite easily. But why would he lie to her, an out-of-town stranger?

Was the security guard in on it too? It explained his readiness to pull a gun on her. On the other hand, his distaste at the mention of Ranger's name indicated otherwise.

She crouched in the forest, less than fifteen feet from the road's shoulder where the men argued. The snow gave the surroundings a muffled quality. She was grateful for the stillness and lack of traffic. Their voices carried further in the quiet. Any closer and they would notice her.

"This is your last chance." Ranger lifted the last two boxes from his truck and handed them to the other man. "You better pull it off this time."

The man grunted. He took the boxes and placed them in back of his truck.

"I mean it, Burt. This time, be on time and make sure nobody's around. We can't have any unwanted attention. Being sloppy like that makes it awkward for everyone."

Awkward how? Pretending the avalanche was an accident when it was purposely triggered? Kat pulled out her cell phone and snapped a photo of Ranger and Burt transferring the boxes.

"Yeah, I know. I never saw her there." Burt dusted his hands on his jacket and climbed into his truck. He rolled down the window and leaned out. "Tomorrow. I'll call you when it's done."

Too bad she had missed the beginning of the conversation.

"Meet me back here at noon."

"Okay, but as long as there's no unforeseen delays or complications."

"Damn, Burt. You make sure of no complications. Get it right this time, no excuses. I can't protect you any longer, so make it happen." Ranger turned and headed back to his vehicle.

Burt's truck suddenly pulled out and headed towards her. She dove into the brush to avoid detection.

Ranger's Land Cruiser followed less than a minute later.

She waited until both vehicles disappeared around the curve in the road. Once certain they were gone, she stepped out from her hiding place. As she climbed back up to the road, it hit her. Ranger's witness reference must have meant her. She had witnessed the avalanche this morning.

All this time she had obsessed over the snowmobile tracks, but for the wrong reasons. The snowmobile was definitely a factor, yet she now suspected it was used to transport the dynamite and whoever had set the charge. The explosion that set the snow in motion had been manmade. Was it Burt? Maybe he and Ranger had met prior to the accident. That could explain why Ranger had been late to meet her.

Large wet snowflakes swirled around as she quickened her pace. Her tiny headlamp illuminated only a couple of feet in front of her, severely limiting her progress. She could barely see. The storm had materialized out of nowhere within minutes.

She shivered and realized she was late. Jace must have finished his session with Dennis by now. He would have returned to the cabin and found it empty. With nightfall, he would be extremely worried about her whereabouts. With no cell phone coverage, she had no way to contact him.

The storm had intensified into a blizzard. So much for checking out the slide tomorrow. She only hoped that Ed kept his promise and had snapped photographs of the snowmobile tracks before the evidence was erased forever. It was now pitch black and she was tired and cold. She brushed away the snowflakes that clung to her eyelashes and exposed cheeks.

Her thoughts flashed back to the avalanche yesterday. Ranger's comments all but confirmed his involvement. Then there was the dynamite itself. Whatever plans the men had, they had to be stopped. There wasn't much time if their scheme was to go down before noon tomorrow. Unfortunately she had no idea where it would happen, only that they planned to blow something up sometime before noon tomorrow.

Time was of the essence if she was to stop them.

Ranger and Burt likely targeted the protestors' planned sit-in in at the mine site. It was obvious in hindsight, since most or all of the protestors would be gathered there. The men could easily rig a trap in such a secluded spot.

Except that Ranger and Burt hadn't brought explosives to the mine site; they had removed them. That implied their sabotage would occur elsewhere. Since the mine had already been inactive for a few years, the protestors gained nothing if they blew it up. In fact, they risked another tailings pond breach. They simply had no motive to further damage the site that caused their troubles in the first place.

Yet she had no doubt the protestors were almost certainly the target of tomorrow's sabotage. Any investigation would point directly to their detractors, including Ranger. Unlike the avalanche, it couldn't be disguised as an accident. Unless, of course, Ranger and Burt staged it that way.

If it wasn't at the mine site, where? The protestor's blockade? They had to meet somewhere prior to the sit-in, and the blockade was a logical place. But the blockade was simply a spot on the road. Aside from blowing up the only road to Batchelor's property, the explosives would be easily spotted.

She refocused on the mine, since it was still the most logical place to target them. The protestors were guaranteed to be there at some point, and the secluded site made it easy to rig a trap. They would be easy prey; however, sabotage would also be obvious. There were easier ways to get away with murder.

Unless the men made it look like the protestors had done it themselves.

The Kimmels' deaths had been staged to look like an avalanche. An accident. The second attack would be similarly planned and constructed.

In a flash she had her answer. Burt and Ranger must have removed some explosives to frame the protestors. They simply had to plant evidence at the homes of one or more of the protestors. A cache of explosives implied they had orchestrated the mine explosion. It was difficult to argue against physical evidence.

If Ranger and Burt detonated explosives near the protestor's sit in, it would appear to be the protestors doing. A terrible accident in which they inadvertently blew themselves up in the process of destroying the mine. While far-fetched, it certainly seemed plausible.

She was so absorbed in her thoughts that she didn't see Batchelor's fence and property line until it was just a few feet away. She sighed in relief. She could finally escape the cold. She quickened her pace and followed the fence line to the driveway. The darkness that had hindered her was now an advantage. Kat cut across the grounds below the elevation rise to avoid detection. She trudged across the driveway, now covered in a thick blanket of snow. She traversed the hill diagonally and smiled when the lodge came into view. The exterior lights cast a warm glow over the buildings and grounds, reflecting off the snow.

She was surprised to see a helicopter parked in the far corner of the asphalt. She realized in hindsight that the squared separate parking area was in fact a helipad. It would be difficult to fly a chopper given the stormy weather.

Batchelor obviously had additional guests. Odd that he hadn't mentioned anything, and the lodge's remote location hardly lent itself to impromptu visits. Given the weather, they must have arrived hours earlier, just after her departure.

She hurried towards the cabin, anxious to brief Jace on her findings and find out more about the unexpected guests. Batchelor was full of surprises. As she had recently discovered, not all of them were good.

# Chapter 12

Kat pulled off her gloves and fumbled for the key in her pocket. Despite gloves, her fingers were numb from the cold and she struggled to turn the key in the lock. Finally it opened. She stomped her feet to dislodge the snow from her boot soles.

All she could think of was a hot bath and sleep. She felt a rush of warm air as she opened the door. "Jace?"

"Where have you been?" Jace paced the floor, his face flushed with anger. "I was about to call for help."

So much for a warm welcome, although she couldn't blame him for being angry. Why hadn't she left a note? "Sorry. I only planned to go for a short walk. I guess I got carried away."

"You can't just take off alone like that, Kat. I had no idea where to even look for you. I've been worried sick." Jace paced in front of the window. The snow had intensified to the point that the canyon was completely obscured.

"I was sure I'd be back before you." She didn't want to spend what little time they had together arguing. She almost regretted even coming on the trip. They hardly saw each other and when they did, they fought. "Besides, I had no way of calling you."

"That's not the point. What if you got lost or hurt yourself? No one would know where to find you."

Kat felt a twinge of anger until she flashed back to her confrontation with the armed security guard. The situation could have easily escalated. "You're right. I shouldn't have left without telling you. I just didn't want Ranger along for the ride. I don't want him planning my every move." Kat wrapped her arms around his waist. "That guy gives me the creeps."

Jace pulled back. "He's not exactly my favorite either, but at least you're safe with him. It's dangerous out there with the avalanche and everything."

"I'm not so sure about that." Based on her discovery, the exact opposite was true. "Ranger is not who you think he is. He's the dangerous one, not the protestors. I understand why they don't like him."

She pulled out her camera and clicked through the photographs. The pictures taken at the mine were dark and underexposed, but it was patently obvious the mine was decrepit and neglected. She advanced the frames until she reached one taken of Ranger and Burt on the highway. It was framed perfectly with Ranger passing a box to Burt. Even the lettering on the box was legible. "Look at this." She handed the camera to Jace. "Those boxes are dynamite."

"Why do they need explosives?" Jace squinted as he held the camera up to the light.

"For blowing things up, obviously. Dynamite has many uses. It even triggers avalanches."

He shook his head. "Mines use explosives. Nothing sinister about that."

"Jace, the mine has been closed for years." She tapped the camera glass. "These boxes are new."

"You don't think Ranger—"

"I don't know what to think." She described her encounter with Ed at the blockade and the snippets of overheard conversation. "It's Ranger we should be afraid of. And possibly Dennis. I'm sure he's involved somehow." She recounted Ranger and Burt's sabotage plans for tomorrow.

"I don't care for either one of them, but that just seems unbelievable. You're sure you heard right?"

She nodded. "Whatever they're planning happens tomorrow morning. I just don't know what it is yet. They've already gotten rid of the Kimmels. Now they can permanently silence Ed and the remaining protestors. We've got to stop them."

"That's crazy. They can't just go around blowing people up and getting away with it."

"Unless it looks like another accident. Like the avalanche."

Jace shook his head. "But why? What's in it for them?"

"I don't know yet, but there must be something. One thing I am sure of—if it looks realistic enough, it won't even get investigated. The Kimmels is a case in point. The police didn't even attend. Search and Rescue tells them it's an accident and the case is closed. Or rather it was never opened in the first place." Certain local people wielded a lot of power, whether overtly or covertly.

She sat on the bed and powered up her laptop. "I need to research everything about this area I can get my hands on. It's got something to do with the land. Apparently Batchelor wanted to build a new road costing millions. Nobody builds a new road when a perfectly good one exists. The current road works fine for accessing his lodge, so why change anything?"

"Unless the road's not good enough for future uses."

"Exactly. The existing road is in good shape. It will last for years and it's barely used. Is the new road needed for more people, more business, or both? Maybe Batchelor wants more land, too. If he drives everyone out, he can buy their land cheap."

"He hasn't said anything about a new development. On the other hand, he never mentioned the road proposal that was turned down, either. You're accusing him of sabotage?"

Kat nodded. "He never got what he wanted by going through the proper channels. His application was rejected. He's resorted to something less savory to get his way. If I can prove it, maybe I can stop another catastrophe."

"If that's what it is. Why not ask Dennis directly?"

Kat frowned. "Why would I do that?"

"Not about the possible sabotage, but about his road building plans." Jace pointed to her laptop. "After all, if he applied and was rejected, it's public knowledge. It's also a valid question for me to ask as his biographer. In fact, I'm surprised he hasn't mentioned it."

"He'll only tell you about his successes, not his failures."

"That's what I hate about this gig." Jace sighed. "It lacks objectivity. I just write what he tells me to. I doubt he'd resort to sabotage, though. But let's put him on the spot by asking him point-blank."

She hadn't meant to depress Jace again. "I'll get my notes together and ask him myself tomorrow. That gives me a few hours tonight to research all the facts."

"I'm afraid that will have to wait. We're expected at tonight's gala."

"Tonight's what?" That explained the helicopter, but a gala on a remote mountaintop in winter? She hadn't expected that.

"Batchelor's invited some dignitaries—flown in especially for tonight—and I have to attend. Some government bigwigs, environmentalist supporters from his younger days. It's supposed to provide part of the material for his 'autobiography'." Jace made air quotes with his fingers. "At least that's what he tells me."

He was still furious about the ghostwriting, not that Kat blamed him.

"I'll stay here," she said. "I've got nothing to wear anyway. Just say I'm still recovering from this morning's avalanche."

Jace grimaced. "I already asked Dennis about the dress code and he said it didn't matter. He expects you to attend, though. Besides, you can't just leave me with all those people. I need you there. You're my excuse to leave early."

She couldn't really argue with that. She owed Jace a big favor after disappearing and making him worry. "But we still have to thwart tomorrow's plans."

"We will, right after we attend the party. You don't have to stay long, just put in an appearance. Who knows, maybe we'll glean some additional information. At any rate, Batchelor's biography is a perfect excuse to ask questions. Like what's up with the warring factions on such a remote mountaintop."

Kat nodded. "Fighting seems so extreme, considering how sparsely populated the area is. But I guess that's the crux of the argument. The locals don't want the land developed, so there's a lot at stake for them. I think they're harmless, though. Angry maybe, but not violent."

"You talked to them?"

She nodded. "After talking to Ed, I can see their point of view. The mine ruined their drinking water and devalued their properties. The mine's offshore owners just ignore them and don't remediate the mine site, or fix the water.  The locals are the ones that have to live with the results. I would protest. So would you in the same situation."

Kat rummaged through her bag for something to change into. She settled on a blue sweater and black pants.

"Batchelor says they're pretty violent."

"I didn't get that impression at all." Except for the guns, understandable given what they were up against. "It sounds like the out-of-town protestors are the violent ones."

She hadn't actually seen the other protest group, just evidence of their handiwork with the blocked trail. Judging by both Ed's and Ranger's comments, they kept a low profile. That was odd, given their supposed penchant for publicity. Ed described them as always trying to upstage the locals. Would they participate in tomorrow's protest?

"There's another group of protestors?" Jace raised his brows. "Batchelor never mentioned them."

"Ed did, and so did Ranger." She recalled the fallen trees that had blocked the trail on their initial snowmobile excursion. "The out-of-town people are professional protestors trying to stir up controversy. They're using the Regal Gold Mines tailings pond as a platform to advance their own agenda and get media attention. It hasn't worked so far."

It struck her as ironic that Batchelor had once been a high-profile protestor. He had used publicity stunts to gain media attention and further his cause.

"Hmmph." Jace scratched his chin.

"What?"

"How did they travel all the way here in winter, with the roads closed? By air, like us?"

Kat shrugged. "I guess so. Flying would be very expensive, though. Non-profits don't usually have money to burn. Must have deep pockets." Winter protests were also unusual, for obvious reasons like the cold. Not only was it uncomfortable for protestors, but the media were unlikely to provide much coverage.

"Very deep pockets. Unless they're financed by someone else." Jace checked his watch. "We'd better head over to the lodge. Dinner's in half an hour."

"One thing I can't figure out," Kat said. "They're clashing with the local protestors, a total waste of time. Why not just join them?"

"Exactly. They're both protesting the tailings pond and the contaminated water. Fighting with each other just detracts from the cause. If the out-of-town protestors want to gain notoriety, there are bigger causes with easier access. What's the name of their organization?"

"No idea." Kat shook her head. "If I knew, I could figure out who's financing them. But I have no idea who they are."

Jace pulled on his boots. "We came here by private plane and we're staying at Dennis's lodge. Where are these protestors staying? They must have flown in, just like us. Someone will know."

Whoever knew wasn't talking. But Jace was right about one thing. There were no hotels nearby, so they were either guests of one of the local residents, or they were staying in a Sinclair Junction hotel. It had to be the latter, since they had worn out their welcome with the locals.

Protestors were, by nature, attention seekers. Yet the out-of-town protestors were practically invisible. Who were they, and why were they so elusive?

# Chapter 13

The party was well underway when Kat and Jace arrived at the lodge. The great room was at half capacity with around fifty people, mostly older couples. The men all looked alike, stout, rosy-faced and stiff in their too-tight black suits and polished shoes. Most of the women wore semi-formal dresses with pearls, the uniform of cash-seeking fundraisers.

Kat scanned the room for Ranger and was relieved to find him absent. A good thing but also a bad thing, she reminded herself. No doubt he was fine-tuning tomorrow's planned catastrophe.

Kat felt woefully underdressed. Even Jace's attire blended in. He wore the dark blue suit he kept for "emergencies", his term for fancy dinners and similar events. They were to be avoided at all costs, except when he covered them as a journalist.

At least he looked the part. She on the other hand, did not. She was easily the most casually dressed of anyone at the party in a casual sweater and pants. She cursed herself for not packing a dress. She never expected to end up at a political fundraiser atop a remote mountain in the middle of winter. She had expected a wilderness weekend getaway, not a gala.

She followed the other guests into the dining room. Three large round tables had been added to the large dining table to accommodate the guests. Each place setting had a name tag and she was surprised to see that she and Jace were seated apart, though they were both seated at the main table. Jace was on Dennis's right, while she was seated between two women at the opposite end. She took her seat, grateful for the chance to hide her casual attire.

The woman on her left wore a formal evening gown of royal blue velvet fabric. It was accented with a sapphire and diamond necklace that strained at her flabby neck. Kat smiled at her, though she wasn't in the mood for small talk tonight.

She remained troubled by the dynamite and couldn't focus on anything else. Where and how did they plan to use it? To trigger another avalanche?

Kat caught the woman staring at her and realized she had spoken. Kat hadn't heard a word.

The woman beside her smiled. "You really are still shook up from the accident. I've heard all about it."

Her companion was vaguely familiar, though Kat couldn't place from where. She glanced at the woman's place setting and instantly recognized the name, *Rosemary MacAlister.*

Of course. Rosemary was almost as famous as her politician husband, George MacAlister. She was a Vancouver socialite and a fixture at many charity events. The power couple were major benefactors and even had a hospital wing named after them.

Batchelor's gala was apparently on their social circuit, despite its remote location. Kat wondered why, until she realized it was a fund-raising event for George MacAlister, Rosemary's husband.

He was running for re-election and this was the first of many events to raise campaign funds.

"I'm still shaken but getting better," Kat was ravenously hungry, a sure sign she had recovered. Her stomach growled at the thought of food.

Jace had mentioned that the party was a thousand-dollar-a-plate dinner, complete with caviar canapés, a whiskey bar, and wine tasting. Kat couldn't imagine paying such a steep price but then again, she and Jace hardly fit the same multi-millionaire demographic as the power couple partygoers.

Even at a thousand dollars a plate, the expenses wouldn't be covered. Batchelor likely footed the bill for the difference. Plenty of undisclosed in-kind donations went on behind the scenes, especially for those subject to political scrutiny.

She was surprised at the number of guests that had managed the winter trek, given the road closure. "I never expected an event in the middle of nowhere like this. Especially with the storm outside."

"Isn't it terrible?" Rosemary tilted her glass and downed the rest of her wine. She set the wineglass down on the table, but it tipped. Red droplets spattered the white linen tablecloth. "Oh dear. I probably shouldn't have had the extra martini on the helicopter."

"You flew up here?" Kat couldn't imagine martinis in a helicopter.

Rosemary nodded. "We all did. Dennis sent his helicopter for us. He couldn't have the guest of honor missing, now could he?"

"There must be at least fifty people here," Kat said. Most of the men clustered around Dennis at the head of the table. That included Jace, who sat to Dennis's right.

Rosemary laughed. "We flew up in batches, four at a time. It was almost like rush hour. We'll be flying back later tonight."

Poor pilot, having to wait around. The conditions weren't exactly ideal for flying. In fact, it was downright dangerous. The snowstorm had turned into a blizzard, not expected to clear until mid-morning tomorrow. But the guests seemed oblivious to the weather outside.

And oblivious to the lack of food. An hour later the first course arrived, brought by tuxedoed waiters. Kat squirmed in her seat. Now she really felt underdressed.

The first course was a tiny smoked salmon and citrus salad artfully arranged on a handful of lettuce leaves. She wondered what portion of the thousand dollars this course represented and whether the ingredients had been flown in as well. Could you spend a grand for dinner and still come away hungry? She hoped their cabin fridge was well stocked with carbs, because this dinner was looking a bit light after her calorie-burning trek today.

Someone tapped lightly on her arm. She turned to see Dennis, also tuxedo clad. Why hadn't he provided Jace with dress code details? This event had obviously been months in the planning. "Glad you could make it," he said. "I see you've already met Rosemary, George's wife."

Kat nodded. The obvious ploy to separate the men and women annoyed her and smacked of sexism. What did she have in common with a society wife thirty years her senior, other than gender? On the other hand, she was just along for the ride, since

Jace was the official invitee. Instead of overreacting, maybe she should just sit back and enjoy the food and drink. Poor Jace had to carry on in his role as official biographer.

Not that Kat was counting, but Rosemary was on her fourth glass of wine and they hadn't even started the second course. She had just swallowed the last of her salad when Dennis had suddenly materialized behind them.

"More wine?" Dennis smiled at Rosemary and refilled her glass from an expensive-looking bottle of Merlot.

He turned to Kat. She shook her head, pointing to her still-full glass. "I'm fine."

Once Dennis was out of earshot Rosemary leaned towards her. "I hate these things," she slurred. "I've got to suck it up and ask for money."

Her neighbor was already tipsy and the event had barely started. Kat scanned the crowd, formulating an exit plan in her mind. "I never expected an event like this here in the mountains."

"Dennis has them all the time. He's not good at much else, but he knows how to throw a party."

Things had just gotten a lot more interesting. Rosemary's opinion of Dennis was apparently less than complementary. "I take it you've known Dennis a long time?"

Rosemary nodded. "We all grew up here. George and Dennis went to school together. I was two grades behind them."

"Here? In the mountains?" It hadn't occurred to Kat that Dennis originated in Paradise Peaks. She just assumed he had moved here to get closer to nature, rather than move back to his roots.

"Not right here, exactly. In Sinclair Junction. But our families all had property up here in the mountains. It's still a real backwater, but we're trying to change that."

"How?" What did she mean by 'we'?

"We need to jumpstart the economy," she said. "Since the mine closed a few years ago, there's been nothing. No industry, no jobs. George wants to change all that, by developing tourism. There are plans for a new ski and vacation resort."

"Really? I had no idea. It's very beautiful around here, and the mountains seem perfect for a ski resort." She flashed back to Elke and Fritz. Perfect for everyone except locals who opposed it. That included pretty much every current resident.

"It will be even better once we upgrade the highway. It's just ridiculously inaccessible in winter."

"What about avalanches? Isn't it too dangerous for skiing?"

"Right now it is, but the resort will use controlled blasts for avalanche control. Just part of regular operations. We're very excited about the new development."

Rosemary downed her glass.

Kat held up the wine bottle and Rosemary nodded. She refilled Rosemary's glass. No need to go anywhere. All the research she needed was sitting right beside her.

"I had no idea a development was in the works." Dennis hadn't mentioned it. Neither had Ranger or any of the locals. "What about the mine property?"

Rosemary's mouth dropped open. "Uh-oh.  I just assumed Dennis told you."

"Told me what, exactly?"

Rosemary giggled. "I've said too much, but now that I've ruined things, I might as well tell you the rest." She nodded towards

Batchelor. "This lodge is just the start. Together with the surrounding property, this is the start of the Golden Mountain Resort, a ten-thousand acre development."

Batchelor's land was just four hundred acres. That meant he needed all the properties that bordered his, as well as additional land. That included Elke and Fritz's land, the mine property, and others. Except the mine site was contaminated, along with Prospector's Creek.

Kat played along. "Now that you mention it, I remember. Dennis said something in passing but I've forgotten the details."

"It's going to be a fantastic community," Rosemary said. "An environmental showpiece, all self-sufficient. Solar power, glacier water, and an organic restaurant featuring 100% locally sourced food."

The glacier water was simply the existing drinking water, since the reservoir was glacier fed. The pristine wilderness was a marketer's dream.

The contaminated water was a roadblock for Batchelor, yet he seemed unconcerned. The tailings pond had to be addressed for the project to go ahead. Since that would cost tons of money, why not build elsewhere? It seemed illogical to choose a contaminated site, but maybe he had already committed prior to the tailings pond accident. Still, it didn't make financial or business sense, and billionaires were known for focusing on the bottom line. There were lots of other places to build resorts, so why here, given all the roadblocks?

Whatever his reasons, it was apparent he needed neighboring properties. Properties that weren't for sale.

"Batchelor's property isn't big enough for a large resort. How can the mountain support that kind of high density?" Batchelor knew exactly who his holdouts were as a result of his unsuccessful application several years earlier. Elke and Fritz were certainly among them. If money hadn't convinced them to sell, had he resorted to other methods?

"It won't," she laughed. "This property is only a fraction of what will be an exclusive, gated community. There will be a thousand one-acre lots, skiing in winter, and a golf course for summer."

"Golf?" Bringing more people didn't bode well for unspoilt nature.

"Just a nine-hole course to start," Rosemary said apologetically. "Phase two will add a championship eighteen-hole course."

"All that for a thousand properties?"

"And the hotel," she gushed. "It will be great when others discover this hidden gem. I can't wait."

It seemed a monumental change from the pristine mountains today. And a significant change of direction for a well-respected environmentalist. Batchelor had sold out.

A good portion of Dennis's profits likely made their way into George's re-election campaign. The project couldn't go ahead without the proper government approvals. Approvals that George, as Environment Minister, could fast-track through government.

Suddenly everything made sense.

The project was worth millions more to a man who was already a billionaire. Was it worth his reputation to turn his back on his environmentalist past?

Was it lucrative enough to commit murder?

# Chapter 14

Rosemary talked Kat's ear off all through dinner, desert, and coffee. The two-hour affair had so many courses she lost track of them. Slowly her hunger disappeared. There was nothing on the menu she considered local, from the wild salmon to the after-dinner cognac. It was all imported and flown in from the coast, no small expense even for a billionaire like Batchelor. The more she discovered about him, the less she knew. His private persona was a stark contrast from his public image.

She would kill to stretch her legs and work off her meal, but she remained trapped. Rosemary sat on one side and the woman on her other side kept interrupting them both to discuss her latest interior design project.

She was dying to return to her cabin to jot Rosemary's comments down on paper. Once she dug into the history of Paradise Peaks unincorporated, she could discover exactly what roles Rosemary, George, and Dennis had played in their hometown. Of the three, only Dennis still had a home here, but that didn't mean that the MacAlister's lacked local connections. Then there was Golden Mountain Resort, the development

Rosemary mentioned. Dennis's rejected development application would provide some clues on his future plans.

She had to talk to Jace alone. He was likely unaware of Dennis's resort plans since he hadn't mentioned them. He had probably reached the same conclusion about the gala as she had. Dennis was buying favors with financial contributions to George MacAlister's re-election campaign. There was another story here, one that almost certainly would be omitted from Batchelor's official biography.

She scanned the room. Most guests stood in small clusters or milled about now that dinner was over. She spotted Jace at the whiskey bar. He was surrounded by a half dozen middle-aged men who had latched onto him. They laughed and swore loudly as they embellished stories about Batchelor. They cast themselves in starring roles in thinly veiled attempts to insert themselves into Batchelor's biography.

Jace wore a tired, irritated expression. No doubt he had his ear talked off, just like she had. But she had at least gleaned some very interesting information. She finally caught his eye and signaled him to meet her in the foyer.

He crossed the room and they stepped out into the foyer together. Laughter trickled out from the party. They were alone, but the cavernous ceiling's acoustics amplified their whispers to an uncomfortable level.

Kat recounted Rosemary's comments. "She's quite entertaining, actually."

"She's very well-connected," Jace said. "Whatever she says must hold a grain of truth."

Kat glanced around but saw no one. Still, with the acoustics, anyone nearby would easily hear their whispered conversation. "Can we go somewhere quieter?"

Jace motioned for her to follow. "I forgot my notebook in Dennis's office. We can talk better in there."

They ducked into his office, a spacious man cave complete with a pool table where a boardroom table might have been.

"Here I thought you were working all day."

Jace grinned. "He's got me working, don't worry. I'm definitely earning my keep. I just have to hold my tongue as I count down the hours."

Kat repeated Rosemary's claims about Batchelor's resort plans. "I don't know what to think. It sounds like Dennis secretly plans to buy up all the land."

"He never mentioned that to me. The MacAlister's are involved too?"

Kat shook her head. "Not in the land buying, but according to Rosemary, Dennis is their biggest campaign contributor. With George as Environment Minister, I wonder if he'll get special favors once he has the land."

"You're jumping to conclusions. Of course they're friends. They all grew up here, and also have a keen interest in the environment. Nothing wrong with them sharing common interests." Jace grabbed his notebook off the table. "Dennis is conniving, but I don't think he's corrupt."

"He stands to make a lot of money if certain things happen. People rationalize their decisions sometimes." Hopefully that rationalization excluded murder. It seemed beyond belief, but with so much riding on the land acquisition, she had her doubts.

Jace scratched his chin thoughtfully. "Like getting the right approvals and permits."

"And getting a new highway built. Even though the other residents don't want it."

Jace grabbed his notebook from a side credenza and handed it to her. "Take this back with you. I can't afford to lose it."

As Kat took the notebook, a stack of papers on Dennis's desk caught her eye. It was letterhead belonging to Earthstream Environmental. The four-leaf clover symbol was identical to the logo on the security guard's cap.

"I recognize that logo." Kat pointed to the papers. "The watchman at the mine had the same emblem on his hat. Maybe he wasn't a security guard after all."

"Earthstream is Dennis's environmental consulting company. I'm surprised the security guard didn't tell you that. It's one of Dennis's operating companies. They do environmental cleanup."

"That's odd. Don't you think Ranger would have mentioned something about Dennis's work there?"

Jace looked puzzled.

"When we went through the blockade? He said the protestors have a beef with Dennis, yet he didn't mention that Dennis's company was doing the environmental cleanup. Another thing—Ranger works for Dennis, and the guard knew I was Dennis's guest. At the very least, you'd think he wouldn't point his gun at me."

"He pointed a gun at you?" Jace frowned. "You probably shouldn't go off on your own like that."

She'd said too much. "It wasn't like that. I knew he wouldn't shoot." An exaggeration maybe, but she hadn't sensed any ill will.

"He had a gun, Kat. No one knew you were there. That right there is enough to worry about."

"I surprised him. He didn't expect to see me on-site. Maybe I'm over thinking things, though. Dennis probably just gave him a hat or something. Who knows?"

Jace nodded. "Dennis doesn't have his finger on the pulse of all his companies. Other people run the day-to-day operations, so he wouldn't necessarily know about his company's work there."

"Even in his own backyard? Everybody knows everybody else in this place."

"I'll ask him about it tomorrow. We haven't really got into his corporate stuff. We're focussing more on his philanthropic and charity work. I agree though. It is odd that he'd have someone at the mine and not know about it."

"He has to know."

Jace grabbed his notebook and turned to leave. "The mining company hired one of the dozens of subsidiaries Dennis owns. So what if his employees forgot to tell him? It's just coincidence that the mine happened to hire his company."

"I don't believe in coincidences," Kat said. "Besides, why would they be working now? The mine has been shuttered for a few years now. It's also wintertime. It's cold and difficult to work when there's snow on the ground." Aside from the guard's age, he simply didn't look the part of an environmental engineer or consultant. "How could he be unaware of his own company operating in a tiny place like this? A place he grew up in? He'd capitalize on the cleanup to win favor with his neighbors."

"You're right." Jace frowned. "And everything's pre-planned when it comes to Dennis Batchelor."

They returned to the great room just as George MacAlister rose from his seat. He stood beside Batchelor at the head of the table and began speaking. It was his typical rally-the-troops campaign speech, the kick-off to his political re-election campaign.

Kat listened politely and planned her getaway. Unlike the other guests, she could escape to her cabin. As long as she timed it right she could leave unnoticed. It was a lengthy speech, forty-five minutes, and it was impossible to exit without attracting attention. Like many politicians, MacAlister was adept at taking a long time to say absolutely nothing of substance. His speech was followed by several supporters who extolled George's environmental wisdom and planning.

She finally got her chance when Batchelor rose to speak. She kissed Jace on the cheek, grabbed his notebook, and left. No one watched her leave other than Jace, who promised to glean whatever information he could on Golden Mountain Resort and Batchelor's connection with the MacAlisters.

She slipped out into the crisp night air and left the warm lights of the lodge behind her. The blast of cold air was surprisingly refreshing. She followed the shoveled walkway rather than the snowy trail back to the cabin, lost in thought.

The avalanche this morning had taken both a physical and emotional toll on her. She could easily fall asleep but she had work to do, and just a few hours left to do it. Little time to waste if she was to save the people of Paradise Peaks.

# Chapter 15

Paradise Peaks' long history of grass roots activism went back to the 1980s. The early protests that inspired Dennis Batchelor to become an environmentalist had come full circle. Batchelor had once led protests; now others protested against him. While the protestors officially targeted the mine, they made it clear they also opposed him.

Kat remained convinced Batchelor was connected to whatever Ranger and Burt had planned for tomorrow. He was smart enough to keep his hands clean by staying one step removed. Ranger did all his dirty work for him.

In order to stop the impending catastrophe, she needed to know what it was and exactly how they planned to execute it.

Paradise Peaks had changed a lot since Batchelor had thrust it under the environmental spotlight decades ago. The media attention brought more visitors, but not necessarily the nature-loving kind. What was good for the local economy came at an environmental cost. The locals' interests were trumped by dollars and cents. Since Paradise Peaks' future revolved around money, what were the odds that Batchelor wasn't involved?

Zero.

Kat flashed back to Rosemary MacAlister's comments on the plans for Golden Mountain Resort. Dennis needed the adjacent properties, including the Kimmels' property and Regal Gold Mines. A chill ran down her spine at the implications of that scenario. The Kimmels had refused to be driven out. Suddenly their lives were extinguished and they were no longer here to fight.

Maybe they weren't crackpots as Ranger and Dennis implied. If the Kimmels' claims were justified, of course Batchelor would discredit them by calling them crazy. Who would most people believe?

She powered up her laptop. As the mystery deepened she needed to document her findings while still fresh in her mind. Even the police might find some of it useful, if and when they finally got around to interviewing her about the avalanche. In any event, her summary might help Jace later on, if he wrote the other unofficial story.

Batchelor benefited directly from their accident because it removed any obstacles to acquiring the land. Since he also needed the Regal Gold Mines property, it made sense that the tailings pond hadn't been fixed. Some of the repairs were unnecessary if the site was repurposed.

The contamination still needed to be addressed of course, but decontamination was less extensive and expensive than rebuilding the entire tailings pond to make Regal Gold Mines fully operational again. Selling the property might be the best solution for the mine's absentee owners, too. After all, the mine had operated for over thirty years and must surely be in its twilight years. Most of the gold, and most of the profits, had already been extracted.

She flashed back to the mine site security guard's cap with the Earthstream logo. The four-leaf clover implied a connection to Earthstream and, therefore, Batchelor. But that might not mean anything in such a small community. Everyone was connected in one way or another.

The man appeared to be well beyond retirement age, so he might not even be a security guard. Maybe he was just informally watching the place. It was unlikely the man was employed as an Earthstream Technologies environmental engineer or other specialist, given his age. Batchelor had probably just given him the cap. But then why was he at the mine in the first place?

She hadn't a clue, but it was pointless to spend more time wondering. It was already eleven o'clock, yet she was no closer to figuring out Ranger and Burt's plans for tomorrow.

She yawned and decided to call it a night. Out of habit she clicked on her browser and was surprised to see that she had a strong Internet connection.

She mouse-clicked to the Earthstream website and scrolled to the company information section. Earthstream Technologies was one of dozens of companies within Batchelor's complicated organizational structure.

Earthstream had a Luxembourg head office. It was owned by a Luxembourg holding company, which was in turn owned by a Cayman Islands numbered company. Numbered companies were anonymous by design, whether to escape taxes, legal liability, or both. On paper, the web of companies and labyrinth corporate organization chart effectively obscured ownership.

However, anyone who followed the maze could see that the ultimate owner was Dennis Batchelor.

Like most billionaires, his holdings were structured by an army of lawyers and accountants. Their sole mission in life was to execute his wishes for maximum profits with limited liability. But just because tax loopholes were legal didn't make them moral.

Any conscientious indignation Batchelor felt for environmental issues didn't stop him from capitalizing on every possible tax and financial benefit available. One thing was clear: the environmental crusader's anti-corporate stance didn't apply to his own corporate interests. The only local cleanup he took part in was in the financial sense to maximize his net worth.

Earthstream's website was also interesting for what it didn't show. The website listed numerous company projects underway, but Regal Gold Mines wasn't one of them. There was likely a logical explanation. Maybe the project was too new, too small, or had been already completed.

Except Regal Gold didn't fit into any of those categories. It was a bigger than many of Earthstream's listed projects. It also wasn't a new project. The tailings pond had collapsed a few years ago and still hadn't been fixed. That raised another question. Absentee owners or not, the government should have forced the company to clean up. It was unheard of to leave a community without drinking water for years on end.

Of course, MacAlister *was* the government. As environment minister, he could overrule decisions or overlook transgressions. That was political suicide if anyone found out, but the stakes just might be high enough to risk that possibility. Could he have some sort of side deal with Regal Gold?

There had to be an explanation why MacAlister, as Environment Minister, ignored the protestors' valid concerns for more than two years. The government should have interceded when Regal Gold's noncompliance became evident. There was simply no excuse for the drinking water to remain contaminated and undrinkable for that long. It also defied logic that two very powerful men with local roots had simply accepted the status quo without protest.

Earthstream's services included environmental remediation, so it could have easily resolved the tailings pond situation. That would have immediately occurred to Batchelor. Had Regal Gold Mines been shamed into finally fixing the problem? If so, that was good news, but why weren't the protestors aware of this development? Given the endless protests and hostility, surely they would be the first to know, if only for public relations purposes. After all, it was a good news story Batchelor could capitalize on.

What could possibly be more lucrative than gaining business for Earthstream?

The one thing more valuable to Batchelor was land for his resort. Land he could buy cheaper in its contaminated state. Was Batchelor hoping to buy the land for a bargain price? If so, had he convinced MacAlister to look the other way?

It was interesting that Jace wasn't aware of the resort plans. Why hadn't Batchelor mentioned any of it to his official biographer? Did he have something to hide?

She checked her watch and realized it was now after midnight. Jace was the only guest not stranded by the weather, but she suspected he couldn't leave the remaining guests. Their return flights were likely grounded until the storm lifted.

She turned her attention to Regal Gold Mines. While it was owned by offshore owners, as a publicly traded company it was required to file regulatory documents. She pulled up the securities information and scrolled through the regulatory filings.

Her eyelids grew heavy as she clicked on each report. The lengthy disclosures and disclaimers were dry enough to put anyone to sleep. She focussed first on the quarterly financial reports, but nothing unusual jumped out.

Regal Gold Mines had been quite profitable right up until the tailings mine incident. Despite the mine's age, it had at least a decade of life left. Every day it sat idle cost the owners' money in lost profits. All the more reason to get it repaired and back up and running. Yet they hadn't.

Something else struck her as odd. According to the regulatory filing, the offshore majority owner had recently sold its shares, yet the local protestors seemed unaware of the ownership change. It was an odd time for a sale with the tailings pond issue. Investors typically avoided companies with undetermined environmental liabilities. Aside from the purchase price, the new owner could inherit millions in environmental levies and face possible bankruptcy. It was a risk few were willing to take.

Sometimes it happened. But the buyer was either a fool—or someone who already knew the outcome.

The majority owner, a Chinese company called Lotus Investments, had sold its 51% majority ownership stake directly to the new majority owner. The new owner then took Regal Gold Mines private, delisting the shares from the New York Stock Exchange.

According to the regulatory filings, the new majority owner was a company called Westside Investments. In addition to Westside, a second company had a significant ownership stake in Regal Gold. It was a numbered company, 88898 Holdings Limited, based in the Cayman Islands. Together the two companies owned 81% of the outstanding shares.

Bingo.

Following the money, and in this case, the mining company's ownership, would no doubt shed light on the transactions. The ownership change was surely the key to unlocking the mystery. She scanned the remaining reports and stopped at the last one. Westside had issued a tender offer to buy all the remaining shares at a premium to the current market price. The offer wasn't all that generous, but it didn't have to be. The shares had lost almost all their value after the tailings pond incident. In fact, they were dirt cheap, valued at pennies a share.

She refocused on Westside Investments. The information on the majority owner was sparse, other than it was in turn owned by 247 Holdings, another Cayman Islands company. All she could dig up were the names of the directors, all lawyers at the same Cayman address. It was a shell company, with the real owners hidden behind a corporate veil. Unlike Regal Gold, it wasn't publicly traded, so ownership information wasn't readily available online.

She tried a different angle. Companies with large ownership stakes always installed their own board of directors at the companies they invested in. Secret or not, they needed to exert control. It was how they influenced operations and protected their investment. At least one or two directors had to be Westside appointees.

She clicked on each of the Board of Directors biographies. Most of the nine directors appeared to be experienced mining executives with decades of experience, including two that were employees of the Chinese company. All the appointees were men, including the sole director who lacked direct mining experience. On the surface at least, it made sense.

Yet none of the directors represented Westside Investments, the current majority owner.

She was right back where she started. Regal Gold's management had been unable or unwilling to re-activate a profitable mine. Yet the mine's lost revenue far outweighed the expense of fixing the tailings pond. Each day's delay cost them money. Why wouldn't they make it operational as soon as possible? What were they waiting for?

More puzzling was why Westside and 88898 Holdings had invested in a mothballed mine with a potentially huge environmental liability. There had to be a payback, but what was it?

One thing was certain: Westside Investments, as majority owner, had to be pulling strings in the background. They wouldn't be content with zero representation on the board of directors with so much at risk.

Where was Jace when she needed him? She often bounced ideas off him, and right now she was stumbling in the dark. He was right about Dennis Batchelor. The man paid well, but his demands on Jace were completely unreasonable.

She returned to her research, this time following the thread for 88898 Holdings. The Cayman Islands company was a wholly-owned subsidiary of Pirate Holdings. Such an intriguing name just begged further investigation. She scanned a list of directors but that got her nowhere. Like many companies in offshore tax havens, the directors were little more than figureheads. In Pirate's case, there were just three. All were lawyers employed at the same company, Meridian Consulting. A dead end.

Or was it? The names seemed familiar. She scrolled back to the director bios on the Regal Gold Mines website. Her mouth dropped open when she saw it. Three of Regal Gold Mine's directors had ties with Meridian Consulting too. The companies appeared unrelated, yet they shared the same directors. Pirate Holdings was represented on the board through Meridian Consulting.

Interesting, but did it mean anything?

She bet it did. Meridian Consulting must be where the ultimate ownership lay. It held the key to the truth. Whoever owned Meridian controlled the purse strings of Pirate Holdings, Regal Gold Mines, and who knew what else.

That answered the question on Pirate Holdings, but who owned Westside Investments? She reread Westside's regulatory reports and sketched out an organization chart on a pad of paper. She penciled in boxes for company names and filled them in with the names she drew from the regulatory reports. The company at the top of the chart was 247 Holdings. It jumped out at her on graphite and paper. Westside Investments and Earthstream were both subsidiaries of 247 Holdings. Dennis Batchelor was the 51% owner of Regal Gold Mines.

Suddenly everything made sense.

Batchelor already had a portion of the land he needed, through his ownership in Regal Gold Mines. But why buy a contaminated mine site that had inflicted environmental damage on its surroundings? Because he got cheap land for his resort, and the lack of drinking water drove out long-time residents.

But it also meant Batchelor had to pay to fix the problem. The on-site contamination would take years—or even decades—to resolve and cost millions. As a new owner, he was liable for any problems, yet it was impossible to accurately predict cleanup costs. The final tally would only be known once the work was completed. Not many billionaires invested in companies with unquantifiable risks. Why would Dennis Batchelor?

Minutes later she had her answer. Everything hinged on Earthstream's environmental assessment, so that must be key to the puzzle. As required disclosure for public companies, the contamination was reported in a regulatory filing. Sure enough, Earthstream's disclosure had resulted in a huge price drop in Regal Gold Mines' share value. Its shares were practically worthless when Westside and 88898 had snapped them up.

While Regal's management had met legal requirements by disclosing the tailings pond accident in their shareholder reporting, they had otherwise taken pains to keep the incident quiet. That was why it hadn't been listed on the Earthstream site. No one had forced them to act—at least not until the protestor group was formed and Elke, Fritz, and others took matters into their own hands.

The protestors never had a chance. They hadn't known who they were up against.

Despite all that, Lotus had still found a buyer for its Regal Gold Mines shares.

Assuming the buyers had done their due diligence, they knew about the environmental disaster they had just inherited. Yet they bought the company anyway, for pennies a share. The offshore owners made no attempt to clean up the site since it would bankrupt them. They were legally untouchable and saw no point in spending money on a worthless mine.

Would a reputation-conscious environmentalist tie his fortunes to a contaminated mine? It seemed extremely unlikely. Batchelor would never risk his personal brand on that.

Yet he had.

Had Earthstream purposely exaggerated the findings in its environmental report just so Batchelor could obtain the land he wanted? If that was the case, Batchelor, and whoever was behind Pirate Holdings, appeared to have acquired the mine through dishonest means.

It was the only conclusion she could fathom. Why else would an environmentalist invest in an environmental disaster? He had to know something no one else did.

One man's trash was another man's treasure. The property was worthless from an operating mine point of view, but was extremely valuable as a resort property if it could be cleaned up. As long as Batchelor got the necessary approvals, he stood to make a fortune. With his friend MacAlister as environment minister, no doubt he would.

The locals had even less influence now that Batchelor owned the mine property, but they didn't know that. Kat still didn't know Ranger and Burt's plans for the explosives, but now at least she knew the motive. Scare the holdout landowners into selling cheap. With the Kimmels gone and the mine property locked up, only Ed and the remaining protestors stood in Batchelor's way.

# Chapter 16

The cabin door flew open and cold air rushed in. Kat shivered. "Close the door, Jace. It's cold in here." Boots stomped in the entryway, then the door slammed shut.

"Jace?"

Silence.

She set her laptop down and rose to meet him at the door.

It was almost one in the morning. She was half asleep and had already dozed off a couple of times while waiting to share her findings. "I know you're exhausted, but you won't believe the dirt I've found on—"

She slid across the floor in her socks and almost ran into Ranger. "What the hell are you doing in here?" She lost her balance as she abruptly turned. They were inches apart and she had nowhere to go.

He grabbed her wrists and pulled her to face him. "What kind of dirt?"

"Let go of me." She snatched her arms back but he was too strong.

He laughed. "Don't bother. No one will hear. You should thank me. I just saved you from falling."

"Don't you knock?" She struggled but couldn't free herself from his tight grip. "Let go. You're hurting me."

He ignored her question but loosened his hold slightly.

"I'll scream."

Ranger released her and walked past her to the bed. He picked up her laptop.

Her heart pounded. She followed and prayed that her screensaver was engaged.

It wasn't.

"What's all this?" He didn't wait for an answer. "Researching the mine, I see."

"You have a problem with that?" She held out her hands for her laptop, but he didn't return it.

"This is the dirt you're talking about?" He turned the screen towards her.

Her face flushed at the sight of the regulatory reports. As long as he didn't notice she'd penciled in the organization chart on the bed, she might be able to talk her way out of it.

Kat crossed her arms. "It's a private matter between me and Jace." Thank goodness she hadn't said anything specific. "Speaking of which, I'd better go get him."

Ranger blocked her passage. "He's busy with Dennis. He'll be awhile."

She wouldn't let him intimidate her. "Why are you here in the first place? What do you want?"

His mouth turned up into a thin smile. "I work here. Never mind what I'm doing. Let's discuss what you're doing."

Kat tugged at her laptop but Ranger pulled it away. She almost went flying as she lost her grip.

He walked to the table and placed the computer on it. He flipped the laptop open.

She breathed a sigh of relief as he ignored the papers on the bed that detailed Dennis Batchelor's global empire. Her hopes were just as quickly dashed as he read her notes on the laptop.

"This is the dirt?" He chuckled.

She shook her head. "Is this how you treat your guests? Give me my computer."

No such luck. He looked up from the screen. "What's so interesting about Earthstream?"

"Just helping Jace with some of his research."

"No you're not. That's out of scope for Dennis's memoir."

"How do you know? You're not writing it."

"You'd be surprised what I know." Ranger's face remained impassive. "Dennis doesn't so much as scratch an itch without checking in with me first."

"Is that right?" That implied Ranger probably did all Dennis's dirty work too. The avalanche and the planned explosion tomorrow were Ranger's handiwork, but at Dennis's bidding.

She took advantage of his momentary lapse and lunged for the table. She grabbed her laptop and shut it. This time he didn't try to get it back. She ran into the master bedroom and shoved the computer in her bag. She stood at the foot of the bed in front of her bag.

"You can't hide anything from me. I'll find out." He stood in the doorway, arms crossed.

"How? By breaking in and terrorizing people? I'll bet Dennis doesn't know you're doing this."

Ranger's lips turned up into a thin smile. "He doesn't need to know the specifics. Nor does he want to."

"Does he know you attack his female guests?"

A split second of uncertainty flashed across his face. "I didn't know you were in here."

She glared at him. "That's no excuse for what amounts to a break-and-enter. You have no reason to be here." She sat on the bed and pulled on her boots. Ranger didn't appear to be leaving, so she had to get out of the cabin, fast.

"I thought you were still at the party." He walked towards the bed and eyed her bag. His eyes shifted towards the French doors to the patio. "The weather's nasty outside. I came to check the window seals."

"After midnight? I don't think so." She stood. "I'm talking to Dennis about this."

He was inches from her bag and she fought the urge to retrieve it. He would just take it from her.

"Go ahead. I'll tell him you're digging up dirt on him."

"So you admit there's dirt?"

His face reddened. "I admit nothing. Only that Dennis asked me to check things."

"You're lying." Kat walked towards him and closed the gap. She hoped he would back away from the bed, but he didn't budge.

He smirked. "I saw you yesterday. At the mine."

Kat's heart pounded. Had he also seen her spying on him from the edge of the highway? "I was out for a walk. You can't stop me."

"Who says I can't?" He smiled, watching her. "I can do all sorts of things."

He grabbed her arm and steered her towards the French doors. "The view is wonderful from here." He opened the doors with his free hand. A gust of freezing air blew in. He pushed her out onto the deck. "Even if it is a bit dark."

An understatement since it was pitch black outside. She didn't need to see the five-hundred-foot drop to the canyon floor below to know it was there.

She jumped as the cabin door flew open, followed by footsteps headed towards them.

Ranger jolted too. He tightened his grip on her arm as he turned to the door.

"What the hell is this?" Jace stood in the bedroom doorway.

She broke free of Ranger's grasp and ran to Jace. "Ranger was just leaving."

She held onto Jace's arm, distancing herself as much as possible from Ranger. She didn't dare tell Jace what had happened with Ranger still in the room. Jace would kill him, and that would be the one crime that wouldn't go unpunished in Batchelor's neck of the woods.

Ranger froze as he sized Jace up. While Ranger was shorter, he was about twenty pounds heavier than Jace. The two men were evenly matched, so there was no guarantee of a winner. Ranger couldn't push Jace off the deck, but who knew what other means he had at his disposal? No matter how things unfolded, Ranger would come out unscathed.

She turned to him. "Are you talking to Dennis, or should I?"

Ranger scowled as he stormed past her. "We'll continue this discussion later."

Surely Ranger had known that anything he said to her would be relayed to Jace. And from there, passed on to Dennis. Maybe it was just a scare tactic. Did Batchelor turn a blind eye to Ranger's tactics, or worse still, condone his behavior?

"What the hell was he doing in here?" Jace pulled back, a concerned look in his eyes. "Are you all right?"

She recounted Ranger's abrupt entrance as well as her findings. "He would have killed me. A staged accident, like I fell over the deck railing." It still seemed unbelievable, but why else had he pushed her outside onto the deck in the dead of winter?

"I'm going after him."

"Jace—no. You can't go after him. At least not right now. Not until we can expose what I've found. You confront him or Batchelor now, and we'll both be in a lot more danger."

"I don't like it." He turned. "You're right, though."

Kat was relieved. They had a lot to do in the next few hours. She grabbed her laptop and pointed to her summary. "There's something sinister going on, and Ranger's a part of it. I'm sure of it. He's after me because I saw him at the mine.

"So what if you saw him. What's wrong with that?"

"On the surface, nothing. I was out for a walk. The problem is that he looked at my laptop. He knows I'm onto something."

"So what if you're looking at Dennis's companies. You're researching for me."

"I don't know how, but he knows, Jace. He must have overheard my conversation with Rosemary. With that and my mine visit, he put two and two together. Just like I did." She hadn't seen Ranger at the gala, but maybe he had talked to Rosemary after her departure. "We've got to warn Ed tonight, Jace. Tomorrow is too late."

# Chapter 17

Kat traced her finger along one axis of the spider web of companies in Dennis Batchelor's global empire. Her diagram depicted just a portion of his vast holdings, but it was all she needed to implicate him.

Batchelor's ownership was invisible to the locals due to his convoluted ownership structure, but on paper it was as clear as day. He owned Regal Gold Mines through Westside Investments. He couldn't hide it any longer. She had stripped away the complicated corporate structure.

Kat pointed to the other significant stockholder of Regal Gold Mines stock on her chart, Pirate Holdings. "I have a hunch who holds the other big ownership stake in the company."

"Let me guess, MacAlister?" Jace leaned forward and traced his finger over the diagram.

She nodded. "Not directly, of course, since it's an obvious conflict of interest with his Environment Minister role. He can't own a company that he's responsible for regulating. He hired some lawyers in the Caymans that serve as directors, just as

Batchelor did. He's structured things so he's invisible and untouchable."

"But no doubt pulling strings behind the scenes."

"Exactly. He's the other majority shareholder."

Jace whistled. "Forget Batchelor's biography. This is way jucier."

Kat nodded. "Batchelor's 51% and MacAlister's 30% give them an 81% ownership stake in Regal Gold Mines. Enough to call the shots. I have a hunch that Earthstream Technologies is about to complete a new environmental assessment. One that gives Regal Gold Mines a clean bill of health."

"He can't do that," Jace said. "Fabricated results don't hide the obvious—people get sick if they drink contaminated water. Batchelor's ruthless in business, but even he wouldn't risk lives just to enrich himself."

"He doesn't have to. The report will be accurate."

"Impossible. Even if you could clean all that water, the groundwater's still contaminated. That stuff takes years to dissipate."

"Unless the contamination never existed in the first place."

"According to the Earthstream report it does. The tailings pond assessment showed a high contamination level—"

Kat smiled. "Don't forget Earthstream is Batchelor's company. That first report said the water was contaminated when it wasn't. He fabricated the results all right, but in the opposite way from what you'd expect. Normally people falsify results to hide something bad. In this case, Batchelor hid something good. There's actually nothing wrong with the water."

"How do you figure that?"

"I couldn't believe he would even consider buying a contaminated mine site. Not just because he's an environmentalist, but because that's not how he operates. He didn't earn billions by betting on risky projects like contaminated mine sites with unquantifiable risks. His other investments are conservative and he looks for sure payoffs. That's how I realized he must have fabricated the whole thing."

"How is that possible? The tailings pond breach really happened. You can't fake that."

"Yes, it did happen." Kat nodded. "That gave Batchelor the idea, since he'd been unsuccessful at buying any land outright. The locals wouldn't sell, and the mine wanted too much money. When the accident happened, Earthstream was hired to assess the damage. He saw a perfect opportunity to make the properties less desirable—and less valuable—by pretending the damage was much worse than it actually was."

"Earthstream's damage assessment was fake?" Jace shook his head. "That seems like a lot of work. Someone would figure it out."

"It's not hard at all. It's just an environmental report. The mine hadn't been operating, so when the accident happened, a local company was hired to deal with the accident. Not only did his company assess the damage, it also performed the work required to stop further damage.

"Earthstream contained the spill before anything leached into the groundwater. But no one told the locals that. Batchelor let them think the water was contaminated when they raised concerns. He also told Regal Gold's offshore absentee owners that the damage was much worse than it actually was."

"All this time the water's been clean?"

"Yes. The spill really happened, of course. Only it wasn't nearly as bad as everyone thought. But the previous owners of Regal Gold Mines didn't know that. They sold the company thinking it was worthless, saddled with a huge environmental cleanup. But that wasn't the case at all."

Jace whistled. "They sold it to Batchelor without even realizing it?"

"Who's going to tell them?" Kat tapped her pencil on Batchelor's corporate organizational chart. "I spent hours poring over dozens of regulatory reports to put this together. It's impossible to connect the dots until you see it on paper. Earthstream prepares the report, but the buyer is another of Batchelor's companies, Westside Investments."

Realization dawned on Jace's face. "And all Regal Gold cared about was assessing the damage and containing the spill. They thought they got off easy."

"Yes. They planned to mothball the mine anyway. It was profitable before the spill, but not enough to justify spending millions to fix a huge environmental disaster. Batchelor figured that out, so he ensured that Earthstream's estimate to fix the damage was higher than the mine's profits.

"It didn't make sense to Lotus Investments, Regal's Chinese owners, to spend all that money. Regal is just one of many investments in their portfolio. After the spill, they decided to just to cut their losses and sell their shares."

Jace nodded slowly. "I see where you're going with this. Dennis had offered a way out of a bad situation for Lotus."

"Yes, the shares were practically worthless once the spill's estimated cleanup costs were known. Lotus knew they wouldn't find any other buyers. The sole offer came from Westside

Investments. 88898 Holdings followed shortly thereafter. Which were really Batchelor and MacAlister, hidden behind offshore companies."

"All based on Earthstream's environmental assessment."

Kat nodded.

"But Batchelor and MacAlister will be exposed eventually," Jace said. "When they develop the land."

"Nope. They'll just set up another shell company that buys the property from the current owners. They'll run it through a few other companies to complicate matters and hide the money trail. No one follows the share transactions of an almost bankrupt mining company."

"Nobody but you." Jace smiled. "I still think it's a bit far-fetched, though."

"I don't think so, and I'll prove it." Kat grabbed a glass from the cupboard and filled it with the murky brown tap water. She held it up to the light and almost gagged as she studied the turbid liquid.

"Don't drink that." Jace tried to grab the glass from her hand. "What if your guess is wrong?"

"It's not a guess." She studied the water. "The water looks bad, but appearances are sometimes deceiving."

"Kat, no! That's a very unscientific way to prove your theory. Let's get it tested first."

"No need." She held the glass out of his reach. "Now or never, down the hatch."

She gulped the water in three swallows and deposited the empty glass on the counter. "It tastes just like the water back home. Better, in fact."

"You're crazy!" Jace rummaged through his duffel and pulled out his first aid kit. "We're in the middle of nowhere without hospital access, and you drink poison water. I can't believe you just did that."

"Somebody had to. Besides, I've never had glacier water before." She smiled. "It's delicious."

Jace grabbed the wine bottle from the counter and emptied the remainder into her glass. He pulled out a small bottle of water purifier from his kit and poured it into her glass. He stirred it with his finger. "Here. Drink this."

Kat smiled and downed it. "If it makes you happy."

Jace shook his head. "For such a logical person, you sure do some crazy things."

"I'm not crazy, and I don't need this." She placed her glass on the counter. "Something's in the water, but it's not toxic. It's just food coloring or something similar designed to make the water look bad. It looks contaminated, so no one even bothered to question it. The cloudy water looked the part."

"Food coloring?"

Kat nodded. "I'm sure there's another name for whatever the ingredient is, but it operates on the same principle. Some non-toxic ingredient that changes the water's appearance."

"But how would anyone get it to come through the tap?"

"Remember the burst pipe Batchelor mentioned? That really did happen. His company, Earthstream, repaired it. It was a minor fix, but the work gave him access to the village water system. It also gave him the means to fake the contamination. He saw an opportunity to profit from it.

"Even the tailings pond breech was no accident. He engineered the whole thing. The spill never reached Prospector's Creek or the drinking water. The whole thing was staged so he could scare people." She described the dead fish and the rest of the scene. "Regal Gold Mines' absentee owners weren't around to know that it wasn't an accident. They didn't want to fix it, so when an unsolicited offer came to purchase the company, they jumped at it."

"Okay, I can see that happening. But how can you prove Batchelor's behind it all?"

"It was hard to figure that last part out. The Chinese owners sold their shares to Westside Investments, a company in the Cayman Islands. At first I couldn't find any connection to Batchelor, until I saw Westside's address in the share sale disclosure. It shared the same address as the other Cayman companies. Westside is owned by another company, 247 Holdings. Guess who owns that?

"Batchelor?"

She tapped Batchelor's company organization chart. "Ultimately, yes. There are a few other companies involved, but that's the end result."

"It's hard to believe the tailings pond breach was triggered on purpose, though. Batchelor really is an environmentalist. Why would he risk environmental disaster?"

"He wouldn't. In fact, he showed his true colors because there was no spill in the first place. He didn't really spill the contaminated fluids or damage the environment. He just made it look that way."

"But the tailings pond wall was breached. Some contaminants must have escaped. It's obvious by looking at Prospector's Creek."

"No, the spill never happened. The wall was breached *after* the containment was put in place. The site is remote and he just used his heavy equipment to make it look like a breach. Prospector's Creek and the land around it were never in danger because the containment was already in place. It's a set-up made to look like a disaster. A disaster that never happened."

"Just like special effects in a movie."

Kat nodded. "Only a few people witnessed the actual tailings pond breach," Kat said. "Guess who those people were?

Jace scratched his chin. "Batchelor, Ranger, maybe the security guard guy—they all work for Batchelor. No wonder they arrived so quickly on the scene to contain it."

"Exactly. It's win-win for Batchelor. He never damaged the environment because it was staged in the first place."

Jace grinned. "And absentee owners wash their hands of it by selling their shares. They can't wait to escape liability. They don't ask questions because they're relieved that someone's taken the environmental disaster off their hands."

"Right. And no one really notices. The stock is thinly traded, and the only ownership change disclosure is in the fine print of a regulatory filing. Nobody cares. The Chinese company avoids environmental cleanup costs. Batchelor graciously takes on that liability as part of the sale."

"He got all that land for a song." Jace nodded.

"Right. But he still needed the Kimmels' property, and they wouldn't sell. That's where things started to get ugly." She flashed back to Ed and wondered if he had visited the snowmobile tracks as promised.

"And now they're dead." Jace frowned. "What happens now?"

"That's what I'm afraid of. The Kimmels' daughter Helen still lives there. She probably doesn't want to sell either."

# Chapter 18

The snow threatened to resume at a moment's notice. Though it was past three in the morning, Kat felt alert and awake. Her findings had got her adrenaline going.

They had so much to do. "We've got to get to the mine and get water samples from the tailings pond and Prospector's Creek," Kat said. "We'll get them tested to prove the water's fine, since the earlier samples were doctored. Once we compare the samples, we can prove the deception. The creek and the drinking water are as pristine as ever, not contaminated."

"You really should have tested it before you drank." Jace scrutinized her for signs of poisoning. "What if you get sick while we're out there?"

She waved him off. "I knew the water was clean. Otherwise I never would have tasted it."

Jace raised his brows. "That's your hunch, but it's still unproven. Your symptoms might not show right away."

"Nothing's going to happen to me. Remember this morning at breakfast when Dennis added ice to his water? His refrigerator dispenser is connected directly to the water supply. He tells us the water's no good, yet he uses ice cubes straight from the water supply."

"Couldn't we just test an ice cube as a sample?"

"No. We need samples at each point in the process: the tailings pond, Prospector's Creek, and the reservoir. We need to show step by step that the entire water supply is clean. Otherwise, there's a chance that someone will tamper with things after the fact as a cover up."

"You mean poison it for real?"

She nodded.

"We need to get off the mountain, too." Jace frowned. "Otherwise the sample is pointless."

"We'll figure it out."

"We'd better warn the remaining protestors. Ranger might go after them."

"I don't know how to reach Ed or anyone else." Even with the Kimmels, the most vocal protestors now gone, the other protestors remained an obstacle between Batchelor and his resort plans.

Kat pulled on her boots just as a light shone through the kitchen window. She stepped over to the window and looked outside. The helicopter pad was illuminated. The rotors whirred to life as the pilot started the engine. A handful of guests stood a good distance back from the aircraft, their luggage on the snow beside them.

She was surprised that the pilot would risk flights in the stormy weather, especially in the middle of the night. He must be ferrying them to the Sinclair Junction airport where their journey would continue on, presumably on Batchelor's private Cessna.

The constant flight departures seriously hampered her plans. It was impossible to sneak out and across the property while the guests congregated outside. Voices drifted through the air. They were too far away to make out their conversation, but the jovial atmosphere of a few hours ago had evaporated. Everyone outside appeared grim and anxious. No wonder, given the inclement weather.

Jace stood by the bed in front of the French doors. "This Ed guy—you don't even know approximately where he lives?"

"No idea. I don't even know his last name." Yet they had to warn him. Whatever plans Ranger and Burt had, they somehow involved the protestors. She was certain of that, even though she had no proof. She had a flash of insight as she recalled their conversation about the snowmobile tracks. "He lives in the direction of the avalanche slope."

"We'd risk a second slide." Jace scratched his chin. "But since it's colder at night, we're probably all right."

"Our only other option is to hold off until morning. We wait for Ed at the blockade site before the protest. He has to go by there on the way to the mine site." Kat stared past Jace to the French doors behind him. The deck was illuminated under the glow of the outside light. Beyond the snow-capped railing, the light dropped off abruptly into icy blackness. She wondered what other secrets the canyon held.

"That's way too dangerous," Jace said. "And I hate to break it to you, but it is almost morning." Jace checked his watch. "It'll be light in a couple of hours."

She sighed. "That settles it, then. No time like the present." They had talked for almost an hour since Ranger's departure. In fact, the helicopter had returned and was loading another batch of guests. Damn, it would likely be another half hour before it loaded up and departed.

Jace glanced out the window. "We can't go yet. We'll be discovered."

"We'll go after the chopper leaves. That gives us at least a thirty-minute window before it returns." The helicopter flights were an unexpected complication. They would trek in the dark and only switch on their headlamps once clear of the property.

Her thoughts flashed back to Ranger and their earlier altercation. "Ranger will tell Dennis everything. What time were you supposed to reconvene with Dennis? If we're not back in time, it will be obvious that we're up to something."

She gazed out the window as a flashlight danced across the lawn. Another guest headed to the chopper. But the flashlight headed towards their cabin instead of the helipad.

She didn't need any light to recognize the profiles of the two men.

"Uh-oh. It's Ranger and he's got Batchelor with him." Judging by their rapid march, they were angry. "Looks like they've already talked."

"I wish I could get on that helicopter," Jace said. "What do I say to him?"

"I don't know, but we have to somehow discredit Ranger." It was their only chance. Their departure was delayed yet again. But, she realized, so was Ranger's. "If we can hold Ranger here…"

"We can delay the explosion." Jace finished her sentence. "I'll think of something."

She realized in hindsight that the helicopter flights were a stroke of luck. If they had already left the cabin, Batchelor and Ranger would have discovered that and tracked them down, thwarting their plan.

She jumped as one of the men pounded on the door. She nodded at Jace and he let the men in.

"Get him out of here!" Kat pointed at Ranger. "He broke into my room and attacked me."

"That's not what happened." Ranger's eyes narrowed as he glared at her.

"You deny breaking in here?"

"I was checking the—"

Kat grabbed her bag off the bed and brushed past the men. "I'm getting on that chopper. The second it touches down in cellphone range, I'm calling the police and telling them what you did. But first I'll tell everyone outside what you did to me."

Jace's eyebrows furrowed, not understanding at first. A split second later he grabbed his bag and followed Kat.

"Wait a minute," Dennis said. "Ranger was just checking the cabin. He didn't realize you were in here."

"And you," Kat pointed at Batchelor. "Your employee attacked me, a guest. What will your other guests think about that?"

Outside the helicopter loaded a few more guests and the pilot shut the door. The dozen or so remaining guests milled over to the driveway, hoping to be chosen for the next flight.

"You can't go out there." Dennis tried to intercept her in the hall.

"What choice do I have? I'm not safe here."

"Okay, okay." Dennis glared at Ranger. His face reddened, clearly furious. He turned to Kat. "He shouldn't have done what he did. I'll deal with him. He won't come near you again, I promise."

Dennis turned and headed outside without another word, Ranger close behind him. She headed to the kitchen window and watched them head towards the helipad. Dennis was in damage control mode, probably looking for Rosemary to grill her on what information she had divulged to Kat.

At least Dennis had promised to keep Ranger away. His promise wasn't worth much, but at least it bought them some time. It also seemed that while Ranger did Dennis's bidding, his methods weren't entirely condoned by his boss.

Most importantly, Ranger had been thrown off track. She and Jace would be alone and uninterrupted for a while, free to sneak out to the mine.

But first she needed to ensure their survival. She couldn't risk leaving everything on her laptop, since they weren't out of danger yet. Ranger or Dennis could still grab it and destroy it. They weren't safe until they were off the mountain, since the two of them were the only ones who knew the truth. A truth that could be easily supressed with another accident.

Jace watched the helipad through the kitchen window to ensure Dennis and Ranger headed back to the lodge. "They're gone, and so is the helicopter."

The helicopter's lights glinted in the night as it lifted off the helipad.

"Just a sec." She copied her findings into an email and pressed send. Jace would be furious if he found out about the email, but she didn't have a choice. Few things were worse to a journalist than a story scoop pulled right out from underneath them, but it was a matter of survival.

Her actions were either a safeguard or the stupidest thing she had ever done. She prayed it wasn't the latter, but she didn't know what else to do.

"It's now or never. Let's go."

She had almost closed her laptop when the error message flashed across her screen. The email hadn't gone through. Damned Internet. Dennis Batchelor's money bought power and privilege, yet Internet connectivity eluded him.

She clicked on the email and tried resending it.

Nothing. Her laptop screen froze. It was still trying to access the Internet connection.

"C'mon, Kat. We'll miss our chance. Put that thing down and let's go."

She pulled on her boots and grabbed her jacket. She grabbed her pack and emptied the contents of the refrigerator.

Jace was already at the door. "We don't need all that."

She wasn't so sure. They might not make it back to the cabin.

Jace was already outside. She paused momentarily then ran back to the table and shoved her laptop in her pack. Leaving it gave Ranger even more reason to destroy them.

One couple had already met an untimely death today and the odds weren't in their favor.

# Chapter 19

Once outside, they circled behind the cabin and crossed the driveway under cover of darkness. From there they headed to the trail at the fence line. The crisp night air shocked her lungs as she adjusted her pack.

The unexpected helicopter flights—and Dennis and Ranger's cabin visit—had delayed their plans. They now had only two hours till sunrise, so they headed to the mine first before the protestor blockade site. Locating Ed was hit or miss with no contact information, but he would eventually appear at the blockade. It was on his way to the mine.

In any event, they needed water samples from the source. Not only for the lab, but also to prove to Ed and others there was nothing wrong with the water.

A wolf howled in the distance, seemingly in the direction they headed. A second wolf answered the call, followed by another and another. Within minutes an entire pack howled, their cries rising in crescendo. Kat shivered.

She hadn't even considered wildlife encounters since it was winter, and it had been quiet outside earlier today. Bears hibernated in winter, but wolves didn't. They were predators, and food was scarce this time of year. Except for the food in her pack, which she had grabbed in case they couldn't sneak back in the cabin. Given the hostile encounter with Ranger, who knew what would happen next?

"We need to pick up the pace," Jace said. "How far is the mine?"

"It's close. But it's hard to walk in the dark like this." Her light wasn't nearly as good as she thought, casting only a dim cone a foot or so in front of her. The straps of her bag dug into her hand. The bag banged against her shin with every stride. Her earlier treks hadn't included a pack, and she had underestimated the added weight. Had she really needed half the fridge contents? Probably not, but it was too late now. It occurred to her that she also carried the scent of food to any predator nearby. She was wolf bait.

"At this pace we'll never be back by morning." Jace paused to wait.

She couldn't ask him for help without revealing the contents of her pack. That meant sharing her fear that they couldn't return to the cabin. There was no turning back, though. Everything had been set in motion with her altercation with Ranger.

The soft flurries resumed. While the snow muffled their footsteps, it also left tracks. Their destination was clear to any pursuer simply by their path. She hadn't factored that into their plans. Whoever planned the trap would also be outside in the predawn morning and inevitably their paths would cross.

She shifted her bag onto her opposite shoulder and tried to ignore the pain, which had morphed into a dull throb. They were fully committed now, since they couldn't turn back and risk discovery.

Whirring rotor blades sliced through the silence as the helicopter passed them high overhead. Back for another load. They reached a fork in the trail. "That one." Kat motioned to the left and they followed the incline to the mine. They were close now. Hopefully the mine watchman was absent overnight. She had no contingency plan if he wasn't.

She slogged uphill behind Jace and after an eternity reached the mine. Kat pointed to the shed. "We'll drop our stuff in there, so we don't have to lug it around. Any problems and we can come back for it later." She couldn't wait to stash her heavy pack, and it was pointless to carry their gear all the way to the tailings pond. Their packs would stay dry and hidden in the shed while they collected the water samples.

She followed Jace to the shed's front door and was relieved to see no vehicles in the parking lot.

Jace fumbled with the padlock. "We can't get in. It's locked. Maybe we shouldn't bother."

"What if we have to make a run for it? At least our packs will stay safe while we get the samples. Besides, it's still a few hours before we can expect Ed to arrive at the blockade. We need to wait somewhere."

"Sure, if I can open it. But I don't have any tools."

Kat stared at the shiny new padlock fastened firmly in place. The watchman had obviously replaced it after her visit. She slumped down against the side of the shed, dejected.

"Now what?" She had also considered the shed as a hiding place of sorts, in case they were discovered. Depending on who they encountered before morning, it might be a necessity.

"Relax," Jace said. "We've got time. Let's look for something to cut or pry it open."

"I'll look around, see what we can find." The snow fell heavily now, everything coated with sloppy wet flakes. She saw plenty of rusted equipment, but no detachable parts to be improvised into cutters or a pry bar.

Glass shattered behind her. She spun around but couldn't see Jace. She peered around the building. Jace had broken the side window with a brick. Now they could climb through the window. She sighed in relief. They had safe shelter, although she hadn't expected him to break a window.

"Sorry, but I figured time is of the essence." He brushed away glass shards with his glove. "And we need a fallback plan. Don't know who we might meet up here."

Good idea too, since a broken or missing lock was a dead giveaway. A side window was less obvious.

She nodded. "I'm half expecting to see Ranger. There's a reason he wanted me out on that deck." Chills ran down her spine as she imagined hurtling down into the canyon below.

She patted her backpack, comforted by the hard plastic edges of her laptop. Everything left behind in the cabin could be replaced.

Jace surprised her by agreeing. "I'm sure he triggered that avalanche somehow. He knows you're onto something, so he's got to silence you. Dennis won't stop him, since it's exactly what he wants. Terrorize people and they'll give up their land."

He motioned her to the window and interlocked his hands to give her a boost up. Kat dropped her bag and climbed up and through the window.

"What's in here? Rocks?" Jace grimaced as he lifted her bag.

"Just a little insurance." She grabbed each bag from him before helping him inside. She stashed their bags in a corner behind some equipment. No one would notice them unless they tossed the place.

He jumped down and brushed off his hands. "I'd call this a one-star compared to our previous accommodations."

Jace struck a match and glanced around the shed. The equipment cast odd dinosaur shadows in the dim light. Other than the matches, they had no lighting. No heat either. It was quite a contrast from the luxurious cabin, and Kat almost wished she had spent more time inside.

He struck another match. "I wish we could build a fire outside." Long shadows fell across his face as he sat in front of stacked boxes.

Matches.

Dynamite.

Jace sat just less than a foot away. She grabbed his hand and blew out the match.

"What was that for?"

A cold gust blew in from the broken window. The sky slowly turned to indigo as dawn approached. She shivered. "Tell you later." Now wasn't the time for panic. "Let's get those samples now." Climbing in and out of the window seemed a wasted effort, but it ensured they had safe refuge until morning. She rummaged in her pack and pulled out a couple of empty water bottles. She handed one to Jace. "We'll go to the tailings pond first."

She didn't have the heart to tell him that their newfound refuge was a shed full of dynamite.

# Chapter 20

The tailings pond was frozen solid. Kat searched for a rock and pounded the ice for several minutes before she was able to break through the glassy surface to the water underneath.

She had just scooped the tailings pond water sample when the helicopter whirred overhead. The chop-chop of the rotor blades intensified as the aircraft drew closer. She froze, waiting for the sound to recede as the aircraft headed to Batchelor's helipad. Instead the beats intensified. The chopper wasn't flying over the mine; it was descending.

"They're coming for us, Jace." Kat tugged on his shoulder. "We're trapped." Ranger and Dennis somehow knew they were at the site, though they hadn't encountered anyone, not even the night watchman. Probably spotted on surveillance cameras. They had come for them once the last of Batchelor's guests had been transported to the airport.

Jace craned his neck and scanned the dark sky. "I hear it, but I can't see anything with the cloud cover."

Kat sprang to her feet. "We'd better go while we can."

"Wait—maybe it's that other protestor group. They can help us."

"There's too many of them to come by helicopter." Ed and Fritz had both mentioned at least a dozen activists. Not only that, but they only protested on weekdays and today was Saturday. "Ranger saw my laptop screen and knows I've uncovered Dennis's mine ownership. He'll know we're here for water samples."

"He doesn't know you've figured that out yet."

"Maybe not, but he knows I'll expose Dennis's sneaky tactics." Dennis had taken pains to hide his ownership in a web of secret companies.  He would do whatever it took to keep his ownership a secret. Even if it involved murder. "Let's go."

 "But where? If we run to the shed, they'll see us cross the parking lot." Jace looked skyward. Helicopter skids poked through the clouds a hundred feet above them, followed by the fuselage.  The parking lot lit up in a dull glow as the light refracted off the clouds. The circle of light expanded as the chopper descended. Wind gusts circled them. In less than a minute, they would be exposed in the helicopter's lights.

They were defenceless without the cover of darkness.

Kat pointed to the mineshaft as the rotors intensified. "Run!"

The helicopter searchlight transformed the predawn parking lot into a strange alien landscape. The blue-white lights danced off the snow, a sub-zero movie set.

They scrambled towards the mineshaft and darkness, but the searchlights followed them.

She felt like an animal in a wildlife documentary, tracked by unseen enemies above. No matter where they turned, they couldn't outrun trouble.

# Chapter 21

Kat doubled over in a coughing spasm ten feet into the mineshaft. Her lungs were on fire from sprinting in the frigid air. She braced one hand against the cave wall. It was dusty and gritty on her palm.

She couldn't see Jace in the pitch-black darkness but she heard his labored breathing.

She was thankful to have dropped her pack, otherwise they never would have made it. But what if they found her laptop? It was hidden well inside the shed, but the broken window was an obvious giveaway to search inside. Her computer contained the only definitive proof of Batchelor's deception, other than the water sample held tightly in her hand. "I think they saw us."

"Maybe, maybe not," Jace said. "Keep moving. We need to get out of earshot." His footsteps echoed in the cavernous chamber. "Sound travels here."

Kat followed his voice as it seemed to get further away. A few feet later she hit a wall. Literally. Her nose hurt from scraping the hard rock and she coughed from the dust. She couldn't just run blindly. Mines were dangerous places.

She swore under her breath. In the darkness she hadn't noticed the abrupt ninety-degree turn in the mineshaft wall.

"Hurry." Jace's voice echoed through the chamber somewhere ahead of her.

The mineshaft air was dank and Kat was blind in the inky blackness. She struggled to maintain her forward momentum, but couldn't see where she was going. "Wait, I don't think we should go any further."

Jace's voice replied somewhere a few feet ahead. "We have to. There's a chance they won't find us. Maybe they didn't spot us outside."

She shuffled forward, unease growing with each step. "They obviously know we're here. We've trapped ourselves." Her face flushed and she felt claustrophobic.

"Kat?" Jace was at least twenty feet ahead now, deep into the mine. "Where are you?"

She was about to answer when footsteps stomped at the tunnel entrance.

Her heart raced. They were cornered. There was nowhere to go. She had to catch up to Jace and fast. She turned on her phone's flashlight and cupped it with her hand to keep the light to a narrow beam in front of her. She looked straight ahead and tried not to notice the narrowing walls and low ceiling. She jumped as a rock fell somewhere ahead.

She exhaled in relief when Jace's back came into view ahead. She scrambled to catch up with him. Her light beam fell upon empty wooden boxes. They bore the same lettering as the ones handled by Ranger and Burt.

Explosives.

"Kat? Shut the light off."

"No. Look at this." She shone her light on the explosives detonator. Too late she realized they had made a fatal mistake. The charge was probably pre-set, timed to go off during the protest. "This place is booby-trapped."

Jace swore softly. "This must be where they planned to do it."

"The parking lot was too obvious." Kat's heart pounded. "Ranger and Burt planned to herd the protestors in here where the explosion will be muffled. No one will hear anything."

They had walked right into their own death trap.

"They'll probably force the protestors in at gunpoint." Jace's voice was low and quiet.

"I see it now." Kat's voice broke. "They'll detonate the charge and frame the protestors by making it look like an accident. Everyone will think the protestors sabotaged the mineshaft by blowing it up, when in fact they were the victims. Looks like we've thwarted their plans."

Her light cast shadows upon Jace's face as she tried to gauge his reaction.

"Now we're the victims." His eyes widened. "They'll blow us up instead."

They had made a fatal mistake. Explosives were used in mine blasting all the time. Business as usual for a mining company, even if they had been inactive lately. Anyone who heard the explosion wouldn't think twice about it.

The mine was mothballed, it was remote, and no one other than their captors even knew they were here.

And there was more than one detonator. Kat followed the wires with her flashlight beam. It ran along one wall out to the mine entrance. The detonator in the cave might be a backup, or maybe it was triggered remotely. She didn't know enough about explosives to know which. And she didn't want to know.

A deep voice boomed through the chamber. "Get out here, now!"

She coughed, an involuntary reaction to the dust.

"Move it."

Kat turned in the direction of the man's voice. He didn't sound like Dennis or Ranger. Her heart pounded as she realized there was no escape. No matter what they did, they eventually had to come out.

That might be a good thing, since it meant no imminent explosion. It bought them some time, gave them a chance to escape.

"Maybe it's the watchman," Kat said, though she wasn't convinced. Though the cave's echo distorted the speaker, his voice seemed younger and stronger than the elderly man she had met earlier today. "That doesn't sound like Ranger. I don't think its Burt, either."

"Whoever it is, we better do what he says." Jace squeezed her shoulder. "No sudden moves till we know what he wants."

He kissed her before turning towards the mineshaft opening. "Follow my lead."

Kat's heart raced as she envisioned the aftermath.

Would the explosion be strong enough to destroy the shed on the opposite side of the parking lot? Someone might find the evidence contained on her laptop hard drive and expose the truth. That was just as unlikely, since anyone on site ultimately worked for Dennis Batchelor. And she had no doubt that Ranger would be all over this place with a fine-tooth comb to remove any incriminating evidence.

She took a deep breath and followed Jace out into the opening. She had nothing to lose, and she wasn't going down without a fight.

# Chapter 22

Jace squeezed Kat's hand as they navigated back to the mineshaft entrance. "Who's there?"

"Jace, it's me, Gord. I'm coming in."

"Gord? What the hell?" Jace was incredulous. "What are you doing here?"

"Kat didn't tell you?"

A beam of light shone into the mineshaft, momentarily blinding them.

"Tell me what?" Jace paused. "Wait—don't come in here. We'll come out."

Kat exhaled in relief. The email had reached its destination after all. Sometimes miracles really did happen.

They reversed course and walked beside the cord that stretched from the detonator towards the mine entrance. It was sloppily laid down and they could have easily tripped on it in the darkness. Would a tug or a pull have been enough to set off the charge? She knew nothing about explosives and preferred to keep it that way.

Jace tugged at her arm. "C'mon. We've got no time to waste here."

He scrambled towards the entrance and she followed. Minutes later she gulped in a blast of icy air. Fresh air never tasted so good.

"Oh man, it really is you," Jace said. "You have no idea how I glad I am to see you."

Gord Dekker stood at the entrance, a high-powered flashlight in his right hand. Technically he was Jace's competition, since he worked for *The Daily Beat* after leaving *The Sentinel* earlier in the year.

Kat rushed to Gord and hugged him. "You got my email! I didn't think it went through." She hadn't had time to shut down her laptop completely when they rushed from the cabin. Her email program had resent the message. The lousy Internet connection must have reconnected long enough for the email to reach Gord.

Gord pulled back and wrapped his arm around her shoulder. "I couldn't figure out why you'd give me a scoop instead of your boyfriend here. I knew you must be in trouble."

Jace wore an expression of exaggerated shock. "You gave the story to Gord?"

"I needed a backup plan with someone we could trust. I knew Gord would fact check and run the story later if something happened to us." She broke from his embrace. "But I didn't think you'd do it in the middle of the night."

"Lucky for you I'm an insomniac." Gord turned to Jace. "Ready to go?"

"Not quite," Jace pointed across the parking lot. "We need to grab our bags out of that shed first."

Kat trailed behind the two men as they headed across the parking lot. Her unease grew as dawn approached and she couldn't wait to be airborne in the chopper. The return trip to the shed seemed to take an eternity. She hoped the chopper wouldn't attract any unwanted attention.

Jace climbed through the window and passed their bags outside, then climbed out himself. "Where'd you get a helicopter?"

"News chopper." Gord grinned. "They let me borrow it. With the pilot, of course, and a couple of refuelling stops on the way. Speaking of which, we need to get a move on. Fuel's expensive."

The chopper's light shone like a beacon at the far end of the parking lot as they headed towards it.

"I started to think we were in for it," Jace said. "We seem to have overstayed our welcome."

"Timing is everything." Gord motioned for Kat's bag and slung it over his shoulder. "Your story's in the morning edition. It's under my byline for now, with both of you cited as anonymous sources. We'll reveal your identities later, once you're safe." He turned to Jace. "I figured you wouldn't want to go public just yet."

"I don't ever want to go public." Kat answered for him. She would much rather stay behind the scenes.

"You got that right. Not until we're out of this place." Jace motioned to the chopper. The rotor blades whirred back into action. "Which reminds me, we don't have much time."

The words were barely out of his mouth when headlights shone into the lot. The vehicle's wheels spun on the snow as it veered towards them.

Ranger.

"Run!" The Land Cruiser accelerated and headed directly for Kat.

The SUV was less than thirty feet away. It closed in and threatened to cut her off from the chopper.

She willed her legs to run to the chopper's open door. Jace was already there, Gord just ahead of her. She fought the wind from the rotors.

"Let's go!" Gord cried. He turned and grabbed her arm.

Ranger's SUV lurched to a standstill twenty feet from the aircraft. He jumped from the vehicle and waved his hands at them. "You can't leave—get back here!"

Kat had barely climbed inside when the chopper lifted off. She was alarmed to see the door was still open as they lurched upwards. She grabbed onto the seat back to steady herself as they ascended ten feet, then twenty, then fifty feet above the pavement where they finally levelled out.

Gord pulled the door shut as the aircraft ascended. Within seconds they were a hundred feet, then two hundred feet above the parking lot. Ranger and his SUV transformed into harmless Tonka-toy specks below them.

Dawn's early light reminded Kat of the precarious weather conditions as the pilot struggled to level the helicopter. Her stomach lurched as she fastened her seat belt.

Minutes later the ride smoothed out as the pilot increased altitude and levelled off. She turned to Gord, anxious to ensure that help was on its way for Ed and the other local protestors.

She spoke but couldn't hear her voice above the din of the aircraft.

Gord handed her a set of headphones and motioned for her to put them on. Gord and Jace followed suit.

"The pilot just radioed the police." Gord's voice crackled through her ears. "They'll arrest Ranger and Burt for the explosives sabotage. They'll contact my editor to get your file. It might take them a few hours to do more, since they'll need investigative assistance from nearby law enforcement. They'll contain the mine site immediately and ensure no one goes up there. Things will swing into full gear once investigators from the surrounding detachments arrive."

Outside help was a good thing, since Batchelor was accustomed to making his own rules in tiny Paradise Peaks. He probably had local officials under his thumb. After all, they had simply taken Ranger at his word rather than investigate the avalanche. They were either corrupt or incompetent.

That gave her an idea. "Ask them to follow up with a protestor named Ed. The locals will know who I'm talking about. His photographs of the avalanche scene will prove it was no accident." She had no proof other than her hunch.

Gord nodded. "Your avalanche notes and eyewitness account of the explosives are enough to question Ranger and Burt on that too. It will be hard to prove the avalanche, though."

"I doubt Batchelor will co-operate," Jace said. "What's to stop him from flying to some other country? He could just move offshore where his money is."

"I think he'll stay. Positive or negative, he loves the limelight. His ego gets in the way," Kat said. "He's confident that Ranger will take the rap for him. I don't think that's the case."

"Why not?" Gord asked. "He's probably well-paid for his efforts."

"It's not about the money," she said. "Ranger felt betrayed when Batchelor didn't defend his actions against me in the cabin. I don't think it was the first time.  Those out-of-town protestors? Dennis hired them to stir things up. And steal the spotlight, so to speak, from the local protest group. They were paid protestors that he controlled.

"At first I thought they were imaginary, another ploy of Batchelor's to scare the locals. Yet Ranger claimed to know nothing about them. He seemed pretty angry about them, though.

"As Dennis Batchelor's right-hand man, he should have known. I realized then that Dennis kept secrets from Ranger. Ranger must have discovered that too.  A guy like him sees that as betrayal. Why should he put his life on the line for Dennis, when Dennis doesn't give him the straight goods? He felt used, and right about now he's probably second-guessing his boss's loyalty. After all, he's the one getting arrested, not Dennis. I have a feeling he'll expose Batchelor's role."

Jace nodded. "He's not going to take the fall for murder. No job is worth that."

Kat couldn't agree more. She gazed out the helicopter window as the sunrise glowed behind the mountains. She was relieved to leave the valley—and trouble—behind.

This was one hell of a weekend and it wasn't even over yet. How ironic that she had made a getaway from her weekend getaway

# Chapter 23

Sunday morning crept in as the dull gray monochrome of a Vancouver December day. Nothing too dramatic, even the mountains hid under the veil of cloud and drizzle. Sometimes dull was comforting. Today felt downright fabulous. Kat watched the rain trickle down the window.

Kat, Jace, and Gord sat in Gord's downtown office at *The Daily Beat*. They had headed straight for his 29th floor office overlooking the Vancouver harbor when their chopper had touched down a few hours ago. She hadn't slept for almost twenty-four hours, but shut-eye was the last thing on her mind. The *Daily Beat* had gone to press with the story of Batchelor's shady dealings as the lead story within an hour of the arrests of Burt, Ranger, and Dennis.

She leaned forward to take a closer look at Gord's monitor. The front-page headline stared back at her:

*Dennis Batchelor—Billionaire Environmentalist Cheat Exposed*

"Couldn't have said it better myself." She was about to glance away when she saw the byline. She gasped at the sight of her name. "But why my name? I thought we were anonymous sources."

"That didn't seem right. After all, it's your story. You exposed the corruption, so I can't take the credit. I just did a few final edits."

Kat grimaced. "Now I'm exposed."

"Everyone's focussed on the culprits in the story, not you." Gord smiled. "Though my boss does want to talk to you. Something about becoming a guest columnist."

Jace groaned.

"I'll think about it." She disliked being the center of attention, and while the job sounded intriguing, she'd had enough excitement for a year. Between almost getting blown up and her unexpected investigative journalism, she had a newfound appreciation for her day job as forensic accountant and fraud investigator.

And plenty of cases to keep busy.

After Christmas, of course.

Gord scrolled halfway down the page to a second story. This one was an exposé on government lobbying and corruption, with just enough juicy details to spark an investigation and public inquiry into Batchelor's business dealings with the mine. Though the story had broken just hours ago, everyone was talking about it. It only confirmed the public's suspicions of political corruption. Now there was concrete proof.

"An in-depth look at George MacAlister's campaign funding," Gord said. MacAlister had already been suspended from office as the government moved into full damage control mode. Criminal charges were also being considered against both him and Dennis Batchelor for corruption.

"When did you find time to write a second story?" Kat asked.

"On the helicopter ride up. You had most of the details. I just added the campaign contributions from the last election."

"Dennis financed almost his entire campaign, just so they could both profit from hidden land deals." Jace shook his head.

Gord nodded. "MacAlister's secret ownership stake in the mine is also exposed. Leaving office is the least of his worries. Aside from the obvious conflict of interest, he'll face criminal charges over the environmental disaster."

"But the water was never bad," Jace said.

"He knowingly misled the people of Prospector's Creek. Crown Counsel's considering the specific charges right now. Whatever the result, there are hefty penalties for falsifying environmental impact assessments." Gord clasped his hands behind his head. "His greed endangered the public as well as the environment."

"Speaking of the environment, what do you think of Dennis's peace offering?" Kat was surprised at the swiftness of Batchelor's response to the bad press. In a desperate attempt to regain public favor, he had announced his intention to donate a remediated Regal Gold Mine property for use as a public park. He had already chosen the name. Great Bear Park didn't appeal to Kat, but the general public seemed to like it. Batchelor's marketers, at least, had struck gold.

"It's just a thinly veiled attempt to buy his way out of trouble," Gord said. "I'm not even sure it's a promise he can deliver on. Lotus Investments, the previous owners, plan to sue to get their mine back. They want the sale transaction unwound since it was based on fraudulent information."

Kat was suddenly overcome with exhaustion. Had she really only spent a day in Dennis Batchelor's world? Today was promising to be more of the same and it was still only morning. "A full day's work and the day's barely started."

"Easy for you to say." Jace sighed. "I've still got another full day ahead of me. I need to finish Batchelor's draft."

Gord was incredulous. "You're not still ghostwriting his biography?"

"Of course I am. My legally binding contract says I'm owed a hundred grand on completion. I intend to collect what's owed to me."

"He'll never pay you," Gord said. "Especially now that he's been exposed."

"He has to pay me once I deliver my end of the bargain. A ghostwritten biography, as per the contract," Jace said. "It probably won't see the light of day with all that's happened, and that suits me just fine. I don't care what he does with it, as long as he pays me. And he better, unless he wants another lawsuit."

Jace was surprisingly nonchalant, Kat thought. "And you thought you'd never write a book."

"Wait till you see my next one," he said. "An unauthorized biography exposing Batchelor's dirty dealings and corruption. Way juicier than the ghostwritten version."

"A sure bestseller," Gord said. "People want to see his secrets exposed."

Batchelor sure had a lot of them.

"I hope Dennis faces jail time, too." Kat said. "He's indirectly responsible for the Kimmels' deaths."

Investigators had found Batchelor's secret plans for the new resort when they searched his lodge less than an hour ago. Once he had all the land needed, he would claim he had remediated the mine and come out a hero. The new environmental report would show the mine site and Prospector's Creek as fully recovered from the environmental disaster that had never happened in the first place.

How tragic that the Kimmels never got to see their hard won victory. They had won in the end, but lost everything in the process.

Batchelor's new road wouldn't be built and the existing highway would not be rerouted either. It would stay where it was, keeping Paradise Peaks off the beaten track and downright inconvenient to get to. The only change was that the village got an upgraded access road with the proviso that the pristine wilderness was maintained.

Everything would regress back in time to five years earlier, before Batchelor had started his schemes. Sometimes the best progress was none at all.

Ed Levine was right to call environmentalism a city word. Words were nothing without substance behind them.

If you walked the walk, you didn't need to name it to do it right. You didn't draw attention to it. Once it was something to blog about, buy or subscribe to, the truth got lost in the process.

Kat stared out at the rainy vista. Even with the snow in Paradise Peaks, she hadn't felt the Christmas spirit until now. She turned to Jace. "You know, I never really did get that weekend getaway you promised. After working all weekend, I need to relax."

"Someplace nice and quiet?" Gord's face betrayed no emotion. "I could send you on assignment to Luxembourg. I hear there's some money transfers that need looking into."

"I think I'll pass." Kat laughed. "Home is looking better all the time."

Snow dusted the tops of the North Shore Mountains across the harbor and suddenly it felt like Christmas. Not that she needed snow to get in the holiday spirit. She didn't need city words or any words at all.

Like Ed Lavine, she didn't need to name it or brand it. She would just enjoy it.


Did you love the *Katerina Carter Color of Money Mysteries?*
Then check out my other books for more suspense and thrilling intrigue!

Get my books at the links at the end of this book or visit my website: **http://www.colleencross.com**

## BONUS! Excerpt from Game Theory

Stay tuned for more stories in the Katerina Carter Color of Money Mystery series by Colleen Cross. In the meantime, check out my other books or read the *Game Theory* bonus excerpt included on the following pages. Game Theory is a novel in the bestselling Katerina Carter Fraud Thriller Series!  Here's what it's about:

## *Game Theory*

Katerina Carter lands her biggest case ever—a massive Ponzi scheme. Billionaire Zachary Barron's business is in free fall, somehow connected to the shadowy World Institute. Game Theory uncovers how the world really works, where a small pool of winners take all. And the players will stop at nothing to get what they want.

Buy the book now or read the following excerpt for more.

## *A Katerina Carter Fraud Thriller Game Theory:*

# Chapter 1

He didn't look like a man about to die. They never did. Part of the thrill was deciding their fates. It just required a bit of planning.

"Back up. Just a little." She focused him in her sights. He was easily twice her age, but surprisingly fit for sixty. He had matched her step for step as they skied and then snow-shoed up the steep Summit Trail. Wanted her in bed, just like every other man. She had decided long ago to use that to her advantage.

He stepped back, moving closer to the cornice slab of snow that jutted out unsupported from the cliff. She'd been careful to take the eastern approach so he wouldn't notice the dangerous overhang. Her pulse quickened as she anticipated what was to come. Whiskey jacks flew past on reconnaissance, the small gray birds circling as they swooped in to scavenge muffin crumbs from the man's outstretched hand.

It was a Wednesday morning and the backcountry was deserted. Another man on snowshoes had passed them in the opposite direction more than an hour ago. They were alone.

"Smile." She zoomed in, clicked the shutter, and felt a rush of exhilaration. Hers would be the last face he would see, the last voice he would hear.

He grinned as he shifted his weight and unzipped his Gore-Tex jacket. The sun shone through the low clouds, creating strange shadows across the snow.

A split second later his face contorted, confidence replaced with unmasked fear. His mouth dropped open as his eyes hollowed with terror. It was her favorite part: the hunter now the prey, and her victim knowing she had something to do with it.

Realization froze on his face as the ground beneath broke into pieces, unable to support his weight. The snow overhang snapped off the cliff, sending him hurtling down to the valley two hundred meters below.

His screams echoed down the canyon. Then silence, except for the whiskey jacks circling back for seconds.

She smiled. Almost too easy. She tossed the camera over the edge. No bullets, no mess. No trace, unless someone came looking before the next snowfall, forecasted to start in a few hours. Even if they found him before the spring melt, it would look like an accident, a tourist unfamiliar with backcountry snow conditions. She scattered the rest of the muffin to the birds. They pecked at each other, fighting for what was left of the crumbs.

Just like she once did. Not anymore. She would get her fair share, even if she had to kill for it.

# Chapter 2

Katerina Carter shifted in the hard plastic chair and tucked her hands under her thighs. Her fingers were crossed on both hands, knuckles crushed into the unforgiving seat. It defied logic, but she did it anyway. What did she have to lose?

Uncle Harry hunched forward beside her, elbows on knees, poised for Dr. McAdam's next question. His first mini mental health exam had been six months ago, right after the accident. The early-stage Alzheimer's diagnosis meant the loss of his driver's license and the independence that went along with it. He'd been depressed ever since, his memory dramatically worsening.

The tiny examination room barely held the three of them. Since the diagnosis, the doctor had insisted a family member accompany him. That was Kat given Aunt Elsie's heart attack and sudden passing a year ago.

"What city are we in, Harry?" Dr. McAdam rolled back on his stool as he waited for an answer.

"Vancouver." Her uncle pulled a hanky from his pocket and wiped his brow. A thin sheen of sweat covered his forehead.

"Good. What is your home address?"

"Easy—418 Maple." Harry beamed.

"All right. What year is it?"

"It's 1989."

"Hmmm. What month?"

"June."

"What day of the week?"

"Saturday."

December 5, 2012, a Wednesday. The Weather Channel finally got it right today. Wet snow, chance of freezing rain tonight.

Kat checked her watch. Most of the afternoon gone with a full day's work waiting for her at the office. Like most days lately—plans derailed, whole days and weeks evaporated in an instant. Keeping Harry safe, fed, and calm was practically a full-time job.

"You better get yourself a calendar, doc. Now will you help me get my license back?"

"Let's deal with this first, Harry." Dr. McAdam pointed to a drawing. "What do you see in this picture?"

Harry cast a furtive glance at Kat. "A watch."

"And this?" Dr. McAdam smiled at him.

"A pen. See? Easy-peasy."

"Now some arithmetic. Starting at one hundred, count down by taking seven off each time."

Harry wrung his hands together. "How is this getting my license back?"

"Just bear with me, Harry." Dr. McAdam shifted his gaze to Kat.

"Uncle Harry, just relax. Take your time." Kat's mother had failed a similar test twenty years ago when she was first diagnosed with Alzheimer's. The mood and memory changes were unmistakable, even to a fourteen-year-old.

Kat's father had accompanied her mother to the appointment. Shortly thereafter, he had walked out on both of them for good. That's when she had moved in with the Dentons. Alzheimer's was a cruel death sentence.

At least Harry got twenty more years of sanity than his sister. Early-onset Alzheimer's like her mom's supposedly ran in families. Did she inherit the gene? She'd rather not know.

"One hundred."

Silence.

"Ninety-three." Harry's brows creased.

Kat squeezed her fingers together as her stomach growled. Kat's lunch plans had been foiled by a two-hour delay to convince Harry to leave the house. Harry had all his meals with her and Jace now, partly because he always forgot to eat on his own.

"Twenty-three."

She pulled one hand free and glanced sideways at Harry. She wasn't that hungry after all. Matter of fact, she felt a bit sick to her stomach. Harry had complained of stomach cramps for the last few days too. Must be that flu going around.

Harry counted down to three and turned his gaze to the door. He hummed under his breath.

"Harry?"

"Doc? Are we done now?"

"Not quite." Dr. McAdam sighed and handed him a pencil with a clipboard. "I want you to draw a clock face. Then draw the clock hands pointing to ten before two."

Easy enough. Harry didn't read or do his morning crossword anymore, but he still knew what time it was. He always chided Kat for being late.

Harry tapped the pencil against his lip and stared at the blank page on the clipboard. Slowly he lowered his arm and started to draw.

A shaky, oblong circle, but it was a circle.

Kat exhaled.

Harry dropped the pencil on the clipboard and brought his hand to his face. He brushed his index finger back and forth against his lip. Finally he picked the pencil up again and pressed the lead to paper. One line. Then a second one.

Upside down, marking 6:35.

"Now can I get my license back?"

"Harry—you remember your car accident?" Dr. McAdam removed a pen from his pocket. "You can't have your license back unless you retake and pass the driver's exam."

Harry had crashed his prized 1970s Lincoln through the front window of Carlucci's Pasta House after mistaking the gas pedal for the brake. Luckily the accident happened just after the lunch crowd had dispersed. No one was hurt, but the damage was done.

His life had spiraled downward since then. He had missed numerous appointments, accused his neighbor of stealing, and most recently, set his kitchen on fire after forgetting to turn the stove off. Luckily Kat had arrived in time to smother it, limiting the damage to a blackened wall. She shuddered to think of what might have happened.

Harry thrust the clipboard back into the doctor's hands. "One accident in almost sixty years! You pulled my license for that? Not fair. I've got the reflexes of a thirty-year-old." Harry motioned to Kat. "Tell him, Kat."

Kat pretended to search her purse for her cell phone.

"Kat?"

"Less to worry about, Uncle Harry. I can drive you to your appointments."

"I don't want you driving me places. I'm perfectly capable of driving myself."

"No, you're not. You get lost and—" The words tumbled out of her mouth before she could stop them. "I just think it would be easier on you, that's all."

"So you two are in this together? Maybe I'm retired, but I'm not dead. Or stupid." He flushed and turned to Dr. McAdam. "Let me retake the road test."

Dr. McAdam pursed his lips. "I'm not sure that's a good idea."

"You're not safe out there, Uncle Harry. What if it happens again?"

"It won't. If you won't help me, fine. Hillary will."

Kat opened her mouth, then caught herself before answering.

Dr. McAdam frowned. "Hillary?"

"Harry's daughter." She shuddered just thinking about Hillary. Her cousin had vanished ten years ago, shortly after reneging on a six-figure loan from Harry and Elsie. They had refused to advance her any more money. Not that they could have, since it had wiped out their savings and taken them years to recover. Harry sure talked about her a lot lately. Alzheimer's stripped away recent memories and regenerated ancient ones, like river rocks eroded underwater.

Dr. McAdam stood and brushed his palms on his white lab coat. "Your troubles are much bigger than driving, Harry. I suggest you get your affairs in order, and soon. Alzheimer's can progress very quickly."

"Alzheimer's? That's ridiculous. I don't have Alzheimer's." Harry jumped from the chair and brushed past Dr. McAdam. He turned at the doorway. "Go to hell. Both of you!"

He threw open the door and slammed it behind him.

The Harry she knew never would have done that. Kat blinked back tears as she stood. She grabbed the chair back, overcome by dizziness as black dots darkened her vision.

Dr. McAdam held up his hand, oblivious to her condition. "Wait—he'll cool off in the waiting room. We should chat anyways. What else have you noticed?"

Kat's vision cleared and the shakiness passed. "He has delusions. Talks about Aunt Elsie like she's still alive. He thinks squatters have moved into his house and are trying to kill him."

"Typical." Dr. McAdam scribbled something on his prescription pad and handed it to Kat. "Have him try these. They could help with the hallucinations and might slow down the progression of the disease. You also need to start exploring caregiving options now, because the disease requires a great deal of expertise and attention. The better places have waiting lists, which you'll need to get on. Call my office tomorrow and we'll arrange for Harry to see another doctor."

"A specialist?"

He stood in the doorway and stared at his shoes. "I won't be able to keep seeing Harry. With his Alzheimer's and all…"

"You're dropping him as a patient? Right when he needs you the most?" Kat swallowed the hard lump in her throat.

"It's complicated. He'll be better off with a geriatrician anyways."

"But he's been your patient for close to forty years. How is seeing a doctor he doesn't know better for him?"

"It's not going to matter much. But I'll recommend someone—just call the office tomorrow." He checked his watch. "I am running a bit behind right now, so if you'll just excuse me…"

"But—"

"Good luck." Dr. McAdam pulled the door shut behind him.

After forty years, that was some goodbye.

# Chapter 3

The afternoon's wet snow had turned to freezing rain with nightfall. It stung Kat's exposed face and hands and soaked through her leather soles. She punched in Jace's cell number but got his voicemail for the umpteenth time. Where was he?

She hung up without leaving another message. She had been purposely vague in her original message, asking only for him to meet her in front of the medical building.

Harry had been alone in the waiting room for less than five minutes. Now he was gone, and it was completely her fault.

"Kat."

She jumped at the voice, barely audible above the driving rain.

Jace waved from a half-block away as he hurried towards her. Even in his bulky ski jacket he was tall and athletic looking. "Sorry—I was out on a call. I got here as soon as I could."

He held her close and kissed her. "Out-of-bounds skier. Broken leg—he's lucky we found him before the snowstorm hit. Never would have lasted the night." As a search and rescue volunteer up in the North Shore Mountains, Jace often had callouts for lost skiers and hikers.

That same weather system in the city meant endless torrential rain. Vancouver rain smothered you in stealth mode, in a chokehold lasting weeks and months. Slow but relentless, west coast weather beat you into submission before you even knew it. It was why there were more suicides here.

The rain roiled diagonally in sheets as the wind circled through the tunnel carved from the downtown high rises. Kat couldn't remember—had Uncle Harry worn his raincoat or his lightweight, non-waterproof windbreaker?

He pulled back to look at her. "What's up? Where's Harry?"

She avoided his gaze. "Gone."

"Gone? What do you mean, gone?"

She broke from his embrace and pointed to the concrete high rise behind her that housed the medical office. "We were at his doctor's. He disappeared from the waiting room."

Jace didn't know about Harry's Alzheimer's diagnosis six months ago. They had only rekindled their romance a few months before that, and she was waiting for the right time to tell him. Only there never seemed to be a right time, and it'd been too easy to hide the depth of Harry's problem—older people are just expected to grow fuzzy.

"Is he still sick? The flu should have passed by now—"

She changed the subject. "He's been gone four hours. I don't know where he could possibly be." Kat explained how she had repeatedly combed the building and the surrounding streets. She had searched everywhere. But no Harry.

Four hours later she had nothing to show for her exhaustive grid search. She was completely soaked, exhausted, and at a loss on what to do next.

She tensed as her stomach cramped. She must have caught Harry's flu.

"Why didn't you mention Harry in your message? I might've got here sooner. Four hours is a long time. He could be anywhere by now."

Kat pushed him away. "You think you can do better?"

Jace's lips pressed into a frown. "No—I'm just saying two heads are better than one. Just involve me, before things get out of control."

She stepped back and crossed her arms. "Things aren't out of control. I can handle it." The more she kept Jace out of it, the better. Men left when things got uncomfortable. Like her dad did after her mom's Alzheimer's diagnosis.

"No, you are absolutely not handling it. You're a wreck." He touched her cheek. "Why won't you let me help you?"

Jace already did Harry's home repairs, grocery shopping, and much more. Would their relationship survive, or would the burden of his care strain it beyond repair?

She shrugged, not knowing what to say. Jace was right. She had just never expected Harry to be out of her sight. Especially since his doctor's appointment was the sole reason for the trip. Now he was gone, a mistake she couldn't undo.

He softened his voice. "Did you tell the doctor how he's been forgetting things?"

Kat nodded. Jace simply thought Harry was forgetful.

The endless crisis management of the last few months wore on her and she was exhausted from lack of sleep. Caring for Harry and running her full-time fraud investigation practice was impossible. She worried she would make critical errors in her work. She couldn't afford to lose clients, or her reputation. More importantly, she couldn't lose Harry.

Kat tucked a lock of hair behind her ear as she struggled to hear Jace over the wind. It whistled through the high-rise towers, the gusts increasing with each passing hour. She grew increasingly worried about Harry. Was he safe?

Kat studied Jace. His inner calm pulled her in and embraced her like an aura. His steady gaze rested on hers as if no one else existed. It was what she loved most about him. Only now his face was tinged with worry, despite his efforts not to show it.

Dr. McAdam wanted Harry in long-term care. Kat bristled at the thought. Harry had cared for her; now she needed to do the same for him. She wanted to hang onto him as long as she could. Kat dropped her gaze from Jace's clear blue eyes and followed the water rivulets coursing down the front of his waterproof jacket.

"I didn't want to bother you. Besides, you were working on your story deadline." She had to raise her voice to be heard above the wind.

"Bother me? I'm not important enough in your life to be included?"

"I didn't mean it that way, Jace. It's just that I—I just didn't know what to do."

"You still should have called me." Jace pulled her closer. Even through his jacket, she felt the strength of his embrace. Her fingertips traced the curve of his bicep as his strong arms encircled her.

One more thing and she would break apart and shatter into little pieces. Pieces too small to be made whole again. She broke from Jace's embrace. "I will. But we can't waste any more time. "

Where would she go if dementia clouded her mind? Home. But Uncle Harry wouldn't remember the way, and it was too far to walk from downtown Vancouver. Not that it would stop him. He wasn't very logical.

"Don't get mad at me." Jace stepped back and turned away. "I'm only trying to help."

Now she felt even worse.

The streetlights cast a cold yellow light on Jace as he faced her, arms crossed.

Gore-Tex and Timberlands, ready for anything, always under control. She felt a twinge of resentment, though she was grateful. No one else dropped everything when she needed help.

"Sorry," she said. "I'm beat. The Barron hearing's tomorrow and I'm not ready." Zachary Barron's future net worth rested entirely on her.

Forensic accountants like Kat specialized in fraud detection and uncovering hidden assets. Or, in high-net-worth divorce cases like his, providing valuations and expert testimony. A nasty divorce battle, a hedge fund tycoon with a short fuse, impossible expectations, and millions at stake meant no room for error.

"You'll be fine."

"I don't know—I've still got hours of work to do." If things went wrong, Zachary Barron could ruin her reputation with a phone call. If, on the other hand, he won—the publicity would be priceless.

"It'll work out."

It always did for Jace. Her mind slipped back to the doctor's office. What if Harry was hurt somewhere, or worse? She would tell Jace about the Alzheimer's—once Harry was safe and sound. She winced as another cramp gripped her stomach.

"Kat?"

"Huh?"

"I said, yes—let's go to the house. But we should call the police first. They'll be much more effective than the two of us on foot. I know you don't want to ..."

Harry had been calling the police at least twice a week lately for imagined break-ins and thefts. Not all cops were sympathetic when called out for what inevitably turned out to be an old man's delusions, a false alarm. Harry wanted to keep living in his home, and as long as Kat kept an eye on him, she figured he'd be safe. Until now. Things were getting much worse, faster than she ever imagined.

"No—it's okay. Call them."

Jace punched in the numbers on his cell phone as they strode to the underground parking garage.

Kat checked her watch again as they headed down the ramp. The hearing was in less than eleven hours.

As they rounded the corner onto the first level of the parking garage, the glare of the bright fluorescent lights played shadows on the gray concrete walls.

Then she saw him. In the far corner, a figure curled up in a fetal position. He faced them, his back nested against the corner where the two walls met. His upper body was partially covered by a piece of cardboard. She couldn't be sure, but he seemed to be wearing a gray windbreaker.

"Uncle Harry?" She broke into a run.

The man sat up and pulled back the cardboard. He grinned.

It was Harry.

Kat reached him and held out a hand to help him up.

"Can we go home now?" Harry said without missing a beat.

# Chapter 4

The judge yawned as Kat finished her testimony. Bad sign. Financial analysis was often the difference between financial windfall and complete financial ruin in high-profile divorces. As a forensic accountant, she knew it was always a numbers game. High stakes were decided by the stroke of the judge's pen. In this case, a bored judge.

No matter how often Kat provided expert testimony, she always got nervous. And felt personally responsible if things went sideways for her client. Zachary Barron's case was no different. She cursed herself for her lack of preparation. She was off her game. If she lost such a high-profile case, she'd ruin her reputation and maybe even her business. It was the last thing she could afford. She needed cash more than ever for Harry's care, and she couldn't blow it over a lack of sleep.

Zachary Barron's eyes bored into hers. Why was her client staring at her like that? Had she missed something? Said something wrong? No. She had to stop second-guessing herself.

Finally Zachary glanced away.

She exhaled. Relax.

In court just ten minutes and things were already out of control.

"Looks like you forgot a few zeros on your calculator, Ms. Carter."

Kat half-expected Connor Whitehall to wink like she'd just performed a parlor trick—a gray-haired lawyer chastising a much younger expert witness. His aging television-anchor looks, expensive suits, and thirty-something years on her created a powerful impression. An impression he used to discredit her.

"I haven't missed a thing." Kat tried not to sound defensive. She clenched her hands together as she sat inside the witness box. The courtroom was empty, save for the warring Barron spouses and their lawyers. Victoria and Zachary Barron sat on opposite sides of the courtroom, studiously avoiding eye contact.

Whitehall shook his head. He shifted his gaze to the judge and sauntered towards him. The judge's head jerked up from whatever he was reading as the sound of Whitehall's footsteps filled the silent courtroom.

Kat thought she saw a look pass between them. The judge probably figured she was stupid too. Maybe that's why he wasn't listening.

What if she had made a mistake? With less than three hours sleep and no time for a dry run this morning, she was hardly on top of her game. She'd brought Uncle Harry with her to the courthouse again, having run out of options. Leaving him home alone was too risky. He was convinced squatters in his house were trying to kill him. This time she'd parked him at the coffee shop in the lobby and bribed the waitress to watch him. She felt guilty about it, but she'd exhausted all other alternatives.

She hadn't missed anything, she reassured herself. Whitehall was just using old lawyer tricks to make her crack. She was the only forensic accountant in the courtroom, and the only qualified fraud expert. Still, tracing a tycoon's assets was never straightforward.

"You've missed hundreds of millions of dollars!" Whitehall spun around as the corners of his mouth turned up into a mischievous grin. "Yet you call yourself a forensic accountant?"

Whitehall paused before strolling back to where Kat sat in the witness box. He leaned in close, exhaling coffee breath into her personal space. Kat held her breath. Why did she feel like the one on trial?

"Objection!" Zachary Barron's lawyer sprang into action. Finally. Kat felt like she'd been left to the wolves, or worse, a predatory lawyer.

"Sustained." The judge's voice was devoid of emotion as he checked his watch. Counting the minutes till lunchtime.

Divorces brought out the worst in people, more than criminal fraud, white-collar crime, or anything else. But these little wars were the bread and butter of her forensic accounting practice, providing steady cash flow.

For once she was on the side of the client with money. He would pay her bill on time, in full. In her weeks of groundwork, she'd identified all the assets, verified the valuations, appraisals, and legal titles, and even turned up a few surprises. She just had to follow through and it would be over in twenty minutes.

Kat glanced over at her client. Zachary Barron sat head down as he thumb-tapped yet another message on his BlackBerry. He was in his mid-thirties, just like her, but with more money than she'd ever see in a lifetime. He could potentially lose most of it in the next ten minutes if Whitehall got his way. So much was at stake, yet he treated the hearing like a distraction. She, on the other hand, was breaking into a sweat, and it wasn't even her money.

"Ms. Carter?" Whitehall asked.

"Are you asking a question?"

"Yes, I'm asking you a question. I'm disputing the valuation you have assigned to the matrimonial assets."

"That doesn't sound like a question." Kat returned Whitehall's stare with her best look of puzzlement and consternation. Cheeky maybe, but two could play at this game.

"Ms. Carter! This isn't Jeopardy. You valued the matrimonial assets at thirty million. Why have you excluded the family business?" He tapped his pen against her exhibit, a little harder than necessary to make his point.

Good. She'd finally got Whitehall riled up.
Even Zachary glanced from the file he was reading and smiled. One thing she was sure of—if she had millions at stake, she sure as hell wouldn't be catching up on office paperwork.

Victoria Barron, Zachary's ex-wife, ex-part-time financial manager, and walking billboard for plastic surgery, sat at the opposing table, crossing and uncrossing her legs. Her expression remained impassive, except for a slight ever-present smile. Kat concluded it was a remnant of too much plastic surgery.

"May I?" Kat asked.

She rose from her seat and strode over to the easel holding her exhibit of the Barrons' assets. Kat focused her laser pointer on the Zachary's side of the financial organization chart.

On Edgewater Investments.

It was complicated. Operating companies, holding companies, and offshore trusts. Zachary had been careful to keep very little in his own name. She spent the next ten minutes explaining the complex web of agreements and relationships amongst the entities.

Whitehall raised his eyebrows, then walked away and slumped into the chair beside Victoria Barron. He crossed his arms and gave Kat a look of contempt.

She smiled back at him. "Shall I go on?"

He glared at her.

Victoria Barron, Zachary's soon to be ex-trophy wife, was gunning for not only half the matrimonial assets, but also half of Zachary's business. A hundred million rode on Kat's interpretation of what was or wasn't included in matrimonial assets. But Zachary had a pre-nup.

"Edgewater Investments is Mr. Barron's business. It is certainly not community property, so I have excluded it from the matrimonial assets to be divided." She traced the pointer above the Edgewater box, to two other boxes, both holding companies. One was owned by Zachary Barron, the other by his father, Nathan Barron.

"Not true. My client is entitled to half of that."

"If that's the case, we should apply the same logic to Mrs. Barron's business."

"That's hypothetical," he snorted. "She has no business."

Actually, she was in the business of getting married. And marriage number three was about to end. "Are you sure about that?" Kat asked.

"Of course I'm sure!" Whitehall jumped up from his seat and marched towards her. "And I'm the one asking the questions, not you."

"You really should talk to your client. According to my records, she has sizable investments, as well as a healthy income. Didn't she tell you any of this?"

Whitehall stepped back, obviously surprised. He flashed an angry glare at Victoria Barron. Her eyes widened and her mouth opened into a perfectly round Botox O.

Kat flipped to a second chart and rolled through the details of Victoria Barron's winning wine and real estate investments, endorsement deals from her plastic surgery reality show, and recent fragrance deal with a cosmetics company. She had hidden it well, with profits funneled to offshore companies in the Caymans. But a spreadsheet was a deadly weapon in the hands of a good forensic accountant.

"Those aren't investments," Whitehall scoffed. "It's personal property."

Kat glanced over at Victoria. Her perfectly sculpted shoulders slumped and her eyes closed momentarily. "A few bottles of wine, maybe. But she made a two-hundred-thousand-dollar profit last year on her wine investments alone. And her real estate portfolio is eight figures. That's some hobby." Her analysis had dispelled the dependent housewife myth—now it was up to the judge to decide.

"It hardly compares to a hundred million." Whitehall's tone was flat and defeated.

"What else isn't she telling us?" Kat turned to smile at the judge, but his head was down, reading the newspaper Kat had noticed earlier. He had hidden it under a file folder on the side of his desk.

Whitehall flushed as he strode back to his seat without saying anything. Flying by the seat of his pants, probably assuming he'd never be questioned. Unprepared. She had him and he knew it.

"That's just one of the dozens of sales she's had over the last year. Or didn't she tell you?"

His face reddened to a deep crimson. Even from twenty feet, Kat saw his knuckles whiten as he dug them into the weathered oak table.

Silence.

"Why don't you ask her yourself?" Kat pointed with her pen. "As you can see here, she actually owes Mr. Barron, instead of the other way around."

No answer.

Zachary fidgeted.

Kat felt her face flush. Had she pushed things too far?

"Not a chance, Ms. Carter. Your numbers are bogus."

Kat took a deep breath and flipped to her final chart. She was about to explain why Whitehall was wrong when the courtroom doors swung open with a bang. She looked up, startled.

"Kat!"

Uncle Harry stood in the doorway and waved his keys.

"You've got to help me! I've lost the Lincoln."

Uncle Harry—again forgetting the accident.

Kat motioned for Harry to sit down. Judges were unpredictable. This was exactly the sort of thing that could turn the tide against her client.

Uncle Harry threw his hands up in the air in an exaggerated flourish, but then slumped down in a seat in the second row. She hoped he could stay quiet for the next few minutes.

"Friend of yours?" Whitehall raised his eyebrows.

Kat ignored him.

Harry's voice rose again, an unfortunate result of the room's acoustics.

"Damn towing companies! Why can't they leave a note or a phone number or something?"

The judge motioned to the bailiff standing at the back of the room.

"Your Honor, I'm sorry. Give me a minute, please." If she hadn't already blown it, she surely had now. She strode towards Harry as fast as possible without breaking into a run.

"Where, Uncle Harry? On the curb?" Kat whispered as she patted his arm. "Ten more minutes. Then we'll search for your car." The Lincoln was safely parked in Harry's garage. She'd disconnected the garage door opener as an added precaution since he'd refused to part with his car keys.

"They could at least call me." He pouted and crossed his arms.

Whitehall turned to face the judge. "Your honor, do we really need to listen to more?"

"No counsel, I don't think we do."

Whitehall gloated.

Kat returned to the witness box. She glanced at Victoria Barron, who was smiling into a handheld mirror, checking her makeup.

Victoria's smile faded when the judge spoke.

"Judgment for three million in matrimonial assets to be divided equally. Case dismissed."

Zachary Barron snapped his file shut and straightened, suddenly at full attention. Like someone had flipped a switch.

Kat should have felt good, but divorce cases always got her down. How could two people fall in love, then hate each other within three years? Money brought out the worst in people. They would die for it, lie for it, and even kill for it. She'd seen it countless times in her line of work.

That's why she'd never get married. Not even to Jace, despite his proposal. They'd had heated discussions about it, even broke up over it two years ago. They'd been testing the waters as a couple again for the last year, and she wasn't screwing that up by getting married.

She shoved her papers into her briefcase and made a beeline for Harry.

"Let's go outside." She linked arms with her uncle and steered him out to the lobby. It was the second time today Harry had thought he'd lost his Lincoln. "Uncle Harry—maybe it's time you—"

Harry held his arm up in protest.

"Will you stop it, Kat? It's my God-given right to drive. I drive better than all those other yahoos on the road. They're the ones creating problems."

"Driving's a privilege and a convenience. But when we get older, sometimes it's better to be—"

"Don't use that 'we' tone with me, young lady!  I might be old, but I will not be patronized!"

Harry's rising voice echoed in the cavernous marble foyer. Groups of lawyers, plaintiffs, and others turned and stared, most giving her suspicious glares.

"Don't be upset, Uncle Harry. I'm just worried about you."

"I know." His voice cracked. "But it's frustrating. What's happening to me, Kat?"

Harry rubbed a hand over his bald head.

"It's okay, Uncle Harry." Kat touched his arm. "You've just been busy. We all forget sometimes."

Aunt Elsie's unexpected heart attack right after the Liberty Diamond Mines case had hit Harry hard. Dr. McAdam figured the stress accelerated the decline in his mental health. Now Kat was his only family to speak of. What might be next on the dementia journey scared her too.

"It's easier to take the bus. No car or parking tickets to worry about." Kat squeezed his hand. "I can drive you wherever you need to go."

"After you drove your car into the Fraser River last year?" Harry pulled his hand away. "No thanks."

His long-term memory was still remarkably intact.

"Kat—wait."

Kat spun around. Zachary Barron emerged from the crowd and marched towards her. People parted on either side, opening a path for him like he was royalty. A clean-cut man in an Ermenegildo Zegna suit whispered success and power. Kat's arm-in-arm journey with Harry a minute earlier had been more like a jousting match, as she elbow-bashed and zigzagged through the crowd.

Zachary couldn't possibly be mad about the settlement. Or could he? Save a client a hundred million and they'd still find something to complain about. He hadn't even seen her bill yet.

"Kat? We need to talk."

"Sure. You do realize you got a very good result. It's hard to—"

"It's not about the divorce." He glanced around to see who was within earshot, then leaned closer. "You handle fraud, right?"

"Yes, of course." Corporate fraud and divorce were both big areas of her forensic accounting practice. But Harry was agitated; she had to calm him down and distract him from his Lincoln.

Harry. Kat spun around, but he had vanished. The lunchtime crowd had swallowed up Harry's path. Her eyes searched the crowd, a life-sized Where's Waldo? puzzle. Nothing. A wave of panic washed over her. How could she find a short, balding octogenarian in the sea of people?

Out of the corner of her eye, she saw him. A flash of gray hair, a beige raincoat. Harry—or at least someone who resembled Harry—disappeared around a corner.

"Zachary—can I call you later this afternoon? Something's just come up."

She pressed speed dial on her cell, trying to call Uncle Harry and corral him back. Even if he had his phone, he probably wouldn't answer, but it was worth a try.

"It's urgent," Zachary said. "I'll come by your office this afternoon. Two o'clock."

It was more of a command than a question. Kat glanced up from her cell phone to protest, but Zachary Barron was gone.

Read the rest of *Game Theory* by purchasing the book and visit **http://www.colleencross.com** for more information on Colleen's latest releases.

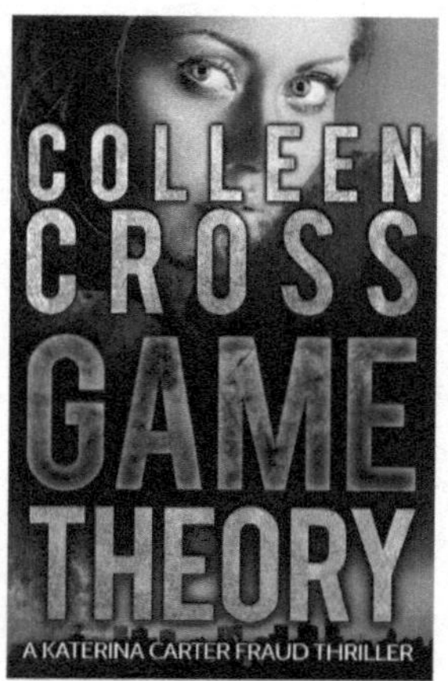

# About the Author

Colleen Cross writes mysteries and thrillers as well as finance and investing nonfiction.

For the latest on Colleen's books, please visit her website. Sign up for new release notification for special subscriber only offers and to ensure you are the first to know about new releases. Emails are only sent twice a year, so don't miss out. Find out more at: **http://www.colleencross.com**

# Author's Note

I hope you enjoyed reading the first three books in the Color of Money Mystery series. I'll keep writing them as long as readers like you enjoy them. Your feedback is important and might even factor into a future plot, so please leave reviews and let me know what you think!

If you enjoyed reading about Katerina Carter, you might also enjoy my full-length novels in the Katerina Carter Fraud Thriller series.

Find out more about me and my books at my website **http://www.colleencross.com** and sign up to be notified of my new releases. You will only be sent an email when I have a new book out.

Thank you so much for reading my book. I hope you enjoyed reading it as much as I enjoyed writing it!

# Also By Colleen Cross

## *Katerina Carter Fraud Thriller Series*

*Exit Strategy*

*Game Theory*

*Blowout*

## *Katerina Carter Color of Mystery Series*

*Red Handed*

*Blue Moon*

*Greenwash*

## Nonfiction

*Anatomy of a Ponzi: Scams Past and Present*